D0375722

For Lyn Hamilton,
fine friend and true woman of mystery

❦

A disordered neighborhood.

❦

"What happened, Emmy Lou? Please tell us."

"I didn't mean it."

"Mean what?" Lilith asked soothingly.

Emmy Lou's green eyes rolled, wild with panic. "I didn't know he was there."

"Who?" I urged.

"I didn't see him."

I glanced around for someone to help. There was no sign of Dwayne's Audi. The Baxters' driveway was empty. Bonnie was nowhere to be seen. No one but Lilith and me to help Emmy Lou.

"I'll go and check what's happened."

Emmy Lou pushed Lilith away. "I told you what happened," she screamed. "I killed him."

I headed for the house. Emmy Lou was hysterical. She probably didn't know what she was saying. But just in case, I started to run.

Tony Starkman was the first sight that greeted my eyes when I opened the door. He was sprawled faceup at the foot of the hardwood stairs. He lay there, unmoving, surrounded by scattered plush toys . . .

PRAISE FOR

Organize Your Corpses

"A comedic, murderous romp . . . Maffini is a relaxed, accomplished, and wickedly funny writer."

—*The Montreal Gazette*

"A fast-moving story." —*Contra Coasta Times*

"Maffini's new series starring professional organizer and amateur sleuth Charlotte Adams is off to a brilliant start with this fast-paced mystery." —*Romantic Times*

The Cluttered Corpse

Mary Jane Maffini

Santa Fe Springs City Library
11700 E. Telegraph Road
Santa Fe Springs, CA 90670

BERKLEY PRIME CRIME, NEW YORK

THE BERKLEY PUBLISHING GROUP
Published by the Penguin Group
Penguin Group (USA) Inc.
375 Hudson Street, New York, New York 10014, USA

Penguin Group (Canada), 90 Eglinton Avenue East, Suite 700, Toronto, Ontario M4P 2Y3, Canada
(a division of Pearson Penguin Canada Inc.)
Penguin Books Ltd., 80 Strand, London WC2R 0RL, England
Penguin Group Ireland, 25 St. Stephen's Green, Dublin 2, Ireland (a division of Penguin Books Ltd.)
Penguin Group (Australia), 250 Camberwell Road, Camberwell, Victoria 3124, Australia
(a division of Pearson Australia Group Pty. Ltd.)
Penguin Books India Pvt. Ltd., 11 Community Centre, Panchsheel Park, New Delhi—110 017, India
Penguin Group (NZ), 67 Apollo Drive, Rosedale, North Shore 0632, New Zealand
(a division of Pearson New Zealand Ltd.)
Penguin Books (South Africa) (Pty.) Ltd., 24 Sturdee Avenue, Rosebank, Johannesburg 2196,
South Africa

Penguin Books Ltd., Registered Offices: 80 Strand, London WC2R 0RL, England

This is a work of fiction. Names, characters, places, and incidents either are the product of the author's imagination or are used fictitiously, and any resemblance to actual persons, living or dead, business establishments, events, or locales is entirely coincidental. The publisher does not have any control over and does not assume any responsibility for author or third-party websites or their content.

THE CLUTTERED CORPSE

A Berkley Prime Crime Book / published by arrangement with the author

PRINTING HISTORY
Berkley Prime Crime mass-market edition / April 2008

Copyright © 2008 by Mary Jane Maffini.
Cover art by Stephen Gardner.
Cover design by George Long.
Interior text design by Laura K. Corless.

All rights reserved.
No part of this book may be reproduced, scanned, or distributed in any printed or electronic form without permission. Please do not participate in or encourage piracy of copyrighted materials in violation of the author's rights. Purchase only authorized editions.
For information, address: The Berkley Publishing Group,
a division of Penguin Group (USA) Inc.,
375 Hudson Street, New York, New York 10014.

ISBN: 978-0-425-22092-4

BERKLEY® PRIME CRIME
Berkley Prime Crime Books are published by The Berkley Publishing Group,
a division of Penguin Group (USA) Inc.,
375 Hudson Street, New York, New York 10014.
The name BERKLEY PRIME CRIME and the BERKLEY PRIME CRIME design
are trademarks belonging to Penguin Group (USA) Inc.

PRINTED IN THE UNITED STATES OF AMERICA

10 9 8 7 6 5 4 3 2 1

If you purchased this book without a cover, you should be aware that this book is stolen property. It was reported as "unsold and destroyed" to the publisher, and neither the author nor the publisher has received any payment for this "stripped book."

Acknowledgments

I would have been lost without the many people who provided help and encouragement behind the scenes with this book. Once again, I owe special thanks to Lyn Hamilton for friendship, support, and advice to me as well as to Charlotte. As usual, Mary MacKay-Smith offered her astute comments and eagle eye. Officer Chris Myers of the Troy Police Department kept me from getting in big trouble with the law. Victoria Maffini, Barbara Fradkin, Linda Wiken, and Janet MacEachen came through with insight and expertise in their own unique areas, while Elaine Naiman and Jan Kurtz helped out in the name department. Bless them all.

I also appreciated the many DorothyL librarians who sprang forward to help with details: Vicki Deem, Serena Brooks, Shannon Jensen, Matthew Kochan, Catherine Brown, and many others who generously offered assistance for future books. Thanks also to professional organizers everywhere, because like librarians, they make life better.

Thanks also to my agent, Leona Trainer, for her on-going enthusiasm for the Charlotte Adams books and to Tom Colgan and Sandy Harding at Berkley Prime Crime for being cheerful and understanding, no matter what. A note of appreciation is due the mysterious copy editor, Caroline Duffy, who yet again has saved my bacon. Naturally, any errors are my own.

On the home front, Daisy and Lily continue to be fine role models for Truffle and Sweet Marie. My husband, Giulio Maffini, does everything he can to help me lead the ideal life of a mystery writer.

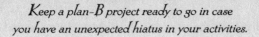

Keep a plan-B project ready to go in case
you have an unexpected hiatus in your activities.

1

"You have saved my life." Emmy Lou Rheinbeck's green eyes glowed with gratitude.

"Oh, not really." I stared modestly down at my patent leather wedge-heeled shoes.

"But you have." A radiant smile lit her face.

I couldn't help smiling back at my latest client. There was something contagious about this woman's emotions. Even so, I felt uncomfortable. I like a pat on the head as much as the next girl. When I deserve it.

It seemed only fair to point this out.

"Nice of you to say that, Ms. Rheinbeck, but I haven't done anything yet." In fact, we'd been chatting in her living room for fifteen minutes, as I listened for some clue to her problem.

She tossed her sleek copper hair. "Please call me Emmy Lou. I get more than enough *Mrs.* Rheinbeck at work. And, believe me, we are not dealing with my work side here."

I'd gathered from our conversation that she had a high-powered management job at a large insurance company. She must have left the city early this Friday afternoon and come directly to our three o'clock meeting. She was dressed for success. The midnight blue fitted suit had a hint of sheen and probably a subtle touch of Lycra. The white satin shirt-style collar and oversize cuffs provided plenty of drama without diminishing her executive look. She might have had ten years on me, and when I get to forty, if I look half that good, I'll be euphoric.

I said, "Okay, Emmy Lou."

"And you *have* helped me, Charlotte. You've come all the way across town to meet me. I appreciate that, considering that I did cancel our first consultation appointment back in the fall."

"You and everyone else. I guess it was all that fuss about me in the news. A lot of people got cold feet."

"I wasn't ready to deal with my problem. So, the fact that you're here has already made a difference."

"Great. I'm happy."

"You have no idea how much you've helped." She wagged her perfectly French-manicured index finger at me. I couldn't miss the flash of chunky diamonds. They reminded me of my own engagement ring, now resting on the bottom of the Hudson. Too bad the cheating so-and-so who'd given it to me hadn't plunged after it. But as they say, you can't have everything.

I resisted the urge to sit on my hands, although I had no clue what this alleged problem was. I glanced around the living room. She'd mentioned a collection on the phone. What kind of collection? Danish silver? Lladro figurines? Christian Dior lipsticks? If she had an organizing or storage problem, there was no sign of it from where we sat. In fact, the Rheinbeck residence, a simple two-story wood-frame home dating probably from the 1930s, could have served as the "after" version on an upscale television renovation show, with its espresso-colored furniture, hardwood flooring, sleek glass, and trendy light fixtures. The butter-soft cognac leather sofa felt as good as it looked. I wouldn't have been surprised to spot television cameras zooming in for a tight two-shot.

She sighed. "It's a bit embarrassing, but I suppose I'd better get on with it."

Taking that first step is always tricky. I was glad I didn't have to push her. You don't want to bully a client, but it's painful for people to get started.

Emmy Lou said, "So, how about a piece of cake?"

I recognized a typical stalling technique. "Not for me, thanks. Maybe we should talk about—"

"Double chocolate cheesecake. I made it myself. It's my signature dish." She spoke like a woman who was used to getting her own way.

Of course, I like to get my own way too. "I'm trying to cut down on sweets."

"For heaven's sake and you're so waiflike. I thought it was just us full-figured girls who fussed endlessly over calories."

I am not waiflike. Okay, short maybe, four foot eleven and holding, but I weigh ninety-five pounds and that's normal for my height. I seem to be able to eat what I want. Of course, I have to be careful who I mention that to, as some people don't find it endearing. And for once I wasn't fussing, simply trying to get started. I knew it would help if Emmy Lou could describe her clutter problem. That didn't seem to be happening.

I smiled obliquely. It wouldn't pay to lose all control at this early stage of whatever it was we would be doing.

"I think I'll have some anyway." She stood up and smoothed her skirt. "Not too late to change your mind."

"Thanks, but no thanks."

As Emmy Lou sashayed toward her kitchen, leaving a subtle trail of exotic fragrance, I wondered if that suit had been custom made for her. It hugged her assets and skimmed over anything that might have needed minimizing. She reminded me of a line from a song one of my mother's husbands used to sing: "Round and firm and fully packed, that's my gal." Emmy Lou had definitely seen more than a few double chocolate cheesecakes in her time. But on her that looked good.

I watched her graceful progress toward the kitchen. I didn't need to walk the length of the first floor to see that the high-grade open shelves held immaculate dishes, artistically displayed. Even from the sofa you couldn't miss the gleam of the granite countertop that separated the dining area from the cooking section. The glimpse I'd had showed a stainless steel fridge with wide double doors. The six-burner gas cooktop was overshadowed by a dramatic range hood. I was betting there was a two-drawer dishwasher tucked away under that granite countertop.

I suppressed a wave of jealousy. My own kitchen occupies a former linen closet. Even as a linen closet, it hadn't been terrific. Never mind, the galley style serves my culinary needs, which mostly involve storing a variety of Ben & Jerry's finest. Normally I love everything about my cozy second-floor apartment, but normally I'm not sitting in a place like this. I did not have a chocolate cheesecake waiting for me at home, although chocolate cheesecake is one of my favorite things.

Emmy Lou's copper bob swung nicely as she moved from the massive fridge to the granite counter, carrying a footed cake plate and a small bowl. She reached elegantly into a cupboard, picked plates, then a *clink* here, a swirl there, and she was ready to go. Apparently, the stunning kitchen was for more than show. She glided back to the living room with two plates, each with a slice of cake. Both pieces were decorated with a dollop of whipped cream and a few pretty chocolate shavings. She placed the plates, forks, and napkins on the coffee table. She raised an eyebrow and smiled.

"In case you change your mind."

Did I mention my mouth was watering? But it was time to get back on task.

I said encouragingly, "So you need help organizing . . . was it a collection?" Just because she was paying for my time didn't mean we needed to waste it.

The smile vanished.

I added, "Because everything in your home looks beyond perfect."

She had a musical laugh, although this was the first time I'd heard it. "I guess there's more to me than meets the eye, Charlotte." She took an elegant bite of her chocolate cheesecake.

I was resisting, but I wasn't sure how much longer I could hold out. Chocolate has always been my drug of choice.

I persevered. "What kind of collection?" Nothing in that room for sure. As far as I could tell, Emmy Lou Rheinbeck was better organized than I was. And that's something.

From the far end of the kitchen, we heard the click of a lock opening, then a door banging. Emmy Lou jumped, dropping her fork on the Berber carpet. Her hand shot to her mouth.

A voice rang out, "It's me, sweetheart. Forgot my briefcase. No point in getting to the bank without that."

"It's in here, honey," she said. Was it my imagination or were her hands shaking?

"Honey" strode through the kitchen. "Sorry to interrupt you girls. I'd forget my head if it wasn't so darn shiny."

"Charlotte, this is my husband, Dwayne." Emmy Lou glowed when she looked at him. I wasn't sure why she was so jumpy, but Dwayne didn't seem to be the cause.

Dwayne grinned. He was shorter than Emmy Lou and had a gloriously bald head. He wore a rumpled sport jacket and casual pants. His tie hung loosely knotted and not quite centered. But who cared? This guy's grin could fill a room. Add to that he had a voice like liquid honey. I could see how a glamorous woman like Emmy Lou could fall head over heels for him. I found myself grinning back. Dwayne looked like the kind of guy you could count on.

Emmy Lou said, "It's on the console. Tuck your shirt in, please, honey."

Dwayne bent to kiss her cheek. Maybe he hadn't noticed the nervous little tic in her eyelid. Funny, because he looked at her intensely, the way my dogs might eye a juicy steak inches out of their reach.

Next he shook my hand. A warm, firm handshake. "Glad to meet you, Charlotte. We followed you in the papers with all that trouble last fall. We figured you'd be just the gal for Emmy's project, didn't we, sweetheart?"

"We did."

"Sure glad you were able to come by. Whatever you decide, it's great with me. Nothing's too good for my lady. You dropped your fork, sweetheart. Can I get you another one?" He sprinted toward the kitchen without waiting for an answer.

Emmy Lou jumped to her feet. "Aren't you going to be late for your appointment?" She turned to me and laughed. "Dwayne owns a restaurant. It's doing so well, he's already planning to expand. That is, if he gets to the bank in time, *with* his briefcase."

Dwayne hustled back with a fresh fork. "Plenty of time. You two keep having fun. And Charlotte?"

"Hmm?"

"Make sure you leave some of that cake for me. My Emmy Lou's cheesecake can't be beat."

He stopped long enough to hand me his business card. I put the card on the coffee table and stood up to shake his hand again.

"Great meeting you, Charlotte. Good luck," he said to me. Emmy Lou got, "See you later, sweetheart," and a kiss that was slightly this side of X-rated. Even though he was at least two inches shorter than she was and his shirt wasn't completely tucked in, there was something very sexy about Dwayne Rheinbeck. Emmy Lou had two pink patches on her cheeks as she sat down again.

"Don't forget to lock the door," Emmy Lou called.

Dwayne departed as fast as he'd shown up, out the front door this time, stopping long enough to turn the key in the dead bolt, leaving behind a hint of lime, delicious, yet manly. The room looked the same, but I felt as though a typhoon had blown through.

I was so distracted by the cheesecake, not to mention the smooch, that I actually forgot to put the business card into my purse. Instead, I admitted defeat and picked up my own fork. "I can't resist anymore. How about I try the cake and you tell me about the project?"

"As you can see, it's hard for me to talk about."

No kidding. However, the cake was so good it practically brought tears to my eyes. Years from now, I imagine I will remember that dark chocolate taste and the velvety, melting texture. Emmy Lou was wasted in the insurance business, however high up. She should have been running some kind of global cheesecake empire.

She said, "It's stupid. You know I have a responsible position. I've worked my way up. I'm educated and competent and in charge of my life. I'm good at what I do. I am not afraid to face anything head-on."

"Mmm." Double meaning, I know.

"I've worked hard to make a lovely home for us. Dwayne and I are late bloomers. We haven't been married all that long. Not even a year."

Okay. That explained a lot.

"He's such a lovely man and he puts up with so much," she said, blushing.

Oh please. What did he have to put up with? A stunning wife, a gorgeous home, and food to die for?

"Well," she said, "I guess there's no point in putting it off any longer."

I put down my fork. The cake would be on the table when we got back. I followed her to the second floor. Halfway up, I stepped on something squishy.

It squeaked.

I gasped.

Emmy Lou shrieked and whirled.

I bent down and picked up a toy lamb, with a tiny smirk embroidered on its fluffy white face. It hung limply in my hand. I can't tell you how much that creeped me out.

She reached out and snatched the limp lamb and tucked it under her expensive silk and wool arm. "Oh! That's where you've been, you naughty boy."

I was pondering that when I stepped on a pair of battered toy cats. Again, Emmy Lou held out her hands for them. "They get out of control sometimes."

From that point on, I held on to the banister. By the time I reached the top stair, I'd stepped on and over more pastel fuzzy toys than I'd owned in my entire childhood. Had there been an explosion?

Emmy Lou said, "Now you see how silly I feel."

"So this is the collection?" More stuffed animals lined the corridor, tiny guards against something. But what was the big deal? They were cute, clean, harmless. I thought we'd have no trouble getting these little guys into some sort of order.

Emmy Lou threw back her head and laughed. "Oh no. Not by a long shot."

She squared her shoulders and sailed down the hall, carrying the stuffies. "We haven't redecorated upstairs yet. This whole level was an earlier renovation from the previous owners. We have great ideas, but . . . we need to get things under control first."

I checked out the hallway. Except for stuffed animals lined up against the wall, three deep, it was pleasant and well appointed. Maybe it lacked the wow factor of the first floor, but you'd hardly call a few toys out of control. Most people would be ecstatic to have a bedroom level like this.

Emmy Lou stopped at a closed door and paused. I found myself holding my breath. She turned the handle slowly and said, "Dwayne has been so good about it. Really, it's for him that I want to get the . . . situation in hand."

"Sure," I said.

The door swung open to . . . what? Santa's toy shop post-tornado? Every surface was covered with something fluffy and huggable in a nontoxic pastel shade.

Emmy Lou bit her lip.

I found my voice. "So, this is . . . ?"

"The bedroom."

"*Your* bedroom?"

"Yes."

"I see. Where's the bed? Oh, there it is. I didn't actually notice it at first because of the giant pandas and all that. Is that a stuffed snake?"

"Cute, isn't it? I think the rainbow stripes are adorable."

I draw the line at snakes, however pastel and striped. "Adorable" and "snake" do not belong in the same sentence. Still, Emmy Lou needed my advice, not a list of my phobias—with snakes as number one. Plus I'm supposed to be helpful, not be a smug, judgmental pain in the butt. I gave the room a second look, trying to assess the large space. The previous owners must have opened up the ceiling into the attic level and installed the cathedral window overlooking the backyard, where an enormous oak tree was starting to bud. It would give wonderful shade in the summer. Under normal circumstances, I would have loved this room.

"Maybe you can sit here," Emmy Lou said, sweeping a family of plush yellow duckies from the only visible chair.

I stayed standing. "I can see why you want to get your collection in hand. This will be a spectacular space when you're done."

"You think we can do it?" By this time she had a bead of sweat on her upper lip. She might love these creatures, but they were giving her grief. Why was she letting this happen? But, of course, that was what I needed to figure out.

I said, "It will be great. We'll have fun."

"Do you think? That's a relief. I've been feeling so overwhelmed."

Emmy Lou was the kind of client I loved: she knew what she needed to do but not how to do it. I could tell she would follow through.

"As soon as we have a plan, you're going to feel better. Let's check out the rest of this level. Is there another bedroom?"

"Oh. Yes, but it's sort of an office."

"Okay, we'll have a look. We might need it for swing space."

She bit her lip. "There's nowhere to swing anything. Certainly not a stuffed cat."

I grinned. "Cute."

She said wryly, "Too bad it's true."

"And how about the bathroom?"

She hesitated. "It's not too bad. Not like this. Now that you're here, I have to look at all this stuff in a new light. I can't believe that this whole collection has gotten so totally out of hand."

I shrugged. "It happens."

She reached out, picked up a toy Dalmatian, and stroked its spotted fun fur. "It feels so lovely. Do you like plush toys?"

Sometimes it's better not to disclose your likes and dislikes to clients. "I have two real dogs. They're pretty overwhelming sometimes too."

"I've never had a dog," she said. "Only these." She pointed toward a pile of cuddly doglike creatures, pale blue, green, and pink. She definitely had a pastel theme going with the stuffies.

"Real ones are a lot more trouble," I said. "Trust me."

"I'm not sure that's true. Do they multiply overnight?"

"Why? Do your stuffed animals multiply overnight?" I chuckled.

She gave a nervous giggle, at odds with her sophisticated look. "They're popping up everywhere. I don't even remember buying some of them. I guess that's when you know your collection is out of control."

"They're not all sentimental purchases?"

"Some of them, for sure. It started when I first met Dwayne. We were on our third date and we were strolling past a toy store. I told him I'd never had a stuffed toy as a child."

Ah, I thought. That might explain a bit.

"So he bought you one?"

"One? You probably noticed that Dwayne is a bit dramatic. He charged into the shop and bought me one of every kind they had. And I loved them, of course. And him too, it goes without saying."

Hmm. Maybe the problem with the overabundance didn't lie with Emmy Lou after all. Good thing we were taking our time getting to know the situation.

"Did he buy all these?"

"Oh no. I was hooked almost instantly. My own kind of crystal meth. He bought me lots and lots, although he's stopped doing it lately. He must have realized that he'd unleashed a monster."

I wanted to put a stop to that kind of negative self-talk, as they call it. It makes the process harder. "Emmy Lou, you're obviously a very capable person. So you have a collection that you love and it's got the upper hand. That's no biggie. You'd be surprised by how many normal people have a problem like this in some part of their life. It's good news for me, because I have to make a living. Once we find a way to manage these fluffy creatures, you'll be happy with them again."

"That's good because I can't resist them. And they're

everywhere, even in the grocery stores, sometimes in gas stations. If you're driving along and you see a garage sale, there are always so many lonely plush toys. But then you don't even have to leave the house, when you have catalogs and eBay."

"And you love every one of them."

"I love the idea of them. But they're not all sentimental, no. Any that Dwayne bought, which would be hundreds, I guess, those I adore. Some of the others, honestly, are still in their boxes; most of them have their original tags on. I must be buying them in my sleep."

"Mmm," I said.

She managed a weak smile. "But they are too adorable for words, aren't they? What kind of dogs do you have?"

"Miniature dachshunds. They're called Truffle and Sweet Marie."

"Wiener dogs, that's lovely. Small and cute. Hold on, I think I have some toy wiener dogs. I saw them the other day."

"Oh, that's okay," I said.

Maybe she didn't hear me. She marched over to the closet and whipped open the door. Naturally, the closet was full of stuffed animals. I had no idea where Emmy Lou kept her designer wardrobe, but it sure wasn't here.

She put her hands on her hips and frowned. "Now where did they get to?"

"Don't worry about it."

"There they are!" She reached onto a top shelf and pulled out a box. "Oh, no, they're mice, not wiener dogs. But they're too cute for words."

She placed the box in my hands. "I'd like you to have them."

"Thanks so much, but I couldn't." Meaning please don't give me a pair of stuffed toy mice dressed as a bride and groom mounted on a foam wedding cake with cheese decorations. They wouldn't last a New York minute in the room with Truffle and Sweet Marie.

Emmy Lou turned on her full-wattage smile. "It would make me very, very happy."

This was obviously stressful for her. No point in making it worse. I smiled soothingly. "Okay, thanks, they're very . . ."

"That's wonderful," she said, clapping her hands. "Now the bathroom. We plan to make it en suite when we get to the next stage. We have some fabulous ideas for it. There are hardly any stuffed animals in there."

I blurted, "Hardly any? You mean there are some?"

Emmy Lou said, "The type that go near water, like frogs and turtles and—"

A loud *thump* shook the cathedral window. Two hideously contorted faces glowered in at us. A flash lit up the window.

Emmy Lou screamed and fell back.

Don't put off unappealing tasks.
They'll multiply and sneak up on you.
Pick one and chip away at it.

2

I dropped my pen. I barely stopped myself from screaming too.

The faces remained pressed against the glass. One had dark eyes, a nose flattened against the window, and an expression somewhere between demonic and demented. The other, paler face grinned like a mischievous troll.

Emmy Lou slumped onto the bed, dislodging a massive stuffed zebra. Her breathing was ragged.

I stumbled over fallen plush toys to reach her side. "Are you all right?"

"I'm fine! I'm fine. Honestly," she gasped. She was far from fine, her face the color of spoiled milk, her pupils the size of dimes.

But what had happened?

I raced over to the window and stared out. "What the hell is that? I mean who?"

"Nothing," Emmy Lou insisted. It would have been more

convincing if her voice hadn't sounded choked. "I'm so sorry, Charlotte. You must think I'm crazy, screeching like a—"

"Crazy? People are banging on your second-floor bedroom window. That doesn't happen every day. It's worth screaming about."

"He startled me, that's all."

Outside the two figures disappeared, shrieking with laughter as they clambered down the oak tree.

"Who was that? Who startled you?"

"It's the boy next door and his friend. They don't mean anything by it. They're playful."

I stared at her. "But they weren't children."

"Poor Kevin. He can't help it."

Perhaps she hadn't seen them clearly. "They looked like men to me."

"Yes, yes, he's an adult, technically, but mentally and emotionally, he's a little boy. There's nothing to worry about."

I must have looked unconvinced. And I was.

She said, "I've known him all his life. The problem is that he had a little oxygen deprivation at birth so that his judgment isn't always perfect. Sometimes his little jokes miss the mark."

This one had missed the mark for sure. I peered down into the backyard. Two grown men were laughing and slapping each other on the back. Kevin, I assumed, and his equally bizarre friend.

She said, "It's nice that Kevin has someone to spend time with now. His life was quite lonely for a long time until he met Tony."

Tony must have been the tall, dark, and dangerous-looking one.

Emmy Lou said, "It doesn't matter if he's silly sometimes. I wasn't expecting to see them there, that's all."

"I'm sure you weren't expecting them at your second-story

window. And with a camera! They were obviously trying to frighten you. They took a photo of you in your bedroom without your permission. I think we should call the police."

Emmy Lou scowled at me. "I don't want to call the police. I told you this is nothing serious. It doesn't bother me. And it isn't any of *your* business."

Huh.

I reminded myself that Emmy Lou Rheinbeck had a serious job, dealt with all kinds of people and problems. She knew whether or not she had cause to worry. I was there to find a way to organize a superabundance of plush toys, not to live her life for her.

"Sorry," I said. "How about showing me the office and the bathroom now? We might need that office for swing space."

She glanced up at me from the bed, where she continued to sit surrounded by fluffy and unlikely creatures. The shock had strained her lovely face.

"Not today," she said.

"I thought you were ready to get started. Was it that . . . ?" I pointed to the window.

She shook her head. Her auburn hair contrasted sharply with her bloodless face. She clutched the lamb, perhaps so I wouldn't notice the tremor in her hands. No matter what she said, that bizarre scene at the window had bothered Emmy Lou. Big-time.

She said, "I can't handle this now. Please. Go."

I headed downstairs, reluctantly. I was dragging my stylish wedge heels because I knew Emmy Lou Rheinbeck's problem went way beyond a few thousand toys.

———

Five minutes later, I was standing on the walkway in front of the Rheinbeck house, remembering the firm *click* of the door locking behind me. I clutched my briefcase and wedding mice. Everything seemed so normal now. Like the interior of the house, the outside was a cut above the neighborhood. Bell Street, only one block long, was lined with modest two-story wood-frame houses. Most hadn't changed much in the seventy or eighty years since they'd been built. In fact, two units across the street were being torn down, probably for stylish new infill housing. One was reduced to a foundation now, and the other half-demolished. Sheets of plywood and boards were stacked up against the chain-link fence of the neighboring property. The honking big Dumpster on the lot signaled a neighborhood about to change. Not surprising. The houses on each side of the Rheinbecks' looked tired in comparison. Even the color of the grass faded out as it left their property. Emmy Lou and Dwayne's reno had obviously kick-started changes in the neighborhood. I was sure there'd be envy over the new stonework and upgraded windows. Their front porch looked like a recent add-on, incorporating a roof and a sitting area. The crisp edges of the lawn and landscaped bed were softened by deep purple sand cherries and low junipers. This landscaping had obviously been done by a pro. I couldn't picture Emmy Lou mucking around in the dirt with that French manicure. She'd be more at home in the new silver Volvo C70 convertible parked in the driveway.

I rubbed my chin and worried. Should I have left? Emmy Lou had definitely given me the boot. But what did it mean? You're fired? Never darken my door again?

My nose twitched. I put that down to pollen from the large white mulberry tree on the property next door. I love trees, but they don't repay me in pollen season.

Maybe I'd pushed too hard. While I was debating with myself, a battered Dodge Colt pulled into the driveway of the saggy blue house to the right of the Rheinbecks' and parked. A tall, lanky fortyish man holding a bag from Hannaford's got out of the car. He glanced over and rumbled toward me, pushing his thinning fair hair back with his free hand.

He shook his fist and shouted, "You leave her the hell alone."

For a second I thought I'd heard wrong. Why was he yelling at me? He did look slightly familiar, but I couldn't imagine what I'd done to bring this on. Maybe he was Kevin's father. He definitely seemed deranged.

"Excuse me?" I said when I regained my voice.

"You heard me."

I pulled myself up to my full four foot eleven and three-quarters. I lowered my voice to its deepest range and said, "I am here at Ms. Rheinbeck's request."

He strode toward me, shaking his fist. Up close, his icy blue eyes gave me goose bumps. Plus he seemed frighteningly tall. "But I wasn't—"

A woman threw open the window of the blue house and called after him, "Forget it, Bill. It's not our business."

"Next time we'll have the cops here," he roared.

"There's no reason to call the police," I said, with my chin high. I held my ground, but only barely.

He dropped the Hannaford's bag, pushed past me, and loped across the Rheinbecks' manicured lawn. Several oranges rolled out of the bag.

I whirled to find him confronting a slight young man with wispy hair, mousy brown, not unlike my own, only without the benefit of highlights. Even if I hadn't been distracted by his vintage tracksuit, I would have recognized the mischievous face from the window.

Kevin.

The oranges continued rolling back toward the car. I didn't intend to get in the middle of whatever was going on, but I could do something useful. I snatched up the oranges and stuck them back in the bag. Bill was busy shaking his fist at Kevin.

I decided to deliver the bag to the woman who had been watching from the window. She seemed to have vanished, but that's what doorbells are for. I wanted to get rid of the bag, then be on my way. If the hostilities escalated and it looked as if someone might get hurt, I planned to call 911.

I kept an eye on the scene on the Rheinbecks' lawn as I carried the grocery bag up the steps.

"I mean it," Bill yelled. "Stop hounding her."

Kevin hung his head slightly but said nothing. I had to admit, he did seem somewhat helpless and childlike. If I hadn't witnessed the scene at the window, I would have wanted to protect him from Bill.

A hulking body appeared behind Kevin. I figured with those sloping shoulders and greasy dark hair topped by an equally greasy baseball cap, he must be Tony. He no longer looked either demonic or deranged, but all the same, I wouldn't have wanted to run into him in a graveyard at midnight. Or in a front yard in the middle of the afternoon. And definitely not in a tree outside my bedroom window. He didn't speak either. Of course, his raised middle finger said it all.

I turned and caught a glimpse of the woman at the window again, peering intently at the action. She called out, "Get back in here, Bill. Remember your blood pressure."

"Come on, Bonnie. I can't let them drive her crazy."

"Yeah right," Tony said, his finger pointed skyward. "You're the one trespassing, doofus."

"Bill!"

He stomped back toward his own driveway, but stopped and turned back to watch the boys as I rang the doorbell. I heard the bell sound inside. I kept one eye on the door and the other on the action so I didn't miss anything. Tony retracted the middle finger slowly. The smirk lingered.

I glanced back toward my client's house. I thought I saw the living room blinds twitch. Emmy Lou could hardly be unaware of the shouting.

What kind of neighborhood hell had I stumbled into?

The dull blue paint on the clapboard was in need of a new coat or three. The front steps had a wobbly banister and two

steps that were overdue for replacement. A few straggly daffodils had pushed their way through the patchy grass by the
stairs. On the plus side, I could smell something delicious
being baked on the inside. Was Bell Street the secret food
center of Woodbridge?

When no one answered, I rang the doorbell again. "Your
husband dropped these," I called loudly.

Bill returned to his own driveway and paced in smaller
and smaller circles, sort of like my pooches when they're
ready for a pee.

Then he spotted me on the doorstep. "And you are . . . ?"

I hate that way of asking a person's name. Normally I
would have introduced myself, but normally I am not caught
in the middle of people bellowing threats at each other. "Charlotte Adams. I was seeing Mrs. Rheinbeck." I smiled.

"Visiting?"

"Leaving." I am used to neighbors taking an interest in
my clients and their projects. Often they want details. Other
people's mess and clutter is almost as interesting as their sex
lives, and just as much not anyone else's business.

He eyed my briefcase suspiciously. Not the friendliest
guy, this Bill.

The woman who appeared at the door was fortyish with
pixie-cut salt-and-pepper hair and a distinctive heart-shaped
face that would be pretty at eighty. Although her pinched
mouth hinted at chronic pain, she managed to smile. I spotted the cane she was leaning on and felt a wave of guilt about
ringing the doorbell until she was forced to answer.

She called out to Bill, who was behind me, "It's true.
Emmy Lou called me a minute ago. Sorry about that little
scene, Charlotte, did you say? I'm Bonnie Baxter and this big
dope here is Bill. And those foolish creatures across the way
are giving Emmy Lou a lot of grief lately. Bill's at the end of
his rope."

Bill extended his large hand. Up close he wasn't scary at
all. Just a pleasant man with a tired, lined face.

"We worry," he said.

I glanced back toward the smirking hulk who was firmly planted in the same place. "Did you say that they've been giving her grief?"

"Harassing her. Peeking in the windows. Phoning. Following."

I'd witnessed the impact of their faces in the window. It had scared me out of my new shoes, even if Emmy Lou had pretended it hadn't shocked her. I was worried too. If that kind of stuff had been going on for a while, no wonder her hands shook whenever she heard a noise. It explained the tic too.

I said, "That's terrible. There are laws against stalking. She should . . ." Of course, it's always easy to say what others should do. I turned toward the house expecting to see my lovely new client wringing her hands, but this time there was no twitch in the blinds.

A comment came from Bonnie, leaning on her cane at the door. "Bill has tried to warn her, but she won't listen. She's such a sweet person. She has to be careful. Those two are obviously not normal."

No kidding.

Bonnie added, "Bill even offered to go with her to the station, but she says to let it be. I hate to see those two making her miserable."

"And getting away with it," Bill added, glowering across the Rheinbecks' yard. An El Greco delivery van had squealed to a halt, and Kevin and his friend collected what looked like the Gargantua pizza and carried it into the house.

He said, "No jobs, but they got money to spend on junk food. There's always a pizza van pulling up in front of that house. So, yeah, maybe Emmy Lou will listen to you. We can't get her to take it seriously. We keep an eye on Emmy Lou, in case."

"In case what?" I said, with a panicky feeling. "Do you think Emmy Lou's under any kind of threat?"

"This Tony is being an ass. The other one, Kevin, he's a bit of sad-sack slacker. But she shouldn't have to put up with the stupid jokes and all. Anyway, if she has anything to worry about, I'll be there in a flash," Bill said, thumping up the stairs. "And Emmy Lou has us on speed dial."

"What about her husband? Wouldn't he take action?"

Bonnie shook her head. "Bill and I have both talked to Dwayne about it. Emmy Lou keeps telling him it's nothing. I doubt if Dwayne's ever seen any of their stupid stunts."

"Hmm. I'm glad Emmy Lou has good neighbors looking after her."

"On one side anyway," Bill said.

I saw no sign of the peculiar Kevin or the thuggish Tony as I climbed into my Miata. They were probably inside stuffing their faces. But I was feeling ambivalent. On the one hand, the job looked good. This client might take a bit of coaxing, but it would all work out. She'd be happy in the end. And it would be a satisfying contract for me, no dirt and no messy murders like I'd had in the past. On the other hand, Emmy Lou was obviously being harassed. Were Kevin and Tony dangerous as well as annoying?

I reminded myself that Emmy Lou was my client, not my friend or neighbor, and that she hadn't asked me to be involved. In fact, she'd asked me to leave. Even so, I sat there chewing my lip. Tricky situation. Whatever I decided, it would probably be wrong.

I felt a wave of relief when a silver Audi wheeled into the driveway beside me. Dwayne hopped out and gave me the victory sign. He strolled toward my car, grinning, and leaned in through the open window. I figured the meeting at the bank must have gone fabulously.

"Hey, Charlotte," he said. "Thanks for coming by. It won't be that easy, but my gal needs someone strong to help her deal with this. Someone who's not emotionally involved. Stay the course."

"Listen, Dwayne, I have to mention that your neighbor

Kevin and his friend seemed to have frightened Emmy Lou this afternoon. She got pretty upset and ended our session."

Dwayne stood up and scratched his shiny head. He stared across his new landscaping. Kevin and Tony must have finished their pizza in record time. They were outside again cavorting with the camera. Dwayne bent down again to make eye contact with me. "Pair of losers for sure. But I don't think there's anything much to worry about."

"I'm not so sure. Maybe you should talk it over with the police."

Dwayne treated me to his contagious grin. "Are you trying to ruin my love life? Emmy Lou's real fond of Kevin. Known him since he was a baby. She'd pitch a fit if I called the cops on Kevin."

I did not grin back. "Not that it's my business, but their behavior was spooky. Your neighbors on the other side seem kind of worried about Kevin and Tony too."

He snorted. "Bill does, you mean. Sorry, shouldn't have said that. Bonnie's a sweetheart, but she has MS and she doesn't get out. She gets Bill's version of everything, and he's seriously paranoid."

"But . . ." I said, trying not to appear paranoid myself.

"Tell you what, I don't want my Emmy Lou upset, so I'll talk to Mrs. Dingwall, Kevin's mom. I feel sorry for the poor lady, but she'll have to keep a lid on Kevin if she doesn't want me to do it for her. And I'll tell her to get rid of Tony the house pest before he causes any more trouble."

*Don't bring anything new into your home
unless you know you have a place to keep it.
Except for books, of course.*

3

At the corner of Bell Street, I slammed on my brakes to avoid hitting a woman dressed in jeans and a pair of Birkenstocks, with a long grey braid hanging down her back. She was walking a black-and-white cat on a leash and had chosen to cross the street, mid-block, in a diagonal fashion without looking either way.

A speeding white delivery van blasted her with his horn. She took no notice. As she ambled toward the second house from the corner, I recognized her as Patti Magliaro, one of the waitresses at Betty's, my favorite diner. Patti was one of the eternal hippies who popped up here and there in and around Woodbridge. Vague and ditsy, but part of the charm of our town.

I did a U-turn and caught up to her in front of the demolition site across the street from Emmy Lou's. I stopped the Miata and called out, "Hi, Patti!"

She blinked and then walked toward me, her Birkenstocks flapping against her bare heels. "Do I know you?"

"Charlotte Adams. I see you at Betty's all the time."

"Oh, didn't recognize you in the car. Club sandwiches, right?"

"That's me."

"And the devil's food special."

"Got me again."

"You look a bit different on the TV."

"Oh well," I said, "those weren't the best circumstances."

"Guess not. You looked taller for one thing."

I paused. "Really? Of course, I am sitting in the car."

"Yeah, and a lot meaner. Like really, really mean and—"

"Beautiful cat," I said. I didn't want to talk about why I'd been on television or how mean I looked now or then.

She lit up. "Princess is special. Everyone loves her."

"I bet. Do you live around here?"

"Yep. Lived here for more than twenty years. Number 13." She pointed to a grey two-story house with a crisply clipped hedge that shielded the view of the demolition site. "I have the upstairs apartment."

"I have an upstairs apartment too. In Jack Reilly's house," I said with a smile designed to make me seem less mean.

"Oh, Jack. Such a nice guy. I knew his folks. Real good people. That was a terrible shame about their accident. I remember when Jack was little and—"

Normally I'm not rude, but I cut in. "That reminds me. Do you know the people across the street?"

She blinked and started off again. "Most of them have been here forever: the Van Loons at the corner must be in their eighties, and the Mrazeks across the street can't be much younger, late seventies anyway. The people in number 14 are in Florida until the end of the month. My landlord Ralph is there too. He lives downstairs from me, and the people who bought 15 haven't moved in yet. There's a new couple in the blue house, number 12. They've only been there about a year. I know him, Bill something. I think she has MS."

"Bonnie and Bill Baxter."

"There's Mrs. Dingwall and Kevin in number 8. And I know Emmy Lou." She pointed across to the Rheinbecks' house. "She grew up in number 7. Of course, I didn't live here then."

This time Patti indicated the well-kept green house with the chain-link fence protecting a pristine garage from the demolition site. It had an oddly regimented garden. "When she got married last year, she moved back, across the street from her old home. That's unusual, isn't it? I've met her husband. He seems like a real gentleman. He's in the restaurant business too."

So Emmy Lou had grown up on Bell Street. That came as a surprise. Although it explained why she and Dwayne had poured a lot of money into a small house on a faded block that hadn't been discovered by the renovators. Yet.

I said, "Did she want to be near her parents?"

Patti twittered. "Probably wanted to thumb her nose at the two of them. Couldn't say I'd blame her. Pair of miserable cheap sourpusses."

Emmy Lou had mentioned that she'd never owned a stuffed animal as a child. There could be many reasons for that, including having parents who were miserable cheap sourpusses. Well, it didn't matter. I wasn't there to pry into Emmy Lou's history. I wanted to know if she'd be all right. "But at least they'd be there if she needed help."

Patti shook her head. The long silver braid swayed. "Doubt it. I don't think she's spoken to them since she first left home. And I bet that's mutual. Told you I was surprised that she moved back. But she could turn to any of the other folks on the street. From what I hear, everyone was crazy about Emmy Lou."

I could only imagine the life and energy Emmy Lou would have projected as a teenager. She would have been gorgeous and she would have lit up Bell Street. "I'm sure. You mentioned Mrs. Dingwall and Kevin. So you know him?"

"Sure, I've known Kevvie since he was this high." She gestured vaguely toward her knees.

"Do you think he's . . ." I searched my mind for a politically correct synonym for crazy and dangerous.

"Kevvie's okay. Not playing with a full deck, but he's sweet enough."

That was good. "He seems to be playing tricks on Emmy Lou. It's probably not my business, but Bill and Bonnie are worried about it."

"Who are Bill and Bonnie?"

"The people in the blue house on the right." I refrained from mentioning that I'd told her that a minute earlier. Her memory wasn't the best, perhaps because of a fondness for illegal herbs.

We both jumped aside as a dark-haired young man wearing a backward baseball cap whipped along the street on Rollerblades. He flipped a fast-food bag and an empty drink bottle into the Dumpster as he passed. We stared at the site.

"Ew!" she said. "I hate that. It's bad enough about all the dust from the demolition site, and the materials lying around, but people throw all kinds of garbage in that Dumpster. Even dog poop. It's supposed to be for construction debris. They only empty it every two weeks. Imagine what that will smell like by Friday. You know, these days—"

Time to get back on topic. "Kevin?" I said.

"Emmy Lou has nothing to worry about with Kevin. He loves her. It's that guy that's hanging around with him that makes my skin crawl."

"Tony?"

Patti hesitated. "Yeah. Tony Starkman. Tony's got a bad aura, for sure."

And I'd thought it was greasy hair. "Do you think he would do anything to harm her?"

"No, or I'd have had to do something about it." Patti knit her brow, obviously thinking hard about it now.

"Well?" I said after a long minute.

She said, "What do you think he might do?"

"No idea. I'm sort of reacting to the Baxters. They were agitated."

"Tell you what, I'll keep an eye out for her when I can. I'm not around that much, but the wife is there all the time. And the guy comes and goes from work."

"You're right. And there's Dwayne."

"Comes and goes too. He works downtown, not far at all. Anyway, it's not like Emmy Lou is among strangers. She probably knows everyone on this block. And I'll let her know she can call on me too."

"Thanks, Patti."

"Glad to help. Don't be a stranger now. Remember the devil's food special."

Something about the way Patti had hesitated when we were talking about Tony nagged at me on my drive home. I shook my head. I needed to get back. My dogs would be late for their afternoon walk. Everything was fine at the Rhein-becks. Dwayne was back in the house. And even when he was out, she could always call Bill and Bonnie if she needed help. Even if she couldn't count on her parents for some reason, she knew everyone on the street. Emmy Lou had been my client for less than an hour. In fact, I wasn't a hundred percent certain she was still a client. And I had no idea what the best course of action was. But I knew who would know.

Pepper Monahan, rising star in the Woodbridge Police, would be up on all the latest techniques for assessing risk in harassment. She'd been through some tricky situations herself. She'd climbed the ladder carefully, stepping on the fingers of some of the old boys as she went. And she'd defi-nitely had her share of bad stuff growing up. Too bad my former best friend wouldn't give me the time of day.

In the ongoing battles between Pepper and Charlotte,

let's say that I am the friendly person who wants to help other people live happier lives and Pepper is the ambitious police officer with the power to interrogate and arrest. I carry a to-do list. She carries a gun and a grudge along with her lip gloss.

But one of my principles is never to put off unappealing tasks.

I pulled over, picked up my cell phone, and called the Woodbridge Police. It's an easy number. I asked for Detective Sergeant Pepper Monahan. The desk sergeant put me through. I got Pepper's voice mail. It was hard to imagine, but her voice mail sounded even more intimidating than Pepper in person. I decided to try again later.

I left the wedding mice in the car. They'd been an unplanned acquisition, and I needed to find a place for them out of reach of Truffle and Sweet Marie before I brought them in. I hustled up the stairs to my apartment, trying to ignore the empty first floor. In the first six months after I returned to Woodbridge, I'd had plenty of time to get used to my old school friend and landlord, Jack. At the end of a typical day, Jack would be lying in wait to ask me about my day and attempting to relieve me of any surplus ice cream, chocolate, and good gossip I might have picked up. Of course, he always had an effective ploy.

At least once a week he'd try to entice me to take another foster dog from the canine rescue group he belongs to. He had effective ploys for that too, but I'd managed not to fall into his traps. He taught Truffle and Sweet Marie tricks and games. Their favorite was Where's Charlotte? That wasn't my preference since it involved me hiding behind doors or in the shower or on the stairs. Never mind, it beat their other fave game, Let's Hide Charlotte's Stuff.

But since Jack had opened CYCotics, the cycle shop of his dreams, he was no longer there to meet me when I got home. I felt a small pang every time I walked past his apartment and up the stairs to mine. I opened my door while holding my breath. I never quite knew what I was going to find.

"Hey, guys," I said, looking around.

Four beady black eyes regarded me with interest. I am the food lady and that's definitely cool. I put my keys in the container on the hall console. That was high enough to be out of their reach, unless Jack had popped in and moved a chair. I glanced around to see if the toilet paper had been unfurled throughout my tiny apartment. Nope. No mountains of white.

I peered into my bedroom. The closet door was closed, as I'd left it, so that meant my shoes and boots hadn't been hidden at the furthest point under the bed. Also good.

The cushions were on the sofa; no dishes lay on the floor. I smiled. Perhaps they were starting to settle in. They'd been with me the better part of a year, a pair of flea-bitten, half-starved siblings abandoned on the median of the interstate. Jack's rescue group had taken the time to clean them up, get them medical attention, and find them a foster mom to rehabilitate and housebreak them. Jack had set out to find a permanent home for them. The three of us owe him.

Our walk was speedy and efficient. The temperature had suddenly plummeted, and Truffle and Sweet Marie do not care for nippy spring afternoons. They are creatures made for summer.

Back in the apartment, I made a place for the wedding mice: the highest shelf in my cupboard. For all I knew Emmy Lou might demand their return. I spooned out dog food and fresh water. Then I left the pooches to it while I checked voice mail, e-mail, and snail mail. All right, I had no snail mail or e-mail, but I did have voice mail.

"Don't forget about tomorrow night," Margaret Tang's voice said.

Whatever happened to hello?

I blinked. I had already forgotten about tomorrow night. That's not like me. I'd obviously been distracted by the drama at Emmy Lou's. Did I have a consultation booked? Time to check my agenda. I keep only one and it's paper. Not fashion forward but it's easy, effective, and inexpensive. I reached for my purse.

Margaret continued. "But in case you have forgotten about it, tomorrow night is Sally's baby shower."

"Oops," I said out loud. "Of course. I knew that."

"I bet you didn't even remember."

"Yes, I did, Margaret," I said, feeling a bit ridiculous fibbing to the voice mail. I skipped the rest of the message and called her back.

She said, "I need your help. This is my first baby shower and—"

"Oh, it is *not*."

Margaret hesitated. "It is."

"Your first? How can that be?"

"Hey, listen, I've been working on getting a law degree and setting up a practice and I haven't been invited to any. I used to be a misfit, worked my way up to being a nerd, and now I'm a full-fledged wet blanket. That's my story and I'm sticking to it."

"But even if you are a wet blanket, not that I'm admitting that, you're good for some shower loot. You surprise me. Even in the city, I got invited to baby showers for people I'd never met. They usually took place the week before the person moved to a smaller community never to be seen again."

"Not that there's anything wrong with that," Margaret said.

"No, especially since that's what we did, moving back to Woodbridge. However, we were able to do it without having to actually produce a child."

"We always did pick the easy way."

"How can it be your first? Weren't you at any of the other showers for Sally? That's amazing."

"I hadn't moved back when Sally had her first three babies."

"Neither had I, but I was tracked down anyway. And NYC isn't that far away when there's a party to be had."

"So, what happens? Is it like in the movies?"

I hated to think about what movies Margaret was watching if they featured baby showers. "It's for Sally, so it will not follow any rules and it will be fun. And we bring something excellent to eat and a present for the munchkin-to-be and that's it. I have dibs on s'mores."

"No games?"

"Nope."

"No hats with bows on them?"

"Not on my watch. Nothing but good old-fashioned gossip, snacks, and laughs."

"Girls only?"

"For sure. That mixed shower trend hasn't hit Woodbridge yet. Anyway, since this is the fourth time, the girls consist of you and me and Sally. So not actually a shower, just an excuse to get together and give her a gift for the latest."

"I can deal with that."

"With your Ivy League education, you will rise to the occasion, challenging as it may be."

"Not so fast. It's the gift that's the hurdle. I have no idea what to get her. I don't know anything about babies. Can we get together to pick out something?"

"Okay. Lunch tomorrow. We'll go to Cuddleship. It will make a nice change from your usual criminal occupations."

"Don't be jealous," Margaret said, getting in the last word before she hung up. "We can't all be struggling lawyers in small towns. Which reminds me, time to get back to work."

Margaret might want to spend the weekend working, but I didn't. For one thing, my main task consisted of figuring out a solution to Emmy Lou's plush population explosion that didn't involve either of us resorting to sedatives. Even though in my business I often work on weekends when people are free, I never give up my Friday night. Friday night is for going out. Plans flexible. Dates optional. After all, I had the dogs.

But the Emmy Lou situation was nagging at me. Before I went anywhere, I tried Pepper's line again.

Damn voice mail.

Looked like I had no choice but to track her down. It was a few minutes after five o'clock. I knew that Pepper could be counted on to work long after hours. Ambition has its price. First I fixed my makeup, which is important when meeting your nemesis. I put on a pair of skinny jeans and a nifty little turquoise sweater that had been waiting for the right Friday-night occasion. I slipped on a pair of Steve Madden metallic high-platform shoes with an ankle strap. Finally I changed my earrings to giant silver hoops. You don't want to go head-to-head with Pepper without putting on your armor.

"Come on, poochies, we're going for a ride."

The dragon had left the den before I pulled up in front of the Woodbridge Police Station.

"You missed her," the desk sergeant said cheerfully, pointing toward the door. Something in his tone told me Pepper wasn't the sunniest disposition on the Woodbridge police force.

"Want to leave a message? I can put you through to her voice mail."

"Been there, thanks. I'll try later."

I pushed Emmy Lou and Pepper to the back of my mind. I needed a small dose of normal, uncomplicated happy human being. Someone cheerful and upbeat. Someone noticeably absent from my daily life since he'd opened his business.

Jack.

I climbed back into the Miata. Sweet Marie leapt into my lap, and Truffle jumped up and licked my ear. I was getting used to that. "Let's go see Jack."

On the way, I stopped at Tang's Convenience for a tub of Ben & Jerry's New York Super Fudge Chunk for me and a tub of Chunky Monkey for Jack. I picked up an extra Super Fudge Chunk in case Jack managed to steal mine. It wouldn't be the first time.

I selected some chew treats for the dogs. As usual, Mrs. Tang appeared not to recognize me. She took my money suspiciously, although she knew darn well I had been Margaret's very good friend for twenty years.

A white Ford Taurus was pulled up next to the Miata when I came out the door. Leaning against it, chatting to Margaret Tang, was Pepper.

"Hey," I said.

Margaret said, "Is my mother her usual merry self?"

Pepper nodded without smiling. "Charlotte."

She'd changed her hairstyle a bit. Usually it was a sleek blonde bob. Elegant to the point of chilliness. This new cut was layered and softer, with subtly different shades of blonde. Very nice. Not the kind of do you could get in the small city of Woodbridge. Pepper would have gone into the city for that. And she would have left a couple of hundred bucks behind her in the salon.

"You hung up on my voice mail," she said.

"Ah." I hadn't realized that she would know that.

"Twice. You have a new hobby wasting my time?"

"I didn't want to leave a message about this problem. It's probably nothing, but I needed a bit of advice." I wanted to shriek, "Don't curl your upper lip at me," but I kept my cool.

"And?"

"Okay, this might sound crazy, but I have a new client. She's a sophisticated, capable woman, maybe forty years old. Very attractive. During our consultation, two guys from next door climbed the tree outside her bedroom window and made noises and faces at her."

Pepper said, "Made faces?"

"Fine, I know that sounds stupid. But it was terrifying for her. They even had a camera and took at least one photo. The neighbors think these guys are stalking her. But my client refuses to call the police. She says one of them is a harmless kid. Her husband seems annoyed but not worried. I didn't know what to do. Maybe it's none of my business. But I can't let it go."

Pepper said, "Officially? Nothing we can do without a complaint from this woman."

"I wondered if—"

"Did it set off your alarm bells?"

"Oh yeah. It seemed creepy."

Pepper pursed her lips. "Sorry to let you down, but we can't go on a fishing expedition."

"Well, I guess *not*," Margaret said.

Pepper agreed. "I don't intend to harass innocent citizens."

"Good thinking," Margaret said.

I stared at her. How dumb was I? Margaret had set up her law practice in Woodbridge, and she would always keep an eye out for the rights of the accused. I hadn't mentioned Emmy Lou's situation to her. Too bad I'd run into the two of them together.

"You know, you might want to take a look at your taillight here, Charlotte," Pepper said. "You'll end up with a whopping ticket if you get stopped by the wrong cop."

I stepped to the back of the Miata with her.

"There's nothing wrong with my lights," I huffed.

"Keep your voice down. Give me the name of the guy and his address," Pepper said. "I'll see what I come up with."

"Oh right and—"

"And Margaret doesn't need to know everything."

I lowered my voice. "Okay. My client's at 10 Bell Street. Her name's Emmy Lou Rheinbeck. Her husband is Dwayne. The kid next door is Kevin something. Dingwall. That's it. And his friend is called Tony Starkman. Kevin lives at number 8, a grey house with a big front porch. The people on the other side of Emmy Lou are Bill and Bonnie Baxter. They think these guys are trouble. Of course, they're a bit odd themselves. Possibly paranoid."

I knew enough about Pepper's upbringing to guess how she'd react.

"Leave it with me."

"Thanks," I said in a normal tone. "I'll get that taillight looked after."

"You do that."

Margaret said, "Gotta go. See you tomorrow. Should be fun."

Pepper said, "What should be fun?"

I don't know who was the more surprised by that: Margaret or me.

Margaret said, "There's a baby shower for Sally."

"Sally's pregnant *again*?"

Margaret said, "One of these days they'll find out what's causing it."

"And there's a baby shower?"

"Not a real shower," I said, feeling dread creep over me.

"Charlotte's bringing s'mores," Margaret added. "I had no idea she could cook."

Pepper snorted and then said, "Is it a surprise?"

"Kind of. Benjamin's at some kind of medical conference, and Sally thinks we're dropping in to keep her company tomorrow night after the kids are in bed."

"Who's going?"

"Me, Margaret. That's it. The old gang of misfits."

Pepper looked me straight in the eye. "I was part of the old gang of misfits."

Who could forget that?

"So, maybe I'll come along to Sally's. It would be great to see her."

An odd expression flickered across Margaret's face, but quickly vanished.

I said, "Sure. That would be . . . fine. About seven."

I whirled as a granite-faced man approached the Taurus. He could only be a police officer. No one else in Woodbridge would be wearing a trench coat. He was carrying two cups of Stewart's coffee. He held one of the coffees out to Pepper.

"Later," she said to me.

"Trouble?" he said.

I answered, "Oh no, we're old—"

"No trouble," Pepper said. "Catching up on the news."

Pepper got back into the driver's side of the Taurus. Tall, dark, and granite took the passenger seat. I settled into the Miata and tried deep breathing. One of these days I will learn not to let Pepper ruin my evening.

Margaret remained standing at the door of Tang's Convenience. She watched the Taurus spin off. She hustled back toward me. "Oh my God. That guy was so hot."

"He was?"

"You didn't think so?"

"Definitely not my type. He's quite a bit older, no?"

"Don't be ageist. And I thought you didn't have a type."

"Thanks for reminding me." I was taking a break from men, particularly handsome ones, for various reasons.

Margaret said, "Maybe he's Pepper's type."

"Come on, Margaret. She's married to Nick Monahan. She's been crazy about him since forever, not that anyone can understand it. She didn't give this guy the time of day. He's good for fetching coffee. Nick. Nick. Nick. Nick's so this. Nick's so that. Nick's such a good driver. Nick's such a marksman. Nick's blah, blah, blah. Who could forget that?"

"It doesn't matter whether I remember Nick the Stick. It's if Pepper does."

I climbed into the car and turned the key. "I can't imagine why she wouldn't. Of course, Nick is dumb as a rope, vain, and a total womanizer. Aside from that he's the perfect husband. Except I'm pretty sure he doesn't pull his weight around the house."

"Exactly. And did you see how that guy looked at her?"

"Like she was a double-fudge glazed doughnut and he hadn't eaten in a week?"

"I was thinking more like if she was a tub of Ben & Jerry's and he was you."

"Doesn't matter. The less I have to do with Pepper the better, and that includes speculating about her personal life."

"We're jealous because she has one. But we're going to have to think about her."

"What do you mean?"

"She wants to come to Sally's shower. That will change our dynamic."

I found myself chewing my lower lip yet again. Pepper had arrested me last fall and done her best to make sure the charges stuck. On the other hand, for all of my teens she'd been my best friend. And she had offered to check out the Emmy Lou problem. Part of me wanted to get that friendship back. That was my heart talking. My brain knew that Pepper was too volatile.

I said, "I don't believe she'll show up. She was bluffing to see our reactions."

"Hope you're right, because if she does show up tomorrow night, who are we going to trash-talk?"

When a new issue of a magazine arrives,
get rid of the oldest one.
If you haven't read it by now, you're not going to.
But someone will be glad to get it.

4

In the last few years, artists and young entrepreneurs have flowed into Woodbridge, picking up bargain real estate and bringing life to the town. For the first time since the collapse of SundNor Technologies in the eighties, Woodbridge was booming. Why not? Less than two hours from New York City and you could afford a "loft" conversion on the water. You could walk to your choice of restaurants, bistros, and bars. Or hit the Hudson in your kayak after work. What's not to love?

On a typical Friday night people jam the cafés and this one was no different. The Woodbridge boom was surely fueling Dwayne Rheinbeck's restaurant success. I wondered which of the many new spots was his.

On the other hand, Jack's cycle shop lurks in the middle of an untrendy strip on Long March Road halfway between the uptown action and the downtown trendiness. His strategy: large space, easy parking, cheap rent, and a huge storefront window that makes CYCotics easy to spot on your way to somewhere else. Bright young guys with BlackBerries are Jack's targets for his pricey European bicycles. He also keeps an eye out for aging boomers with empty nests and full wallets.

Despite the trends, CYCotics is never jammed. Not that it matters. Jack has enough of an inheritance from his parents to weather the growing pains. I worry about location, location, location, and lack of same. If Jack's bicycles don't sell, he can always market optimism. Which is a good thing.

I arrived in a surly post-Pepper mood. Truffle and Sweet Marie were in charge of happy. Jack worked alone, hunkered down next to boxes of Italian bike parts that must have arrived on the late Friday delivery. For once, he didn't have a foster dog with him. He stood up and grinned, resplendent in his yellow and green Hawaiian shirt. I won't say anything about the baggy khaki shorts.

"Hey," he said.

"Hey. I thought we could give you a hand with all these boxes. Oh wow. It's cluttered in here. How is anybody going to get to the cash register with all these obstacles in the way? How about if I—"

A crash from the rear of the shop told me that the dogs had knocked over a tower of boxes. From the sound of it, there was metal in those boxes. Both dogs came racing back to the front, tails tucked between legs.

"I have to do this stuff myself, Charlotte. I need to check out the items, figure out where they're going, or if they're what I ordered. Reconcile orders with invoices and invoices with contents. Then match them up with the right customers."

"Speaking of customers, I notice you don't have any. This is not surprising. How is anybody going to find this place?" I said. "It's not like people are going to walk by."

Jack gave me a puzzled look. "It's a destination store."

"Is that why it's empty?" I said.

"Hey, who's a bossy little organizer tonight? Got some problem you want to get off your chest? Or did you come over to rain on my parade?"

"Sorry, Jack. I ran into Pepper again and I was taking it out on you."

Jack looked me straight in the eye. "You've been home long enough now. You should be getting used to Pepper."

"I should be, but I'm not."

"*Okay*. Have some ice cream. You'll feel better."

"Maybe."

"And CYCotics isn't empty. Not when you and your dogs and Ben & Jerry are here. Even if you are whiny and grumpy."

"Mmm."

The ice cream calmed me down. Or maybe it was Jack. Whining and bad moods don't stick to him. Somehow this is catchy.

"So," he said, "how come Pepper upset you so much this time?"

"It's a long story."

"Like you said, no customers here. Start talking."

"I have to begin at the beginning." Jack's always patient, so I took a deep breath and filled him in, from the Emmy Lou situation to the encounter with Pepper outside of Tang's. "So I didn't want to leave that kind of message with names and everything and she was ticked off that I hung up on her machine, but anyway, when Margaret wasn't listening, Pepper said that she'd look into it."

"That is a long story, but I must have missed something, because I don't see any reason to be upset with Pepper. Is that because I'm a guy? And we don't understand stuff?"

"I didn't finish my long story yet. The worst part was that Margaret blabbed about Sally's shower and now Pepper wants to show up and ruin everything."

Jack's spoon paused midway to his next mouthful of Chunky Monkey. "Sally's having a shower?"

"Yeah."

"No one told me."

"Listen, Jack. You're a guy. You admitted it."

"Who's organizing this shower?"

"Margaret. And me."

"And who's going?"

"Margaret. And me. Sally too, of course. And, now, apparently Pepper."

"Huh."

"What do you mean, 'huh'?"

"You know what I mean. 'Huh' is fairly unequivocal."

I shook my head. " 'Huh' can mean anything."

Jack said, "In this case it means that I go every bit as far back with Sally and Margaret and Pepper as you do. But I don't rate an invitation."

"But I told you it's girls only."

"You'd rather have Pepper than me?"

"Of course not. You're not scary, not even a little bit. And you're my best buddy. You are so good to me. But as I keep explaining, you are also a *guy*."

"Got a calendar on you?"

"Why?"

"I wanted to check the century, that's all. I thought it was the twenty-first. But I could be wrong on that. You know how vague I am."

"Fine, it's nothing to do with equality of the sexes, but if it makes you happy, you can come to the stupid shower."

"Great, thanks. The more the merrier. Hey, what happens at a shower anyway?"

"We were going to talk girl talk and eat and give Sally something for the new baby. It's not even a proper shower."

"Now we have to talk people talk."

"Exactly. And a word of warning, Jack. That means no, count 'em, no sports references, including cycling statistics of *any* kind, and, do not slip up here, not one single reference to obscure European thinkers of the nineteenth century. Also, a little bit about rescued dogs will go a long way."

Jack said, "But what if—"

"No buts, no what-ifs. It's the price of admission, Jack."

"I can do that. So was that all that was bothering you? Because if it was, maybe you need more of a life, Charlotte."

I considered that. I was eating Ben & Jerry's out of the container in a cycle shop with my old school friend and a pair of dogs. On Friday night. "I guess I always overreact about Pepper. Thanks for pointing that out."

"Maybe it's time to put the past behind you."

"Maybe. But it was more than Pepper. I am bothered by this situation with my client."

"Professional organizing is a pretty safe occupation. You know that. As a rule, I'd say your biggest danger is developing a dust allergy."

I nodded.

Jack continued. "Last fall was an anomaly. It's unlikely that you'll have another project where people die. You don't need to worry so much. Don't get me wrong. You did the ethical thing to contact the police about this. I'm proud of you. And you can talk to your client again when you see her next."

"If."

"You said you spoke to her husband. And he's there tonight?"

"I think so. And the neighbors are on the alert."

"So tomorrow talk to her about keeping safe."

"I realize there's not much I can do, but I can't stop worrying about Emmy Lou. She's such a big, strong, capable, lovely woman, and yet, underneath, she seems frightened and vulnerable. You and Pepper weren't there. You didn't see the effect this stupid joke had on her. And she was already pretty nervous. I have a bad feeling about it."

"I hear you. Where's the shower tomorrow?"

I sighed. "Sally's place, after the kids are in bed."

<hr>

Okay. Friday night. Ten thirty. Spring was in the air. What could be better? Well, almost anything if you have enough residual adrenaline in your system and no outlet for it.

After I left Jack at the shop, dealing with some inventory horror story, I whipped through my apartment like an undone balloon. I did the kind of things that I usually enjoy. I cleaned my winter boots and packed them away. I updated my contact list. I made a schedule to call back potential clients. I looked over my strategic business plan to see if I was meeting my benchmarks. I checked that my spices were still in alphabetical order.

The list of projects I had scheduled after Emmy Lou included the usual garages in disarray, estates needing to be sorted out, family rooms with no room for the family, and home offices drowning in seas of paper, technology, and wayward wires. My bread and butter. I love that stuff. I enjoy helping people get their homes or businesses back on track. I bask in the gratitude of clients. I had one client waiting to have her linen closet overhauled, a small but amusing job. I could slot her in ahead of schedule if Emmy Lou decided to stall.

Once Emmy Lou's project was over, everything else looked promising. But of course, I was bugged by this one. Not the toys. Every week I dealt with far worse than that. Plus Emmy Lou knew she had a problem. That was half the battle. Sure she had zillions of plush toys, but they were new, clean, and indoors. There might have been a few on the stairs, but they didn't block fire exits. They didn't involve crawling through basements, or getting rid of the dusty detritus of a lifetime. There were no rodents except for the stuffed ones in the box in the Miata. Emmy Lou's collection didn't stink of mildew or worse. Piece of cheesecake, I would have said normally.

But something was out of kilter at the Rheinbecks'. It didn't seem to be the stuffies. After a lot of thought I had to admit it was Emmy Lou herself. That mass of emotion under her elegant exterior wasn't about the toys. It wasn't because she was worried about Dwayne. I sat back on my sofa, closed my eyes, and tried to relive the afternoon at her home. I recalled the nervous tic below her eye. The way her gaze jumped from one spot to another. The fact she couldn't sit still even in her lovely, tranquil living room. The way she insisted that Dwayne lock the doors.

Emmy Lou was scared to death of something. Could it be Kevin and Tony? They seemed hopeless and goofy, yet she'd flipped when they showed their faces in the window. Because they had been harassing her? Or was it something else?

Whatever was wrong, Emmy Lou was taking it very seriously. I decided that I'd better too.

※

By midnight, I was huddled under a quilt with the dogs. At least they were able to sleep. I was worrying. And I'd moved on to worrying about why I was worrying so much.

When Truffle signaled that he might need a midnight outing for personal reasons, I thought it might be a relief to catch a bit of fresh air. And I could pick up those stuffed rodents from the Miata and put them on the shelf. No point in procrastinating about that. Once the project was over, if Emmy Lou didn't demand them back, I could donate them to a day care or a shelter.

"Come on, guys. One last walk before bedtime." I threw a fleece jacket on over my Kermit pajamas, grabbed my keys, and thudded downstairs in my fluffy pink slippers. I tucked one dog under each arm. They played along, acting like overcooked noodles.

After the briefest of dog business, I unlocked the Miata and reached for the box with the romantic rodents. I hesitated. What the heck. I couldn't sleep anyway.

I tucked the dogs into the passenger seat. They curled up and were asleep before I climbed in and shot off into the night. By the time I reached Bell Street, I was having third thoughts. How could my life have changed like this? Once I was a hip young financial analyst in the city, eating in trendy restaurants, meeting friends in the hot clubs, shown off by my studly fiancé. Now I'd turned into a wacky woman in Kermit pajamas, curb-crawling along a residential street looking for trouble.

A lot can change in a year.

I geared down and rolled along the street. The downstairs lights were out in Emmy Lou's house. Dim lights glowed from the upstairs windows.

Normal, normal, normal.

Unlike me.

Time to head home to bed. As I pulled away from the curb, a large shadow loomed out of the side yard to the left of Emmy Lou's house. Make that two shadows, one large and one scrawny, both wearing baggy pants, giant runners, and dark hoodies, with the hoods covering the back of their heads. I couldn't see faces. I squinted as the shadows moved along the sidewalk. Kevin and Tony? Would they turn into Kevin's house?

They turned right toward Emmy Lou's.

I exhaled. Nothing to get excited about. Two young men walking along the sidewalk in a neighborhood at just after midnight on a weekend. No big deal. They weren't trying to be furtive, for sure. The larger one had a swagger and the scrawny guy more of a scurrying walk. Every now and then Big would slap Scrawny on his skinny back.

I drove along, picking up speed as I went. I glanced into the rearview mirror as I passed them. They paused under a street lamp. I got a clear view of Kevin's pinched face and Tony's thuggish features. Where were they off to? To frighten some other woman?

Tony was laughing, and for some reason I felt a rush of rage. Emmy Lou was miserable, her neighbors worried, her husband on edge. I was having a craptacular Friday night and why? Because of these two losers and their stupid frightening games at her expense.

I slammed on the brakes at the corner and gunned the Miata

in reverse. To hell with the engine. I rolled down the window as I reached them. Kevin jumped backward and shrieked when I called his name.

At the sound of my voice, Truffle and Sweet Marie woke up barking.

Kevin jerked around, then broke into an awkward dash across Emmy Lou's lawn.

He might have kept running, but Tony shouted, "It's all right, Kevin."

Don't be so sure, I thought.

As soon as they caught sight of Tony, the dogs added snarling and teeth baring to their look. They hate hats and hoods.

Kevin edged back toward the sidewalk. His long baggy pants and supersize running shoes made him seem even more awkward.

"This message is for you too, Tony," I said.

Kevin said, "What do you want?"

"I want you both to know that Emmy Lou might let you get away with harassment, but other people won't. Not only the Baxters, but anyone who finds out about what you're doing."

Kevin said, "But what are we doing?"

"The police know about you and that stunt in the tree outside Emmy Lou's bedroom window."

Kevin stammered, "Hey, that was a joke."

"And they know you had a camera. Maybe this would be a good time for you two to visit the library and learn a bit about the laws on stalking."

Tony said, "The library? But—"

"Or maybe you have a probation officer."

Kevin's chin trembled. "We don't have probation officers."

"If you don't have one now, there's one in your future if you don't leave her alone. There are very serious penalties."

Kevin squeaked, "I wouldn't do anything to Emmy Lou. Neither would Tony."

Under normal circumstances I might have believed him. But I had witnessed the so-called joke and seen the impact it had on her.

I said, "Leave her alone. Or you will be very, very sorry."

I'm not sure if they even heard me, but as I revved the engine, I could see the whites of their eyes.

A man strolling on the other side of the street ignored me and turned into the green house with the garden. The porch light switched off. Patti Magliaro was walking toward her house. She must have been getting home from her shift at Betty's. The diner stays open late on Fridays. She stopped and waved.

I waved back, a surprisingly ordinary gesture considering what I'd done. For some reason, my Ms. Rambo routine had made me feel worse. But at least I'd achieved something.

Kevin and Tony had both been nicely frightened.

5

Emmy Lou called Saturday morning while I was at the dog park. She left a message about scheduling another session. I returned her call and got her answering machine. I suggested that she call me on Sunday to set up another appointment.

My first commitment was shopping for the so-called baby shower. Under normal circumstances, I would see if the mom-to-be was registered and save time getting something she'd selected. But it wasn't a real shower, and anyway, Sally doesn't believe in registries. She likes surprises much more than I do. Maybe that's why she was about to have her fourth child.

Cuddleship is a fine location for anyone who wants something out of the ordinary. Margaret had never seen anything like it. She was waiting for me when I arrived.

She gazed around the shop in wonderment. "I can't believe places like this exist. Everything in here is the exact opposite of the way I was raised."

"What do you mean?"

"Extravagant, indulgent, amusing." She looked down. "Speaking of which, nice ankle boots, Charlotte. I like the black leather bows." She managed the compliment with her usual lack of facial expression. No legal opponent's ever going to read Margaret's mind. But lately, she's become chattier. That's a good thing.

"These boots were a replacement for my red stilettos. I miss those. I may never get over their loss, but I thought these might come close to mending my broken heart."

"Whatever it takes. What about these little pajamas? What do they call them?"

"Sleepers. And no thanks, I think I'll stick with the shoes."

"Very funny, Charlotte. I meant for Sally's baby shower."

"I knew that. But a person has to work hard to find humor in a baby shower."

Margaret said, "I don't know what to get her. It's not like she needs anything. And Benjamin brings home the bacon."

"And Sally likes to laugh, so no pajamas. Fun gifts only."

Margaret reached up to a high shelf. "What about those little yellow ducks for the bathtub? I never had anything like that when I was small."

"You're kidding. What did you have in your baths?"

Margaret said, "My mother didn't believe in baths. Waste of water. Showers only."

"Huh."

"It's one of the reasons I appreciate having my own place. Bubble bath, scented bath oil, refreshing bath crystals, candles. Not that I don't get pressure to move back in with the folks."

"Don't give in. Especially if you've gotten used to taking baths."

She gave the largest duck a little squeeze and chortled. "Among other things. Yes, I think these ducks will do the trick."

"Sally's kids already have some. Why don't you get them for yourself?"

"I have to get the shower gift out of the way before I pick out anything for me."

"Why are you obsessing about the shower? It's an excuse to get together and eat."

She rolled her eyes. "It's the whole baby thing, I guess. That's all my parents can think about: get Margaret married so they can have grandchildren. I told them I had to work tonight so I could get away from family dinner. Even though I have my own place, Mom will be checking anyway. I'll call forward my office number to throw her off. She has boundary issues."

"Apparently. Couldn't you tell them the truth?"

"No *way*. I could never mention a baby shower. Babies are their big agenda. I never use the words 'man', 'male', 'married', 'baby', or 'child' in front of them. I can't bring myself to joke about it."

I hoped my full opinion wasn't written across my face. "I'm surprised that your mother wants grandchildren."

Margaret raised an eyebrow. "You mean, since she's about as nurturing as a block of ice?"

"I didn't say that."

"I would definitely say it. Your mother is glamorous and fun and interesting. She always let you get away with anything you wanted."

"There are two sides to that, you know."

"Like the great trips you had to Europe and getting out of school and not having a curfew?"

"How about all the divorces and never meeting my father and never knowing when she was going to be home and all that?" I sputtered.

"Count your blessings. At least she's not hounding you to reproduce."

I had to laugh out loud at that. "And she never will. She'd hate the idea that anyone would think she was a grandmother. All that Botox wasted. But your mother was different. Her family was everything to her."

"Overbearing? Traditional? Controlling?"

I lowered my voice, as other people in Cuddleship seemed to find our conversation fascinating. "I don't want to argue about which one of us has the most dysfunctional mother, because I will win, hands-down, every time."

Margaret nodded. "Sally and I would dispute that. The only one of us who had a normal home was Jack."

"Speaking of Jack, he's talked his way into the shower."

She dropped the yellow ducky. "What? Jack's coming?"

"He pointed out that he's one of Sally's oldest and dearest friends. It's going to be Sal, you, me, and Jack. And possibly Pepper."

"I thought you said it was girls."

"It was until I stupidly told Jack that Pepper might be there. He's never been to a shower either. Apparently, that bothered him. Anyway, it will be like old times."

Margaret said, "You mean back when we the biggest losers at St. Jude's?"

"Exactly."

"That's cool. I can handle it." She reached to the back of a shelf with pastel fuzzy animals on it and snatched one. "What about this floppy bunny?"

"Nah."

"But it's so cute. And it's completely useless." She stroked its ears.

I said, "After yesterday, plush toys are off limits. You heard about my project."

"The guys in the window sound weird, and your client does too, actually. But, in fairness, the stuffed animals themselves seem pretty harmless."

"Maybe."

"You don't think Pepper will show up tonight, do you?"

"She's bluffing to see if she can get under my skin. She hates me, remember? She's ticked off that she didn't get to keep me in jail."

"Okay. I didn't mean to upset you. Your face is all—"

"I'm going to get this collection of Beatrix Potter books. Look, *Jemima Puddle-Duck*! And *Mrs. Tiggy-Winkle*. All the kids will like that. Sally too."

"You're upset." Margaret hadn't let go of that bunny.

"Fine. I suffered at her hands, remember? And I think you should get those blocks over there instead of that ridiculous rabbit."

She raised her voice. "The blocks are boring. And it's not your fault Pepper's slimy husband has the hots for you after all these years."

I glanced around in a panic. I whispered, "Please don't say that, Margaret. What if someone hears you?"

"You mean Pepper? She's not here."

"Everyone knows her." And everyone in the shop was definitely listening.

"Funny, I don't remember you being paranoid before."

Time for a distraction. "People change. How about this crib mobile? The ladybugs are great."

"Whatever. Back to Nick the Stick. I saw him make the moves on you in the police station the last time we were there."

"I've never encouraged him even if she believes I did. And I do everything to avoid him. Let's finish up here. I'm getting the Beatrix Potter books. I've got to arrange the s'mores too."

"Arrange the s'mores? Aren't they the easiest thing in the world to make?" Margaret picked up the bunny and made for the cashier.

Sometimes a little lawyer goes a long way.

———— ✷ ————

By seven, the gift was wrapped and the card signed. I'd thrown in a set of washable bath crayons for the other kids. I figured the phone call was Margaret ready to be picked up.

"This is Emmy Lou Rheinbeck. I'd like to apologize for yesterday."

"Please don't; you have nothing to apologize for."

"I do. I had a ridiculous overreaction to a silly prank. I think my emotions had more to do with anxiety about dealing with my collection than anything else. I am sorry to have wasted your time. And I was rude to you too. Naturally, I'll pay you for that visit. I'd like you to come again. This time will go better. I guarantee no stalling on my part. And no panic. That's a promise."

I said, "Don't worry about it. Panic and stalling are part of the process. And you'll be glad to know they're purely temporary. But I have to admit I was worried about Kevin and Tony. Your neighbors Bill and Bonnie were too."

She sighed. "Bill is such an old woman, and poor Bonnie's fragile, so easily upset. I know these boys. They don't."

Bonnie was easily upset? Emmy Lou had been a zombie yesterday after the bedroom window incident. But I bit my tongue.

Emmy Lou talked on. "And I feel much more in control today. So could you come by?"

"Definitely."

"Wonderful. I'll put the coffee on. Unless you'd prefer a glass of wine."

"Oh, you mean *now*?"

"Of course."

"Sorry, Emmy Lou, but I'm on my way out to a baby shower."

Disappointment dripped over the phone line. "It won't take long, a few minutes to decide on the next steps. Before I lose my nerve."

"I wish I could," I said firmly. I was remembering how Emmy Lou liked to have her own way. "I'm picking someone up in a couple of minutes. She's probably standing outside waiting for me. And we're bringing the food."

"Oh. We must meet on the weekend, because I'm often at the office late weekdays. Friday was an anomaly."

My call-waiting beeped and I saw Margaret's cell phone number appear on the display. Time to go. "That's fine. How about tomorrow?"

"I guess that will have to do." Someone was pouting, for sure.

"I'm glad you reconsidered. Name the time," I said.

"How about midafternoon. Two thirty?"

"I'll be there. Looking forward to it."

"Thank you." Despite the thank-you, Emmy Lou's voice carried the disappointment of a woman who'd had her Saturday-night organizing session squashed.

On the upside, she sounded firm and strong and back in control. I decided she didn't need me worrying about her.

———

I had managed to wedge the gift, the basket with the graham crackers, chocolate, and marshmallows, and, of course, the dogs into the Miata when my cell phone rang.

"Dallas is throwing up," Sally shrieked. "And Madison and Savannah are starting to complain about their tummies."

Howls and wails echoed on the line.

"Oh boy. What can I do?"

"Nothing, thanks, Charlotte. But it won't be a good night here. I'll be doing the bucket-and-mop routine. And the kids will need my attention. We'll get together when they're better."

"I'll call Margaret. Let me know if you need anything. I'll come by."

A loud wail erupted in the background. Sally said, "Nope. It's probably wildly contagious. I don't want you on my conscience. Gotta go." She hung up with a clatter.

"That was a close call," Margaret said when I reached her. "Imagine if we'd been there. Yuck."

"No kidding." Of course, poor Sally was there, without any help.

"I can use the time at the office. Let me know when the

new night is. Oh yeah, and, Charlotte, are you going to call
Pepper?"

I left a message for Pepper saying that the so-called shower
had been postponed. As soon as I hung up, I realized that Pepper might not get that message from her work phone in time.
That is if she intended to go to Sally's. Maybe she'd been
yanking my chain. She does like that game.

Now what?

Once I'd known Pepper's home number by heart. But
now I had no idea what it was. I figured most police officers
don't list their phone numbers for obvious reasons. They
don't want perpetrators to have their addresses. But I knew
where Pepper lived. Nick Monahan had told me one time
when he'd spotted me before I spotted him. He'd leaned in,
stared down the front of my blouse, and breathed the news
as I backed away from him. That was Nick. The perennial
horny adolescent. Only now he and Pepper had bought a
house on Old Pine Street.

"How about that," I'd said. "Just like a grown-up."

"I hear ya," he'd said with a sigh. "I'm not so crazy about
the house thing. But Pepper sure wanted it. And what
Princess Pepper wants . . ."

My eyes had already glazed over when he told me about
the separate lot and the double garage he'd had specially
built for his car and his truck. "That's the reason I went for
the place. Got it all," he said. "Made of brick. Motion detec-
tors. Dead bolts. Video surveillance. Alarms. No son of a
bitch is going to mess with my blah, blah, blah . . . Anytime
you want a drive, Charlie, let me know." He waggled his eyebrows.

As if I could give a crap about Nick the Stick's Mustang
convertible and his Dodge Ram and his fear that they would
be stolen from under his nose. All to say, I'd missed the detail
about the house number in the fog of boring words.

The good news was, I was sure I could figure out which
one it was. This was a pleasant but ordinary street. How

many houses would have a separate lot with a brick garage with such elaborate security on them? I could swing by the new house on Old Pine and tell Pepper. I wouldn't have to let her know how I knew where she lived or that Nick had told me about his precious garage and big toys and asked me for a drive. Any word that I'd been within a block of Nick might set her off. If she wasn't home, I could leave a note. I was pretty sure she wouldn't have shown up at Sally's anyway, but this way I could pretend to be nice. Or at least nicer than I was.

———

Pepper was wearing a pricey pair of skinny jeans and a cream cashmere sweater when she answered the door. Her shiny blonde layers looked perfect. She was heading somewhere, for sure.

I was glad I'd taken the time to put on capris and a filmy flowered blouse.

"Nice place," I said politely.

"What are you doing here?"

"The shower's been postponed. I wanted to let you know. You'd said you might come by."

Her lip curled perceptibly. *"Postponed?"*

"Sally's kids are sick."

"The kids are sick? Is it serious?"

"A tummy bug, I think. But she needs to be with them. Anyway, she wouldn't feel much like partying when the little guys are hurling. And she said it might be contagious."

Pepper made a face. Unconvinced.

"We're disappointed too. We'll reschedule," I said. "Do you want us to let you know when?"

"Whatever."

"I'll call you and you can see if it, um, fits your schedule."

Her eyes narrowed, more dangerously this time. "How did you know where I lived?"

"Someone told me you bought a house near here. I was

worried you'd drive out to Sal's. Anyway, I recognized your car in the driveway." Close enough to the truth. "While I'm here, I wondered if you followed up on those two guys next door to Emmy Lou Rheinbeck."

She frowned. "Of course I did. There's nothing in the system about either one of them. Not as adults anyway. Not so much as a traffic ticket. Nada."

"I guess that's good news."

"Could be they haven't crossed the line yet."

"Thanks for checking. And caring about it." For a fleeting moment I catapulted back in time, back to when Pepper was my best friend and there was nothing we wouldn't have done for each other.

I swallowed. After a silence that was beyond awkward, I turned to go.

"Charlotte?"

I turned back. "Yes?"

"Let me know if anything more happens there."

"Thanks. I hope I'm not wasting your time. Today my client insists it was a joke. Says she's not worried."

"I'll see that there are a few more patrols on the street."

I nodded. "I appreciate this, Pepper. Thank you for taking it seriously."

She nodded. Mrs. Tough Guy.

"I'll call you when the coast is clear for Sally's. Look forward to seeing you there."

"Yeah. I'd like that." A half smile formed.

From the back of the house, I heard a rumbled question. "Who's there, sugar?"

You can always count on Nick the Stick to ruin a beautiful moment.

The half smile vanished.

"Nobody," Pepper said as she shut the door in my face.

6

Oh terrific. So now a nothing Saturday night was about to follow my dreary Friday. Was this what being single and thirty was all about? Where was the fun, the glamour, the nights to remember? I was determined not to crap out on this night too.

I called Jack to say the sort of shower was canceled. And to suggest that we eat out somewhere fun. Before I could make the suggestion, he said, "Sorry to hear about the rug rats being sick, but I just got a call from WAG'D. They need someone to drive a Great Dane to a foster home in Poughkeepsie. I'm the only one available."

I knew that nothing came between Jack and his canine-rescue volunteer stuff. Welcome All Great Dogs, better known as WAG'D, could always count on him. I also knew there'd be no room in Jack's ancient mud-colored Mini Minor for me plus the Great Dane.

Never mind.

I called Margaret's office to suggest that, on sober second

thought, it wasn't such a terrific idea for her to work. I suggested dinner at Wet Paint. I'd wanted to go there since it opened. Supposed to be a very hot atmosphere with cool jazz, intriguing art on the walls, and sometimes a chance to meet the musician or the artist.

I left that as a message. That's the thing about Saturday night. If your plans fall through and you don't have a plan B, it's a night of voice mail hell for you.

Perhaps Margaret had been captured by the folks and dragged off to a combined family dinner and baby propaganda session. In which case her Saturday night would be spent in a lower circle of hell than mine. Although not quite as low as Sally's.

I called Sally.

"Can I help? Do laundry? Let you rest? Pick up a new DVD?"

"Thanks, Charlotte, but you'd better stay away."

Fine. Maybe Sunday would be the new Saturday. Meanwhile, I had stuff to do.

First I researched stalkers. After all, what did I know about this phenomenon? After prowling on the Web for a while, I was more worried than ever about the connection between stalking and violence. I took some comfort in a description of a type of stalker with poor social skills and sometimes limited intelligence who selected targets, hoping to form a relationship. Apparently, this type had, in addition to inappropriate behavior, a short attention span and could move on quickly when things didn't work out. Which they wouldn't. Tony and Kevin might fit that profile, I thought, although it wasn't clear which one thought he'd win Emmy Lou's heart by making faces in her bedroom window.

Of course, I'm not a psychologist and you can't trust everything you read online. I knew that I needed to talk to people who actually worked in the field. Pepper wouldn't want to hear from me again, and anyway, she was aware and stepping up patrols. I called an acquaintance who was a social worker and another woman who was the administrator at a shelter to see if they could offer advice. Voice mail again. Naturally on the weekend.

I made a note to ask my librarian friend, Ramona, to do a literature search for me when the library opened on Monday. Why hadn't I done that earlier in the day when she would have been in the reference department? I gave myself a mental kick.

It was now nearing seven and I had nothing better to do than work. Of course, I'd caught up on that the night before. But there was one thing I could do. I put aside my concerns about Kevin and Tony and gave some serious thought to Emmy Lou's organization problem. I decided to draw up a plan. Plans are my best thing. Normally I would have had one ready by now, but normal seemed to have flown out the window.

Once I had a commitment from her, we'd need to sort and pack up the plush multitudes before reorganizing her space to display the special ones and set up some kind of storage for the overflow. Then there would be the dreaded decision about which, if any, to discard. I reminded myself to bring man-size tissues.

Emmy Lou was a busy executive, and I had only one pair of hands. Emmy Lou would make the decisions. I would coach. Someone would have to pick up the bins and haul off the surplus to the Goodwill and the local shelter. We'd probably need to consider installing custom shelves, display cases, or a more complex storage system. I would suggest my friend, Gary Gigantes, a carpenter who was as reasonable and unflappable as he was meticulous. Margaret and I always said, too bad he was married. I in turn would point out that he was also fifty-eight years old. Margaret would merely shrug.

Emmy Lou and I would sort out who would do what when we agreed to go ahead. Meanwhile, I called the perfect ally for the sort, pack, and move portion: Lilith Carisse.

To my amazement, she answered her cell phone.

"It's Charlotte. Are you free?" I said.

"Finished my shift at the nursing home."

"I have a little job for you."

Lilith is putting herself through college by working a variety of jobs, some odder than others. She solved her rent problem when she moved in with our friend Rose Skipowski. Now Rose has live-in care with Lilith, and Lilith has a whole floor to herself and all the cookies she could ever eat. Jack's last foster dog, Schopenhauer, has found a permanent home with one disabled dog lover and one lively young dog walker. Win-win.

"Whatcha got?"

"It will take a bit to explain it." Not strictly speaking true. I could have summarized the whole thing efficiently in two dozen words. But it was getting late. I was getting hungry. Plus I enjoyed Lilith's company and I knew she was broke. "How about trying Wet Paint? I've been wanting to go there."

"Are you kidding? I can't afford that."

"It's my treat. Part of the job."

"Don't feel sorry for me. I can pay my own way, if it's Mickey D's or Betty's even."

"I make it a policy not to feel sorry for starving students who are working three part-time jobs. Since I want to get a little information and advice from you, I should be willing to pay for dinner. No?"

"Information?"

"When we get there."

Lilith Carisse usually makes an impact in public. It used to be because she had purple hair, but now that she has turquoise and black hair in stubby ponytails, it is more the nose ring and the face piercings. Or perhaps the tattoos. I don't care. It's what's inside that counts. And behind that metal and those tattoos, Lilith is kind and honest with a marshmallow center.

At Betty's Lilith draws stares the way a porch light draws moths. In Wet Paint she didn't raise an eyebrow.

"So, Lilith," I said when we took stainless and leather chairs in the corner, near a glowing red wall, "how would you like to get paid to play with stuffed animals for a couple of days?"

"Sounds good. I'm trying to build my tuition fund. I've been offered an extra shift for a couple of weeks in the cafeteria of the nursing home. They find it hard to get people to work on the weekend. And Jack said he could use some more help at the bike shop. But this sounds a lot more fun. Are you flexible about the hours?"

"Sure. Here's the situation. My client, Emmy Lou, has an incredible number of stuffed animals. We're talking thousands. They're taking over her house. They've captured the bed, and if she's not careful, they'll move downstairs and maybe even follow her to her office."

"Like science fiction."

"She wants them organized."

"I'll bet she does."

A whippet-thin server arrived at our table with the hand-drawn menus. He grinned at Lilith.

"Hey," he said.

"Hey."

Apparently they knew each other.

"Specials are on the front," he said, handing us each an oversize menu.

For a fleeting moment I thought Lilith was blushing. I shook my head. Such a thing was not possible. Flaming cheeks did not go well with turquoise hair.

"Something from the bar?" he asked.

Once he left to get Lilith a glass of water and me something called a martini primavera, I said, "So I guess sideburns are coming back."

"Hmm," she said, studying the menu.

"Interesting look with the fauxhawk," I said.

"He's in one of my classes," she murmured.

"That's a coincidence."

I was impressed by her expression of exquisite boredom. "Between jobs and school, I meet a lot of people in Wood-bridge."

I figured that was the end of that, so I got back on topic. "The problem is she's pretty emotional about it. She wants to deal with them today and she might not tomorrow. So I have to act fast. That's where you come in. The usual sifting, sorting, packing, and disposing."

"You said emotional. What happens if I turn down these other jobs and then she weasels out?"

"I'm meeting her tomorrow with a plan and a contract. We'll have a cancellation clause in there so you'll get paid for two days anyway."

Lilith nodded. She obviously approved of that tactic. "Charlotte, you drive such a hard bargain."

"I know. I'm a beast."

"Count me in. This is too good to miss. Let me know where and when."

I gave Lilith the address on Bell Street and waited until she wrote it down.

"Assuming it's a go, I'd like to get started Monday after-noon when Emmy Lou's at the office. That work for you?"

"Even if it didn't, I can't wait to get a look at thousands of plush toys. You know what, it sounds kind of freaky."

I grinned. "It's peculiar but sweet, except for the striped snake. Sorry to disappoint. I bet you'd prefer freaky."

She grinned back at me. "You know me."

"If freaky's your thing, then you might want to get a look at her next-door neighbor and his friend. They're part of the reason I want to get on this right away."

"Hold on," Lilith said. "These guys are freaky how? You-show-me-your-AK-47-and-I'll-show-you-mine freaky?"

I shook my head. "A pair of overgrown misfits who seem to be a bit obsessed with my client, that's all. She might be a bit afraid of them but also unwilling to admit it. In my opinion it's a form of stalking. The neighbors are worried." I thought about Patti and her comments about Kevin. "But not all of them."

"Call me crazy, but isn't that the point where you call the police?"

"I did mention it to Pepper Monahan. She said she can't do anything without a formal complaint."

A sneer crept over Lilith's face. "That's cops for you. Hassle people minding their own business if they're poor or on the street, but they don't mind waiting until they kill someone if they live in a decent neighborhood."

One of these days, I hoped I would learn about Lilith's former life. But I knew better than to push. "Pepper cares about things like that."

"If you say so."

"I want you on the job so that we can do this over a couple of days and my client won't be there alone. We'll have time to figure out whether there is a real problem."

"Rose's daughter is actually visiting from California this week, so I don't have to worry about her. So I could even stay overnight if that would make a difference."

"Thank you. I'll let you know if that's what we need. To tell the truth, these guys are sort of pathetic and goofy. I'm not completely convinced they're dangerous. I'd like to be reassured. I'm worried about it on one hand, but on the other they seem incapable of doing any real harm. I mean, they scare easily."

She chuckled. "How do you know that?"

I snapped open the oversize menu. "Let's order and I'll tell you later. But first: new idea. I'd like Emmy Lou to meet you and learn what you'll be doing. I think it will help her stay committed to the project. Can you show up around three tomorrow to meet her?"

"I'll be like the old ball and chain?"

"Exactly. You're perfect for it. It's a metal theme."

Business out of the way, we got serious about that menu. When our server returned, Lilith ordered the grilled vegetarian medley and I chose the seared scallops with a citrus salad.

"Excellent choice," he said to her.

"So," Lilith said, once he'd zoomed off to the kitchen, "what's the information you need?"

I filled her in on the details of Kevin and Tony and their weird behavior and even my stupid action the night before. Lilith had spent some time as a street kid before she managed to pull herself together. She didn't talk much about those experiences, but she survived because she'd become a good judge of people.

"What do you think?" I asked. "Do these guys sound dangerous to you?"

"Hard to tell. Sounds like developmental issues. Maybe one of them has a thing for Emmy Lou."

"She is a beautiful woman, but she must be nearly twenty years older than they are."

"Don't count it out."

As we chatted and caught up on what we'd each been doing lately, our eyes were drawn to a lovely young woman with luxurious long dark hair and a slinky red dress. She crossed the restaurant floor as if she owned it and the rest of Woodbridge. She opened a door along the side of the room and vanished inside. I figured every male in Wet Paint sighed with disappointment. Except for our server, who had eyes only for Lilith.

Our food arrived quickly and perfectly. As it did, the light went on by the piano.

"I hope you like jazz," I said.

I turned as a commotion erupted across the room. The girl in the red dress stormed back in. A short bald man in a rumpled Hugo Boss suit raced after her and grabbed her arm. She pulled away from him and kept going. He followed her through the front door and out onto the street. The girl kept walking with her arms folded over her chest, shaking her head, long hair swinging behind her. Whatever he was arguing about, she wasn't happy. She shook her head and continued up the hill. He kept pace until they turned the corner and they both vanished from view.

I knocked over my water glass. "Holy crap. That's Dwayne."

Lilith used her napkin to start mopping. "Who's Dwayne?"

"He's Emmy Lou Rheinbeck's wonderful loving husband." I couldn't believe it. If I'd actually read his business card instead of leaving it on Emmy Lou's coffee table, I might not have chosen his restaurant for my get-together with Lilith.

Lilith said, "Oops. Your client? So she may be beautiful, but I'm betting that girl he's chasing is not even twenty-one."

7

Sometimes nothing but a bubble bath will do. I love them. Truffle and Sweet Marie are always fascinated. I ran the tub and poured in a double helping of coconut-mango-scented bubble bath and settled in for a long soak. But instead of relaxing, I found myself reliving the scene with Dwayne pursuing the girl in the red dress. Maybe it hadn't been what it looked like.

Let's just say, my mother had run through four husbands and a lot of also-rans and usually if my spider senses tingle, I'm right.

But what would that mean for Emmy Lou?

After half an hour, I had managed to unkink and stepped out. I wrapped myself in my favorite big, soft bath sheet and prepared to finish off the perfect Saturday night.

"That's it, we're turning in," I told the dogs. The blast of the phone near midnight came as a shock. Another shock as an angry voice hit my ear.

"What the hell is wrong with you?"

"Hello, Pepper," I said. "I'm not sure what you're talking about."

"I'm talking about you harassing people."

"What?"

"You heard me, Charlotte Adams."

"Who am I supposed to have harassed?"

"The same people you told me to investigate. You had me digging around to see if there was anything in the system about them, and now I hear you're threatening them with violence. You'd better not get me caught in any of your crap. Or you'll have a lot more than messy closets to worry about."

"But I never threatened them with . . ." The scene on Bell Street played in my head. Kevin had been frightened. I'd been pleased about that, even though I felt bad after.

"What? You've gone quiet. You did, didn't you?"

"No. Not really. I chastised them. Told them to leave Emmy Lou alone."

"The complaint said yelling, threatening, and foul language. Acting crazy."

"Does that sound like me?" My heart was racing now. What happened when someone made a complaint against you?

"The crazy part does."

"Listen to the language. Kevin and Tony didn't use those words."

"It doesn't matter who called it in. You can't go around threatening people."

"Don't I have the right to know who's saying these things about me?"

"You have the right to mind your own business and to leave other people alone. Remember that in future."

Pepper likes to be the one who slams down the phone. But first she said, "They might seek a restraining order against you. One more bit of vigilante hooliganism and you'll be hauled before a judge.

I said, "But . . ."

There wasn't enough coconut-mango bubble bath in the world to counter the effects of a call from Pepper.

But who had made the complaint? And why had they picked Pepper to call?

———※———

I was feeling my lack of sleep Sunday afternoon as I spun along Long March Road, heading for Bell Street and my appointment with Emmy Lou. I was still fuming over who had made that complaint when my cell phone rang. The number was blocked, but I took the call in case Emmy Lou was attempting to cancel.

A man's deep voice said, "Charlotte Adams?"

"Yes."

"This is the Woodbridge Emergency Services." The voice was calm.

I gasped. "It's not true. I wasn't harassing them. I don't care if someone—"

"Take a deep breath, ma'am."

When did I hit "ma'am"? I'm only thirty. "I did not threaten those boys."

"Not sure what that's about, ma'am. But we have a report of a fire at your home." Chills ran down my spine as he said my address. "Second floor?"

"Yes."

"The trucks are on their way."

"The dogs! Please make sure my dogs are okay." But the phone line was dead.

I made a U-turn and spun back toward my place. Jack was home. He would let the firefighters know about Truffle and Sweet Marie. I hit speed dial, but Jack's cell phone went straight to message. What if Jack had been overcome by smoke? What if almost everyone and everything I cared about was dead?

The Miata may be cute, but it's also very fast; I put the petal to the metal and broke a few laws getting back home.

I squealed into the driveway.

No fire trucks.

No smoking ruins.

No tiny charred bodies.

The beautiful old two-story Victorian with the white gingerbread that Jack had grown up in and that his wonderful parents had left to their only son was the same way I'd left it. Jack was in the driveway, vacuuming out the Mini Minor. Something to do with the Great Dane.

I sat in the Miata and shook with relief. Jack ambled in my direction, grinning amiably.

"What's up? Meeting canceled?" he said. "That's great because we can hang out. Have some fun. Better late than never. Sorry about last night."

I got out of the car and gave him a bear hug and got the front of his blue and orange Hawaiian shirt wet with a few accidental tears. In turn, he patted my head.

"I thought you were dead. I thought the dogs were toast. I thought the house was burned down."

Jack said, "Huh?"

You'd think that someone so close to getting a PhD would be more articulate in highly emotional moments. The bear hugging and head patting went on for a while, until Jack said, "What made you think there was a fire?"

I filled him in on the phone call. Of course, before the words were out of my mouth I realized how dumb that was. Woodbridge Emergency Services would not have my cell phone number. And even if they had it, it was highly unlikely they would call people in their cars and tell them their houses were burning.

I stumbled upstairs, my knees weak, and staggered into

my apartment. Truffle and Sweet Marie were in the middle of their second or possibly third afternoon nap and were less excited about seeing me than I was about seeing them.

"I've been had," I said.

"I guess so," Jack said. "You should probably have a bit of ice cream to settle you down after the shock."

I said, gathering up the dogs, "It was a very upsetting few minutes."

"Weird kind of practical joke. Who would do something like that?"

"Oh, I have a pretty good idea." A vision of Kevin and Tony making faces in Emmy Lou's window flashed in my mind.

"Who?"

"Two people I can't even speak to, because I've been accused of harassing them. And the police, in the person of Pepper, told me to back off and leave them alone."

Jack stared at me. "Are you making this up? Possibly to get ice cream?"

"No, I am not making this up for any reason. And the ice cream is mine, in my freezer, paid for with my cash might I add. I don't need to make up traumatic experiences to get it. I can eat it out of the container if I want to."

"That sounds good. I'll join you."

"Actually, let's save it until I'm back from my meeting."

"I'll be here."

I left a message for Emmy Lou explaining that I'd been delayed because of an emergency. I chewed my lower lip as I drove toward Bell Street. Why wasn't Emmy Lou answering? Had she decided to blow off the meeting? I tried to reach Lilith too, but, of course, she would have been waiting outside Emmy Lou's house, wondering where the hell I was. I figured her cell phone had been turned off, or being Lilith and often broke, maybe she'd run out of minutes.

Kevin and Tony, I imagined, would have been somewhere

nearby laughing their hooded heads off. Although in the back of my mind, I wondered how they could have pulled that one over on me.

—◆—

Even as I turned the corner to Bell Street, I could see the commotion. Emmy Lou Rheinbeck was standing in the middle of the street, clutching an armload of stuffed toys. She looked like a large deranged child. Today her sleek red bob was a tangled mess. Lilith had her arms around her, holding her back from . . . what? Patti Magliaro was loping across the street toward them, her flowered peasant skirt swirling and her long grey braid flapping behind her. Princess, the cat, struggled against the leash. A man in his late sixties stood staring across the street at the fracas.

I heard the wail of sirens in the distance. I squealed to a stop and jumped out of the Miata.

"What's wrong, Emmy Lou?" I shouted.

She sank onto the pavement with a wordless, eerie wail.

"Did something happen?"

Emmy Lou doubled over on the road, weeping.

Lilith urged her to move. "Come on. Let's get out of the street."

I said, "Did someone hurt you? Please, Emmy Lou, tell us so we can help."

She whispered. "No one can help now."

"I'm sure that—"

"Just leave me alone." She stared down at the toys in her arms and shuddered. "Take them away! I don't want them."

She thrust the stuffed animals into my arms. A yellow toy rabbit tumbled to the ground. I managed to hold on to a couple of plush pooches and an oversize red squirrel. I stepped back and met Lilith's glance.

I mouthed, "What's going on?"

She whispered back, "No idea. I got here a bit early and

I was waiting for you. This red-haired lady drove up and went in the house a few minutes ago. Then she ran out the front door a couple of minutes after, screaming and crying. I've been trying to get her back on the sidewalk before someone comes speeding down the street."

By this time Emmy Lou was trembling visibly, her pupils dilated, her mouth gasping.

Patti's hands fluttered. "What can I do to help?"

"I'm not sure. We'll see," I said, taking off my jacket and putting it on Emmy Lou's heaving shoulders. "It's okay. We're here."

"Noooo," she howled. "Please say it didn't happen."

Lilith and I exchanged glances. Lilith put a calming hand on her shoulder.

"Let's get you inside," I said. I couldn't imagine what had triggered this emotional reaction. What had those foolish boys done now? Or had she found out about Dwayne and the girl in Wet Paint?

Emmy Lou pushed me away, screaming, "Not inside. I can't go there."

"Did something happen? Sounds like the police are on their way. Everything's going to be all right."

"It's not going to be all right! You aren't listening."

"We are trying to help."

"He's dead. No one can help."

"What happened, Emmy Lou? Please tell us."

"I didn't mean it."

"Mean what?" Lilith asked soothingly.

Emmy Lou's green eyes rolled, wild with panic. "I didn't know he was there."

"Who?" I urged.

"I didn't see him."

I glanced around for someone to help. There was no sign of Dwayne's Audi. The Baxters' driveway was empty. Bonnie was nowhere to be seen. The man across the street turned and walked back into his house.

"Patti, could you take Emmy Lou to your place and get her wrapped up and give her some tea or something? Lilith will come along with you. I'll go into the Rheinbecks' and check what's happened," I said.

Emmy Lou wasn't going anywhere. She pushed Lilith away. "I told you what happened," she screamed. "I killed him."

I dropped the toys on the side of the road and headed for the house. Emmy Lou was hysterical. She probably didn't know what she was saying. But just in case, I started to run.

Tony Starkman was sprawled faceup at the foot of the hardwood stairs, like a rag doll on the dark polished wood floors. He lay there, unmoving, surrounded by scattered plush toys. Could anyone survive having their neck bent at that angle? His beady black eyes stared in shock. Blood pooled from the back of his head, stark against the pastel fur of a fluffy blue cat. It spread slowly on the dark floor. This time Tony had been on the receiving end of the nasty surprise.

I knelt down and tried to take his pulse. I wanted to be wrong. How could this happen in the Rheinbeck foyer, elegant, spotless, and smelling slightly of citrus? I couldn't feel a pulse. His wrist felt warm. Maybe he was in shock. There are medical miracles. I dialed 911.

Mona Pringle answered, cheerfully. As usual, she recognized my voice. "Charlotte Adams? That you?"

"Someone's dead, Mona. Number 10 Bell Street. He fell down the stairs, I think."

"Hey, finding bodies is getting to be a habit with you, isn't it?"

Mona's been doing her job a bit too long in our small town. She lacks a certain gravitas in the face of disaster. "This is serious. Send the ambulance."

"No need to snap," Mona said. "You can relax, Charlotte. They're all on their way. You're the fourth person to call this in. Of course, no one else mentioned a body."

*Keep a small Ziploc bag for receipts
and business cards in your purse.
Don't forget to file them every night.*

8

I looked up to see Pepper staring down at me. She was wearing a cotton hoodie, chinos, and sneakers. Her hair was pulled back in a ponytail. She'd obviously been at home, on call. She was not wearing her happy face. Behind her, the tall, craggy detective waited silently. He looked as though he'd been at a golf game. He obviously did not possess a happy face.

As I had been kneeling by Tony Starkman's body, my face probably looked pretty unhappy too. Neither Tony nor I got too much sympathy.

"What the hell are you doing here?" Pepper said.

I got to my feet, somewhat shakily. "My client said that he was dead. I came in to see if he was all right and I called—"

"Client? What are you, pretending to be a lawyer now?"

"Emmy Lou Rheinbeck. I told you all about her and—"

"Okay, that one. She's outside screaming her head off."

"She was hysterical when I got here. That's why I came in."

"Yes. And that brings me to my next point."

I looked straight into her eyes, even though it meant tilting my head. "And that would be?"

"That would be what are you thinking, contaminating a crime scene?"

"A crime scene?" I squeaked.

"Does that come as a surprise to you?" Pepper motioned me out of the way.

At that moment a man and a woman wearing white paper suits, blue booties, and latex gloves were making an appearance. One of them had a camera and began to take pictures of Tony. My stomach lurched as the full impact began to sink in.

"I'm sure it was an accident, Pepper. Emmy Lou said . . ." I thought back. Oops. What exactly had Emmy Lou said?

Pepper said, "I heard her shouting, 'I killed him.' Guess what I think."

"She's hysterical."

"Did you hear her make that exact statement?"

"I don't think that Emmy Lou could possibly—"

"This is not about what you think. This is about a homicide. Did you hear her say it or not?"

"I suppose, but she couldn't have meant it. Maybe—"

"Maybe nothing. And yet, here you are, mucking up my crime scene so we'll have that much more to contend with."

Pepper was scowling down at Tony now.

I said, "This is Tony Starkman. He is one of the two guys I told you were harassing Emmy Lou."

"The same two you threatened?"

I let that slide. "I thought he was probably pretending to be dead. I told you the kind of stunt he and Kevin were pulling: showing up in her window, yelling and making faces and taking pictures. He was quite capable of using fake blood to freak her out."

Pepper said, "Any truth you asked people to take her away?"

"Yes, it is true. I asked Lilith and Patti Magliaro to take her to Patti's and give her some tea or something. I thought she was in shock. But she didn't want to go."

"Bad things happen when you try to think, Charlotte. Now what you've done is cause a pile of trouble."

"Look at the stairs. There are toys scattered everywhere. I almost tumbled to my death yesterday. That's why I was called in. To help Emmy Lou deal with her toy collection. They're everywhere. Tony must have tripped on some of them."

"Oh take a breath, Charlotte, and pull yourself together."

I took enough breath to start again. "You can't believe that Emmy Lou actually killed Tony. No matter what she's saying."

"I believe this: you might have even screwed up our case, stomping in the blood, telling witnesses to leave, and I can't imagine what else."

"There's nothing else," I said huffily.

"I have half a mind to charge you."

I drew myself up to my full height. "With what?"

"Obstructing government administration. You mucked up my evidence."

"What evidence?"

"How can I tell what evidence? You've been in here contaminating it. Look, you even have blood on your shoes."

"But they're my favorite loafers!"

As the words tumbled out, I realized it was ridiculous to worry about shoes when a person was lying dead in front of me.

Pepper rolled her eyes. "Yeah and now you're going to have to hand them over to the evidence technicians."

"They're all yours," I said, stepping out of the Cole Haan loafers that my mother had sent me for my last birthday. No point in telling Pepper that. She'd enjoy it more.

The male evidence technician took my shoes and bagged them. At least *he* didn't smirk. Unlike Pepper.

"I didn't like them that much anyway. Now I'm going to offer Emmy Lou a bit of support," I said with as much dignity as a four foot eleven inch person standing in her stocking feet could manage.

Pepper snorted. "You are *so* not going to do that. Mrs. Rheinbeck is being taken in for questioning."

I gasped.

Pepper said, "Since she keeps shouting out confessions, I imagine we'll keep her until she's off to county jail to wait for her preliminary hearing."

"Sometimes you are so unfair," I said.

Pepper's professionally sculpted eyebrows rose. "Unfair? How fair is it to kill your neighbor?"

"We don't know that. She's a lovely, gentle woman. I think the shock of seeing him got to her."

"You know what? You get to me. I've had enough of little Miss Charlotte Adams, girl detective. You're out of here now." She pointed to the front door.

"Fine, I'm going."

"Head for the nice officer and give him your statement."

—♦—

Outside I gulped in the fresh air. I must have been half holding my breath all the time I'd been near Tony's body. A pair of uniformed police officers stood guard at the front of the house. For some reason at the sight of the police officers and the crowd my knees gave out and I sank down on the front steps with a thump. My jaw dropped when I saw Emmy Lou handcuffed. She was being placed into the back of a police car. Two other officers seemed to be in charge of that. One put his hand on the top of her head. She bent into the vehicle without an argument as I stared, amazed.

A small crowd had assembled in the middle of Bell Street. The crowd turned to watch the police car accelerate away. The red and white roof lights gave a merry flash.

Everything seemed to be happening in slow motion. It took me a moment to become aware of the fuss next door at the Dingwall home to the left of the Rheinbecks'.

A tall, sturdy woman with white hair flung open the door. Her yellow apron flapped in the breeze. She thundered down the stairs, crossed the lawn, sank to her knees, and stretched out her arms. That was the first time I noticed Kevin. He was kneeling on the grass, his head in his hands, rocking furiously.

Lilith spotted me and pushed her way toward me. A uniformed officer turned and told her to stay back.

"Are you all right, Charlotte?" she called out. Behind her Patti Magliaro's pale eyes blinked.

I nodded but couldn't quite manage a smile. "I'll be fine. Give me a couple of minutes to get my head straight."

Turned out that was a conservative estimate. Anyway, I needed to talk to Pepper again, but I knew better than to walk back into the house. I was prepared to wait. In the meantime, both Patti and Lilith were corralled to give separate statements to one of the young officers. I gave mine next. Trust me; it is much easier to be a witness than a suspect. I managed to keep calm and sensible. I hoped I offered a crisp, well-organized account of what I'd seen and a reasonable explanation of why Emmy Lou Rheinbeck would confess to something she hadn't done. No one reacted in the slightest to my theories. Or my lack of shoes.

"What is your problem?" Pepper said when she finally emerged from the house much later, followed by her tall, silent shadow.

"It's not my problem, Pepper. It's my client's problem. And I think you need to talk to Kevin next door." I pointed to the pathetic figure of poor Kevin, keening in the grass. It was hard not to feel sorry for him. He most likely held the key to what had happened. His mother stroked his hair, oblivious to everything else around her.

Pepper shot a black look in my direction.

I said, "He's obviously distraught because his friend is

dead, but once he calms down, he might know what Tony was doing in Emmy Lou's house."

"And I, as a detective, would never be able to figure that out without you. Is that what you're saying?"

"Of course not."

"It would never occur to me to take statements from the neighbors and friends of the victim."

Oh boy. I suppose I should have kept my mouth closed. That's not always easy for me. "I know that Emmy Lou couldn't kill Tony, and I bet Kevin could tell you what Tony was up to."

"Now you're a forensic psychiatrist. The case is pretty well wrapped up then. Tell me, Charlotte, are you trying to take over my job *and* steal my husband?"

I didn't want Pepper's job and I definitely didn't want her husband. It would be all right to tell Pepper that I didn't covet her horrible job. She might even believe me. But, if I turned up my nose at Nick Monahan, she'd be totally ticked off. There was no winning that one.

"Sorry, Pepper. I'm not trying to interfere with your job. And as for Nick, it wouldn't matter if I was after him; he's head over heels for you. You know that."

She smirked. Indicating she knew it.

I was glad she couldn't read my mind. Nick is pretty hot, if you like your men long on looks and short on brains. Pepper must; she married the jerk. Of course, that hadn't stopped him from coming on to me every chance he got.

Definitely, there'd be no explanation for Nick's behavior that she'd care to hear.

"Why are you still here?" she said. "What do I have to do? Arrest you?"

"I'm on my way," I said.

On the far side of the house, Kevin, kneeling, continued to rock back and forth. At least he'd stopped howling. Except for his mother who sat in the grass beside him, her hands now holding his, no one paid much attention to him.

I pulled out my cell phone. For once in her life, Margaret picked up the first ring.

"You are not going to believe this," I said.

———————

Jack was more than willing to find some footwear in my apartment. I didn't care what shoes he selected, as long as they were from the same pair, and I had stipulated that. Shoes are an important part of my mental health. I know that sounds ridiculous, but you try standing up to the police in your sockies and see how you do.

While I was waiting, I needed to do something useful. I reached into the side pocket of my handbag. I keep a plastic bag there for business cards I pick up during the day. Where was Dwayne's card? Someone needed to call him. He'd handed me his business card on Friday, but I remembered that I'd put it on the coffee table. Emmy Lou had turfed me out, and I'd never returned to the half-eaten chocolate cake and the card. That memory made me think: despite her vulnerability, Emmy Lou had shown a flash of temper and an unreasonable side during that initial meeting. And again when she'd called me and expected me to drop everything and hustle over to meet her on Saturday night with no notice. Was I wrong about her?

As Jack pedaled down Bell Street with my espadrilles in his backpack, the Baxters' elderly Dodge passed him and edged into their driveway. Bill stumbled out and stood briefly, openmouthed at the sight of police cars, and the crowd, standing around speculating. He stared at Jack too, when he hauled my espadrilles out of his backpack.

I noticed with horror that the WINY vehicle was pulling onto the street too. And worse, following in a white SUV were the teeth that walked like a man: the dreaded Todd Tyrell. Of course, it was Sunday and not a regular Todd Tyrell day, but like Pepper, he'd always show up when the moment was right. I did not intend to find myself on television again.

I gestured to Jack to hurry up while I hotfooted it across the lawn in my stocking feet. The Rheinbecks' lawn felt smooth and silky with its spring grass. The Baxter side was dryer and rockier, with patches of sharp weeds.

Ouch. That hurt. My nose twitched and I bit back a sneeze. That miserable mulberry tree.

Bill said, "I've got to get inside. Bonnie will be freaking. What happened?"

"Long story," I said as I scrambled up the stairs behind him, before Todd Tyrell spotted us. Jack came barreling along after us as Bill fumbled with the double dead-bolt locks on the door and pushed it open.

"This is my friend Jack Reilly," I said as Jack dropped his Italian bicycle on the Baxters' lawn. "I hope you don't mind if we stay for a couple of minutes. I don't want to be on television."

I wasn't sure if Bill had heard me, but I waved Jack in anyway.

Inside, the Baxters' house smelled oddly delicious. Vanilla mostly. Bonnie was sitting on a kitchen chair, breathing raggedly. Her heart-shaped face grey as a dirty sheet. Bill leaned over her, worry written across his gaunt face.

"You okay, Bonnie?" Bill said, running his hand nervously through his pale shaggy hair. "Why are the media all over Bell Street?"

"What's happening?" she said.

Bill said, "I don't know."

She was going to find out anyway and it wasn't going to get any prettier.

"There's no easy way to say this. Tony Starkman is dead. He was found in Emmy Lou's house this afternoon."

This time Bill sat down with a thump. He reached over and squeezed Bonnie's hand. He turned to me. "Did that fool fall off the roof or something?"

Bonnie gasped. "Bill!"

I said, "I have no idea. He was at the foot of the staircase. Perhaps he tripped. He may have been pulling some stunt on Emmy Lou. I'm not sure why he was in the house in the first place. It's a terrible thing that he's dead but—"

Bill said, "He was hounding that poor woman. You know that."

But despite his actions, Tony's death had shaken me too. I wasn't sure what I thought anymore. "The worst part is that Emmy Lou is saying that she killed him."

Bonnie's hand, delicate and artistic, shot to her mouth. "Oh no!"

Bill jumped to his feet. "That's nuts. She couldn't hurt a fly. That loser's dead and can you believe it? He can cause trouble anyway."

I said, "Of course, she couldn't have done it. I know that and so do you, but she was shouting that she did. The police are taking her seriously."

Bill opened his mouth again and then spotted his fragile wife. Bonnie had started to shake. She said, "I can't believe that could happen. Not here on this safe little street. We've been so happy here. We are starting to get our lives back on track," she said in a strangled voice. Tears coursed down her cheeks. Bill put his arm around her protectively. "Emmy Lou's going to be all right. You know you're not supposed to be stressed. We're going to relax now. How about I take you upstairs and you can have a nap?"

Not supposed to be stressed? Bill was like a series of firecrackers going off at unpredictable intervals. I wasn't sure how much stress Bonnie could avoid living with him.

She shook her head. "Oh, Bill. Do you think I could sleep after hearing that?"

Jack stood watching, tall, gangly, and resplendent in Hawaiian shirt, espadrilles in hand. He cleared his throat. "Would you like your shoes, Charlotte?"

Both Baxters blinked at this. Bill reacted first. "Who the

hell are you?" He balled his hands into fists. I wouldn't have wanted to get in the way of one of those.

"*Bill,*" Bonnie said.

Jack held out his hand, "Jack Reilly. CYCotics bike shop. Don't you run Nerd on the Spot? We're neighbors on the same block."

Of course, the computer shop in the sad little strip on Long March Road that Jack had rented for his shop. No wonder Bill had seemed familiar. I must have seen him a dozen times coming and going from Nerd on the Spot.

"Yeah. But why are you here?" Bill glowered. Surprises were obviously not his best thing. Not a great attribute in a computer technician, I suspected.

By the time we got through all the explanations—friends, landlord, shoes—Bill had lightened up and Bonnie had pulled herself together. She seemed slightly less grey, which meant I might not have to worry about calling 911 again.

"How about some cupcakes?" she said.

I blinked because that was kind of surreal.

"Sure," Jack said.

"What flavor would you like?"

"Charlotte likes anything chocolate," Jack informed her. "I'm more open."

Was I dreaming? Soon Tony Starkman's body would be wheeled out of Emmy Lou's house. Emmy Lou was in some interrogation room in the bowels of the police station. To me, cupcakes seemed supremely irrelevant. Not that anyone else noticed.

"This is the Magic Cupcake, official headquarters. I have chocolate pecan. And lemon. Or cherry. And coconut cream. And—"

"Wow. They all sound good," Jack said. "It would be hard to choose without tasting them. I bet they'd help us to calm down."

"Jack, show a little restraint," I hissed.

"No need for restraint in this kitchen," Bonnie said. "I've got ten different flavors. Why don't you try one of each?"

That explained why the Baxters' house smelled so good. Vanilla, almond, lemon, strawberry, chocolate. Bonnie moved toward the counter where a cluster of cupcakes sat cooling on a rack with a clear plastic dome over it. And for the first time I noticed that the kitchen in the run-down little house was set up restaurant style. Long counters for production. Two large ovens, a professional-style fridge, and of course, the huge table in the middle. Cardboard boxes were stacked high in the corner. It might have been professional and spotless, but unlike the magazine quality of the Rhein-becks', this kitchen was definitely unglamorous. Bonnie's cracked vinyl dinette chairs had all been patched with duct tape.

As Bill lifted a slat of the kitchen blinds and peered out the window at the television crew, I noticed a couple of the blind slats had been patched with duct tape too. Whatever money the Baxters had, had gone into professional equipment. I approved. I say put your cash where your career dreams are.

Bill turned and said, "You can't give away all your products, Bonnie. You've got paying customers."

"Someone died, Bill. And Emmy Lou's in trouble. We're serving our guests cupcakes like normal people and we're not going to argue about it."

Huh. So Bonnie had a specialty cupcake business. I liked that. She also had more than her share of spine. I liked that even better. Although I would not have gone so far as to call Jack normal people.

Bill grumbled but gave up.

I accepted a chocolate pecan number. It was beautifully iced and decorated. Bonnie's delicate, artistic fingers were perfect for this work. Jack seemed to be going for one of each. Bonnie said, "They all have buttercream icing. And the flavorings are completely natural. No artificial products."

"I should hope not," Jack said approvingly.

"If you are looking for a love slave, Bonnie," I said, "you may have found him. Plus he can keep your bicycles tuned up, if you have any, and bring you shoes as required."

"Hard to resist," Bonnie said with a half smile. "Makes me wish I could still ride a bicycle. Oh look at that." She grabbed a paper towel, dampened it, and wiped off the big table. "With that darn demolition across the road, we have dust everywhere all the time."

It was a pleasant, if slightly weird, interlude following the horrible events of the afternoon. It reminded me of the more obscure European film society showings I'd sat through in university. Come to think of it, Jack had suggested most of them. The sight of Bill peeking through the battered slats of the blind at the television vans every few minutes made it that much weirder.

"I suppose we'll find out sooner or later what really happened," Bonnie said as she slipped Jack yet another cupcake. Possibly he was trying for some kind of international record.

"Don't count on WINY for the facts," I said. "And speaking of finding out, did you see anything odd today at Emmy Lou's place?"

Bill turned away from the blind. "I was out making deliveries. And I have a big one yet to make." He pointed to one of the stacks of cardboard boxes.

Bonnie said, "I was busy in the kitchen. Bill, why don't you check out the upstairs window and see what they're up to."

Bill bounded up the stairs.

Bonnie said, "That should distract him for a minute. He's so overprotective and hyperactive. Sometimes I need a break from all that nervous energy. It's because of my MS. He'll do anything to help. We're trying hard to make a go of two new businesses, but it's tough starting all over."

"Tell me about it," I said. "I started my organizing business last year too. You need a buffer to get by."

"We don't have much buffer left, but we're coping."

Of course, I had wondered what happened to bring them there. Some questions are better off not being asked. I nodded. Usually that's all it takes. People are always telling me their life stories.

Sure enough.

"Bill was in high tech. His business went belly-up when the tech bubble burst a few years back. Since then he's invested in a couple of start-ups, but none of them survived infancy."

"I'm sorry to hear that," I murmured.

She shrugged, and I sensed a world of weariness in that. She continued. "That's the way it is in that business. You can bounce back when you're young, and sometimes you can make a fortune. The weird thing is that we both love what we're doing now. I live for cupcakes, and Bill gets a big charge out of helping old ladies get on the Internet."

"Woodbridge is a great town," I said.

"The price is right too. We figured we could live cheaply here after I was diagnosed. And our rent is reasonable for the house and the shop. But Bill's feeling the pressure. He's a wonderful man and I wanted to explain that, but not in front of him."

Bill thundered downstairs again. "They're everywhere," he scowled. "We're going to have trouble with those deliveries."

I decided to help Bonnie in the distraction game, since nothing would be gained by having Bill get us all worked up. "These cupcakes are fabulous. I can't believe it's a new business. What did you do before?"

"I was an accountant. Can't say I miss it. This is something completely different. It's great for me, because I can take a break when I need to. I can take only the number of orders I can fill, depending on how I'm feeling. So far the worst part is having to deliver them. When we make it big, we'll get someone to do that for us," Bonnie said with a grin.

I think watching Jack toss back those cupcakes had helped her regain her composure.

It did seem weird to be chatting about careers after what had happened, but sometimes it's good to give the brain a rest. The distraction was short-lived though. Bonnie asked, "About what happened at Emmy Lou's. We didn't notice anything. What time did it, um . . . ?"

I said, "I don't know. I was supposed to meet Emmy Lou at two thirty, but I had a prank call about a fire at my place and I had to race home."

"A fire!" Bonnie's newly regained color faded.

"As I said it was a prank call, so I was about a half hour late, and when I got here, she was outside shrieking that she'd killed Tony. It was at least three."

Jack mumbled something.

I made the international signal for "Don't talk with your mouth full."

He tried again, "Someone didn't want you to make your meeting with Emmy Lou."

I frowned. "Maybe you're right. But who would do that? And why?"

Bonnie said, "I can't believe any of this. Why would Emmy Lou do something like that? If Tony was bothering her, all she had to do was call the police. Poof! He'd be gone. I can understand that she didn't want to involve Kevin, but Kevin wasn't there."

"He wasn't?" I said.

"I saw him and Mrs. Dingwall leave while Bill was loading the car. Around noon. They often go out on Sunday. He looked a bit more respectable than usual. She told me once that she and Kevin go to visit her mother over in New Paltz or somewhere like that on Sundays."

"And Tony?"

"I didn't notice him, but Bill said Tony was already in the car. Bill always keeps an eye out for him. You may have noticed he's a bit obsessive."

Bill barked, "Tony was already in the car, sitting like a big ugly lump while that poor woman hauled out this big basket of stuff. Kevin was standing around staring at his shoes. I was relieved that big jerk was leaving with them, because Emmy Lou was outside puttering in the garden. And Dwayne's car was gone. I didn't want him bothering her or worse, coming in here when Bonnie was home alone. How's she going to defend herself?"

Bonnie protested, "You worry too much, Bill. The doors are locked, and there's such a thing as 911. I don't want to be treated like a helpless incompetent. Anyway, this is Woodbridge, you know, not some inner-city danger zone."

"You told me I was being ridiculous. Now look," Bill said.

"I was wrong. He must have attacked her or something. That's the only possible explanation."

Jack picked up another cupcake.

Bill said, "You have to admit, there's been something wrong about that place since we got here."

Stuck on a tough problem?
Set your subconscious to work on it while you sleep.
Won't cost you anything.

9

It was early evening by the time Todd Tyrell's SUV and the WINY truck pulled away. Bill announced their departure after one of his regular squints through the blinds.

"Cops are hanging around. They got tape all around the place."

I said, "I'm sure they'll be there until late tonight."

Bonnie bit her lip. "But you can make our deliveries, can't you?"

"Sure thing, babe," he said, giving her shoulders a squeeze.

Bill and Bonnie got ready to complete their schedule. I think Jack hated to say good-bye to the remaining cupcakes. He left carrying a small cardboard box. He tucked the box in his backpack and picked up his bicycle. I reclaimed the Miata. I'd left the keys in the ignition for the first time in my life. Must have been the shock of seeing and hearing Emmy Lou hysterical in the street. A small pile of stuffed animals occupied the passenger's seat. I stared at them. I certainly hadn't put them there, but someone had obviously picked up the toys that Emmy Lou had been carrying and stuck them in my car. One more little bit of weirdness, but the least of my problems. I couldn't wait to get away from Bell Street and back to normal.

Of course, the events of the afternoon kept swirling through my mind. As I was nearing my street, I had a sudden thought: Since Emmy Lou was acting so out of character, had she told anyone to contact Dwayne? Or a lawyer? Even though I knew it was ridiculous for me to worry about this, I swung by the police station, which was between Bell Street and mine, so not entirely lunatic on my part. There was no sign of Dwayne's Audi.

Emmy Lou was on her own.

Unless someone had contacted him about Tony's death and Emmy Lou's trip to the police station, I figured Dwayne would be at work. My next stop was Wet Paint. Woodbridge restaurants are just as busy Sundays as Friday nights. Especially on lovely, warm early evenings in late April. It was warm enough that some had already set up their outside patios. Wet Paint was one of those.

Dwayne was in the bar area schmoozing with a couple of customers. There was a good crowd inside and outside tonight. Dwayne obviously knew his business. His broad grin broadened when he saw me enter the restaurant. Obviously, he hadn't heard. "How'd it go?" he said. The grin faded as he took in my expression.

He didn't say a word as I filled him in on Tony's death and Emmy Lou being taken away in the police car. I left out the handcuffs.

When I finished I waited for a reaction.

Dwayne appeared to be stunned. Then the pudgy schmoozer vanished. He loomed over me. "Is this some kind of sick joke? Because you'll wish you hadn't made it."

I recoiled. "Of course not. And I realize she didn't do it."

Dwayne slammed his forearm down on the counter. A row of wineglasses clanked dangerously. "Of course she didn't do it. How dumb is that? Emmy Lou is the sweetest woman in the world. Too sweet sometimes. She couldn't hurt anybody."

"But why would she say she killed Tony?"

He stared at me, his hands balled into fists. "She actually said she killed him?"

"She was shouting it. On the street."

"Impossible."

"You have to believe me about what happened. When I got to your place, Emmy Lou was in the middle of the street hysterical. We all heard her. Including the detective who is probably in charge of the case."

"Are you sure about this? Maybe she said, 'Somebody killed him'?"

I shook my head.

"My God. They'll throw the book at her."

"I can recommend a good lawyer, unless you already have someone."

Dwayne hunched his beefy shoulders. "Who would we have? We don't know any criminal lawyers. I don't know anyone who would have a criminal lawyer."

"You know me. I have a friend who is a lawyer. Her name's Margaret Tang. She helped me a lot when I was falsely accused last year. Remember all that stuff in the news about me last fall? Margaret stayed with me during interrogations and she kept the media at bay, mostly, and she got me bail. I'll give you my card too in case you need anything, and, um, I seem to have misplaced yours."

He blinked at me, dazed, and slipped my card in his pocket without a glance. He handed me one of his. This one I put in my plastic container. He was on autopilot judging by his expression, but I kept talking. "It worked out all right for me. Margaret did an amazing job."

"This is incredible." He kept patting his pockets, feeling for his keys maybe. "I gotta get out of here. Where the hell are my keys? I have to go to her. I don't want to be rude or anything, and I'm real sorry for yelling at you, but I can't talk anymore."

I stood my ground. "Margaret could be there with her too. She's smart and she's tough and she knows how the detective in charge of the case thinks. She'd help both of you." I handed him Margaret's card.

He stuffed the card into his pocket without glancing at it either. "Once I talk to Emmy, we'll find a way out of this nightmare." He grabbed his jacket from a nearby chair and fished out a set of keys.

I said, "Please don't forget to give Margaret Tang a call. She's . . ."

But Dwayne had pushed past me and had already shoved open the restaurant door. Just as I got back to the sidewalk, his silver Audi flashed past me in a swirl of dust.

I decided that was good.

—◆—

I was met at the head of my stairs by Truffle and Sweet Marie, who flung themselves against my legs. That's dachshund talk for it's nice and warm out, and it's late so let's go out and bark at the world. When it's time to walk the dogs, everything else has to wait. Overall, that's probably a good thing. Takes you out of yourself and your problems, minor or major. I brought a shopping bag and picked up the plush toys from the car on the way back.

"Okay, let's see what devilment you got up to today," I said.

They had no problem with that. Once again, the apartment seemed to be in pretty good shape. No big misadventures. I could see two dents on the bedspread where they'd spent the day sleeping in the sunny spots, moving to warmer places only when the stripes of spring sunlight moved. I wrestled the bag of stuffed animals toward the closet. Truffle and Sweet Marie followed me to the cupboard. They looked up as I stuck the toys up with the wedding mice on the top shelf and closed the door.

The dogs cocked their heads.

Their legs are only four inches long, so maybe they were puzzling over where to get a ladder. Two pairs of black inquisitive eyes watched speculatively. I could almost read their tiny minds: hey, those fuzzy toys would be great in a tug-of-war.

I said, "You won't be getting near these toys. They'll be on the top shelf of this cupboard until Emmy Lou gets home."

I wondered when she would get home, or if. And if she did, would she ever want to see those toys again? You think you're equipped with life skills, but then when murder strikes, you realize all the stuff you don't know. It doesn't matter how organized you are, murder's going to throw you off your game.

"Okay, slow down," Margaret said when I called her from the safety of my sofa.

I took a breath.

She said, "And then this toy-collecting client killed her next-door neighbor's friend. Do I have that right?"

"She says she did, but I don't believe her."

"I see. She says she did, but you think she might be making up a murder confession."

"Yes."

"Why?"

"I'm not sure yet. I don't know her that well. But she's a very nice woman and she certainly doesn't seem like the type to kill someone, even a horrible ugly man whom she disliked and who harassed her. I told you about that before all this happened."

"Boy, I can't wait to mount a defense for this one."

"Maybe you could go and talk to her."

"I'm not allowed to muscle my way in to see a suspect and ask that suspect if I can represent her. I'm sure you know that."

"I do, I guess. I'm a bit scattered about all this."

"Murder's like that. Messy, unsettling, makes you reevaluate people you thought were nice and harmless."

"I don't have to reevaluate Emmy Lou."

"Doesn't matter, because I can't represent her."

"Can her husband ask you to represent her? I told him about you. I gave him your card. I'm surprised he didn't call you already."

"It can take hours to find out anything when you're dealing with the police. Give the poor guy time. He can ask her if she wants me to represent her. He might not want to. Or she might not want to. If she's *able* to make that kind of decision. Do you think she's of sound mind?"

I hesitated. "I would have said absolutely before, but now I'm beginning to wonder."

"Until they can demonstrate otherwise, she gets to make her own decisions, one of which might have been to kill her neighbor."

<hr />

Lilith and Sally left messages while I was taking the dogs out for their last walk of the day. I picked up Lilith's first. "Sorry, Charlotte. I had to dump those toys in your Miata. Did you know you left your keys in the ignition? Anyway, I didn't want to leave the toys by the side of the road. I figured they'd get ruined or stolen. And the cops wouldn't let me put them in the house, because it was a crime scene. I tried to tell them the stuffed animals belonged to Emmy Lou, but your *friend* Pepper threatened to charge me. Anyway, Patti and I didn't want to find ourselves looking like felons on TV so we took off after we gave our statements. I hope you were able to outwait the vultures from WINY.

Anyway, I'm going to work now. I'm on the night shift. I hope your client's okay."

Sally's exhaustion seeped into her message. "I can't believe what I'm seeing on television! It must be a big deal if poor Todd gets dragged out on the weekend. If I wasn't stuck here with this houseful of vomiting children, I'd get over there to give you a big hug. Sorry I can't be much of a friend to you today, but I'm letting Benjamin take over for a while and I'm going to try to get some sleep tonight."

Oh man. Speaking of not being much of a friend, I'd let Tony's death and Emmy Lou's trouble with the police drive Sally's situation out of my mind. I hadn't even checked to see how, or if, she was surviving and whether the kids were getting better. Now it was too late to call her and show a bit of sympathy. In spite of all she'd been through, she'd managed to call me. I felt like a jerk. Of course, Sally never misses a broadcast with Todd Tyrell because she harbors secret, inappropriate fantasies about him and has since we were giggling ninth-graders and he was a superheated senior. Never mind. I believe it's her only flaw.

I put Sally on my to-do list for the next day and went back to worrying about how to help Emmy Lou.

The hardest part of being involved with a death is not being able to do anything. The police had access to information. I didn't. I was just plain stuck. I hate that.

I spent a frustrating evening trying to get my head around what had happened. It would have been better for sure if I hadn't turned on the television set at eleven.

Todd Tyrell's teeth blared at me. Behind him the camera zoomed in on the Rheinbeck house.

Woodbridge Police continue to be tight-lipped about a suspicious death today on Bell Street. A twenty-seven-year-

old man was found dead at this home. Police have not re-
vealed the identity of the deceased pending notification of
next of kin. However, sources reveal that the homeowner,
forty-one-year-old Emily Louise Rheinbeck, is being inter-
viewed at police headquarters. So far no charges have
been filed.

A stock shot of the Woodbridge Police Station replaced
the image of Emmy Lou's house. At least the cameras hadn't
been there to capture her hysterical confession or the humil-
iation of the handcuffs. So it could have been much worse.
That didn't take long: my own picture flashed on screen. It
was one of the ones from last fall where I was being marched
into the cop shop wearing my pink fluffy slippers and an air
of utter culpability. Plus Patti Magliaro was right. I did look
mean.

WINY has learned that the body was found by thirty-
year-old Charlotte Adams. Adams was at the center of
the bizarre Henley affair last fall that shook Woodbridge
to its very core. Stay tuned as WINY promises to bring
you up-to-date images of this shocking crime.

I unplugged my phone and went to bed.

——✦——

Sometimes it's good to set your sleeping mind to work while
you get your rest. Efficient and inexpensive and no harm
done if it doesn't work. Of course, if it does work, you'll
probably find yourself wide awake dealing with whatever
info gets dredged up. I certainly did.

My clock said three fifteen. But there was no way I could
go anywhere and for a long time that included back to
sleep.

My subconscious had sensibly asked me who might have
pulled the prank about the fire and why. A man had called

me. That meant the man had known who I was and how to reach my cell phone. That narrowed it down to any of the thousands of people who might have read my Organized for Success brochures. I'd blanketed Woodbridge with them and used my cell number. But my brain wanted to know why that prankster had picked that exact time to play his miserable gag. For one thing, if I hadn't responded to the call and raced home in a panic, then I might have been at the Rheinbecks at the time that Tony was killed. Perhaps I might even have prevented it. Or I might have witnessed it. So the question became, who had wanted to keep me away?

Perhaps the person who'd killed Tony.

The voice had been deep, possibly disguised. Was there something familiar about it? Or was my mind playing tricks on me?

I drifted back to sleep after an hour or so of replaying the prank call over and over in my memory. I slept until my subconscious sent me another urgent memo: Why would Emmy Lou pretend to have killed Tony if she hadn't?

Once again, my eyes popped open.

I had asked myself the same question more than once when I was wide awake, but my sleeping brain had a few suggested answers. I had nothing better to do than to lie there and try to reconstruct what must have happened. This might have been more effective if I'd been at the scene, but I worked with the material I had. I closed my eyes and imagined the inside of the Rheinbeck residence. The straight staircase, dark hardwood, solid, new sleek wood banister. In order to fall down, Tony must have been upstairs, or at least at the top. Why would he be upstairs in Emmy Lou's house? For no good reason that I could imagine. Kevin had gone out with his mother. Tony had been seen in the car with them. Had he come back early? Why? Dwayne was at the restaurant. Emmy Lou was expecting me at two thirty. Would she have invited Tony into the house? Not impossible, I decided, but highly unlikely. But even if she had, she never would have encouraged him to go upstairs. I couldn't buy that for a minute. Therefore, if he had been upstairs, and he must have been, it had been without her knowledge or without her permission. I decided to work through both of those scenarios: What if he'd decided to play one of his little tricks? What if he'd thought this time it would be amusing to hide and give her another scare? With or without a camera.

This time I got out of bed. The dogs opened their eyes as if to say, "Have you lost your tiny human mind?" They immediately went back to sleep. I made my way to the entrance to my apartment. I opened the door and stared down the long, straight staircase. Not so different from Emmy Lou's. Maybe I couldn't be in her home, but I could approximate what might have happened.

Emmy Lou's bedroom was roughly in the same position relative to her staircase as my kitchen was to my own stairs. It was also across a small section of hallway roughly the same size. I scooted back to my bedroom and picked up my pillow. I moved back to my tiny kitchen and stood there. Suppose I was Emmy Lou and coming out of the bedroom, getting ready to come downstairs. And suppose I came face-to-face with Tony, hulking, greasy, and unpredictable. What would I do? Suppose he lumbered toward me? Instinctively my hands shot out. Emmy Lou was a substantial woman. She was also in a state of nerves already because of Kevin and Tony. Could she have pushed him away in a panic? She'd be strong enough. I tried my reenactment with my pillow. It bounced off the walls and tumbled toward the first floor, hitting the newel post and flopping on the floor. Damaging if it had been a person. I hurried down the stairs, grabbed the pillow, and raced back up. I worked out several possible reconstructions: perhaps she'd been in the bedroom and he'd come up behind her. She'd scream and try to fight. He might have panicked too and tried to get her to stop screaming. She'd struggle to get away, give him a shove . . .

I closed my eyes and tried again to imagine the whole

space. Of course, unlike my staircase, hers was littered with stuffed animals. Some had even been scattered under Tony's body when I found him. Their pastel fur had been spattered with blood, an image I was hoping to forget soon. Perhaps she'd screamed and he'd run away, but tripped on a stuffed duck or a kitty cat and tumbled to his death.

One final theory: What if Emmy Lou had been heading upstairs and spotted Tony at the top? The same thing could have happened for sure. Maybe she hadn't done anything. Tony was clumsy and shambling. He could have been hurrying down the stairs or up the stairs, and merely tripped on those animals. I knew how easily that could happen.

So if any of these propositions held water, it was definitely not murder. An accident. Or worst case, self-defense. Emmy Lou must have been overcome with guilt and remorse over Tony's death. And she'd been emotionally on edge for days because of Tony and Kevin. She'd probably felt like killing him. That would explain her bizarre confession.

I felt better.

Emmy Lou hadn't murdered Tony. And she hadn't lost her mind. Of course, once the police interrogated her, they'd figure that out themselves. They'd probably already released her. She was most likely sleeping soundly beside Dwayne and a giant stuffed zebra at that very moment.

No problem. I walked down to the foot of the stairs and picked up my pillow for the third time. Jack, wearing pajama bottoms, opened the door to his apartment and stood blinking nearsightedly without his glasses. His sandy hair stood on end. He looked like the world's tallest seven-year-old.

"Why do you keep thumping up and down the stairs? Is there something I should be aware of?" he said, stifling a yawn. "Do you need any help with that pillow? I'm good at pillows. Pillows fear me."

"Long story. Probably has a happy ending. Don't worry about it, Jack. I'm heading for bed."

I also planned to call Pepper with my theories as soon as she got to work in the morning. I climbed back into bed with a big relieved smile on my face and flaked out almost immediately. I slept until five thirteen, when my subconscious sent a supplementary message: don't forget that prank call.

*Charge your cell phone next to your bed at night.
It will be where you need it in case of emergency.*

10

Monday makes the week. So I wanted to get off to a good start, after the third worst weekend of my life. As awful as events had been, I didn't want to get dragged down by them. I had people, and dogs, depending on me.

The pooches found themselves having a brisk early morning walk. The timing didn't suit them, but I reminded them that I was in charge, no matter what they may have been led to believe. They were too sleepy to argue. As we hiked up and down the residential streets in our neighborhood, Truffle and Sweet Marie kept an eye out for squirrels. I enjoyed watching bright tulips opening in the spring air. Nothing beats spring for improving the spirit. The walk cleared my sleepy mind.

At home, I fed the dogs, made a coffee, and somewhat reluctantly flicked on the TV. WINY has only one star: Todd Tyrell. If Todd isn't on duty, some unsung hero does the voice-over while Todd's teeth grin at the world. Todd has three expressions: serious, happy, and stunned. I'm pretty sure stunned isn't one of the official ones. Todd was wearing his serious face as he stood outside the Rheinbeck residence. From the gathering of people and police cars, I could tell that this was recycled footage of yesterday's news flash. The voice-over informed viewers that as of this morning, Mrs. Emily Louise Rheinbeck of 10 Bell Street in Woodbridge had been remanded to county jail. A preliminary hearing was scheduled for Thursday. Pepper's picture flashed on screen as WINY congratulated the police on fast action in this case. As you might expect, she looked good in her dress uniform. Todd Tyrell's lips kept moving for a few seconds after the voice stopped.

Once again WINY producers had fished out the guilty-as-sin-uncombed-hair-and-bunny-slipper shot of me from the previous fall and flashed it across the screen. The casual viewer could be forgiven for thinking I'd been arrested for killing Tony and who knew how many other innocent by-standers. I lifted the remote and snapped off the news, before the voice-over guy spelled out my name.

Okay, I told myself. Never mind. Get moving.

My first call was to Pepper. I figured she should have been in by that time, but I got her voice mail. This time, I left a message. Next up was Dwayne Rheinbeck. I figured he wouldn't have slept much either and that he'd have plenty to do if Emmy Lou hadn't been released. Better to call early.

Unlike Pepper, Dwayne did answer. He blurted out, "Emmy Lou doesn't want to see that lawyer you recommended. She has waived her right to legal counsel. They assigned her a public defender. She wouldn't even talk to him. And she stared through me in court. Like a stranger. It was horrible."

"That's bad," I said. Bad? It was beyond bad. It was totally craptacular. I knew how awful it could be dealing with the police even if one of them had once been your best friend and even if you did have Margaret Tang by your side. What was Emmy Lou thinking?

I heard his voice catch. "Unbelievable. A nightmare."

"There must be something we can do. Can you talk to her again? Can you see her in the county jail?"

"I don't know what good that would do. Emmy Lou can be . . ."

"Stubborn?"

"I was going to say resolute. Stubborn sounds wrong, and Emmy's not usually wrong. In fact, she takes pride in being right. So maybe she should waive counsel."

Oh man. "I doubt that. This is murder. Emmy Lou may be first-rate at her job and is obviously a wonderful wife, but she'd be way out of her depth dealing with police and jail. Especially if she leads off by insisting she did it. You can see that as a strategy that would have pitfalls."

"Agreed. And I'm way out of my depth myself."

"And I came in to help her organize these toys so that you would be more comfortable about the collection from hell."

"More comfortable about the collection from hell?"

"Yes. I can see how they would bother you, but we were planning to fix it."

"Didn't bother me. I never noticed them much. It's my fault in a way. I bought her a few when we were dating and that started an avalanche, I guess. I was living in a bachelor pad with two other guys. My home is a thousand times better than that, even with plushies everywhere upstairs. They sure beat empty beer cans and pizza boxes lying around. Anyway, they made her happy. So no biggie. Why would I ask her to get rid of them?"

"Sorry, she didn't say that you'd ask her to get rid of them. I thought that . . . well, sometimes I jump to conclusions."

"Don't worry about it. I'm glad you want to help her. After yesterday. I saw you on television, and, well, all I can say is that I'm sorry you got dragged into all this. And I apologize for yelling at you."

"Not your fault. You'd had a shock. But I believe if she's

behind bars for a while, there's a good chance she'll change her mind about the lawyer. The confession too. You could keep working on that."

"Emmy's not one to change her mind. But I'll keep trying."

"This might be crazy, but I had a thought last night. Emmy Lou might feel responsible because Tony died. Maybe he tripped on the stairs or something. That might be what she meant."

"She's not the type to feel guilty. She does what she has to. And she doesn't waste time second-guessing her decisions or changing her mind."

I wished I was more like that myself. I am way too inclined to worry about what people think and whether I've let anyone down. I said, "Emmy Lou must have a chink in her armor somewhere. She needs us to figure out what it is. The cops like an easy solution. The DA likes a quick result, and the media likes a good villain, as you can see. Emmy Lou is probably quite photogenic so they'll appreciate that. Who can help us change her mind about the lawyer? Doesn't have to be Margaret, but she needs someone."

Dwayne sighed, a waft of hopelessness drifting over the phone line.

I felt like screaming: be a man! You say you love this woman. Work with me here. Instead, I said, "What about her parents?"

"No way. Emmy doesn't want anything to do with them."

"But you could—"

"You know something? We've been married a year and we've lived in this house nearly that long and I've never even met those people."

"What about brothers and sisters?"

"No idea. She never said."

"You don't know if she has any siblings?"

"Weird, I know, but we didn't talk to her family and we didn't talk about them. They must be something, that's all I can say. Emmy's like an angel with my parents, kind to them, thoughtful, remembers their birthdays, visits them. She's the perfect daughter-in-law. My brothers love her. My sisters-in-law love her. My nieces love her. Everyone thinks Emmy walks on water. My parents are going to be devastated. How am I going to tell them?"

"I'm not sure, but you better do it soon, before they see it on the news. Look at it this way: you said they love her. They'll believe she didn't do it. I met her for the first time on Friday and I know that. I'm sure they'll support you. Maybe even have some ideas for getting her to accept legal help. And, you have my number. I'll see what I can find out in the meantime."

—◆—

"I see the light at the end of the bucket, so to speak," Sally chirped when I checked in. "Dallas is back to normal, and Madison is starting to feel better. I think Savannah will turn the corner soon." In the background a steady wail continued. Where did she get the strength? And what would it be like with four? Of course, they wouldn't be sick all the time, but even so.

"That's fabulous," I said, stifling a yawn. I wasn't at my best after only a few hours' sleep.

"Not exactly fabulous," Sally said dryly, "more like barely endurable. Small mercies and all that."

"Can I get you anything? Bring over a latte? Do you want me to watch the kids and give you a break?"

"Thanks, but no thanks. The slightest change sets them all off. They even screamed when Benjamin took over last night. Not that it kept me awake. I'll let you know when the time's right to get together. By the way, speaking of the right time, an acquaintance of mine has a problem."

"What kind of problem?" Of course, I should have known better than to rush Sally when she's trying to explain something. You have to sit back and wait. I sat back and waited.

"More an acquaintance than a friend. I met her at Moms and Tots swim class."

"Hmm."

"She's having problems keeping her mudroom under control. She keeps yammering on about it. I have three plus kids, and Benjamin, and I don't have a mudroom, so . . ."

"You're thinking about getting a mudroom?"

"Hardly. Apparently, they're nothing but trouble."

I love mudrooms, but I didn't have a husband and multiple children, so I kept that to myself. And anyway, I had a lot on my mind that morning and none of it had to do with my organizing business.

"Anyway, I got tired of listening, so I told her about you."

"Oh thanks, I—"

"Don't thank me. She's kind of a flake. But I saw on television that your client's in jail."

"It's all a mistake."

"Okay, whatever. But you need new clients if you want to pay your rent and eat quality ice cream."

"That's probably true. But I have lots of other clients already scheduled and others waiting for cancellations. I'm booked for three months."

"Let's hope you can hang on to them after the local media has you tarred and feathered, which would not be a good look for you. I'm thinking you should sue over some of those shots. They have to be bad for business. Anyway, I thought you'd be at loose ends today and you might need a distraction, so I told Bernice you'd drop by around nine thirty. She owns a jewelry boutique uptown, but she opens late on Mondays."

—❧—

I checked my watch. It was just after nine. According to Sally's directions, Bernice lived two blocks from her. That's the thing about Woodbridge: nothing's far. I had a bit of time to kill before I could call Lilith anyway. By this time, I'd left three messages with Pepper, and I needed something to take my mind off the fact there was little I could do for Emmy Lou. Sally was probably correct; a mudroom might be what I needed for a moment's distraction. I swung by to see Bernice after her two older children left for school.

"Oh," she said, "you caught me. I thought Sally said you'd be by tomorrow." The side entrance to her house, aka the mudroom, was strewn with papers, sneakers, jackets, and what looked like a half-eaten tuna sandwich.

I jotted down a few notes, took a quick count of the sneakers in the corners and the jackets and discarded fleeces. I added soccer balls, baseball, bat, and gloves. School supplies, notes. I assumed that more backpacks and books would return with the two kids who were in school. Perhaps carting more stuff than we single, childless people could even imagine.

Bernice whinnied, "Oh no, what are you writing down? Is it that bad that you have to write things down?"

"Part of the job. I always do it. Helps me remember."

She continued to chew her lip. "I wanted to clean up before you saw what it was like here."

"It's better if I see it like this. I can get an idea of what you need." I whipped out my digital camera and started to take a few pictures.

"What are you doing?" Bernice gasped. "I don't want a record of this!"

"I don't have to take pictures if it makes you uncomfortable. I should have asked first. Sorry about that. But no one else will see them, and they'll help me when I'm doing my plan."

"Kids," she said. "Kids are a problem for me. With their school papers and projects and their stinky footwear and their old lunches."

"Never mind." I grinned. "I wish we'd had shoes like that when I was in grade school. I am retroactively jealous."

"They each have three more pairs. Of course, we're not sure where those are. Might be missing or stolen."

"Ah. Mind if I open the closet?"

"Do you have to?"

"Yes." Sometimes it's better to make up rules. What the hell. I opened the door cautiously. More shoes, more paper, more jackets. Scarves and mittens tumbled out. I lifted a few items and discovered another pair of lunch boxes underneath.

"Oh dear," Bernice said, biting her lower lip. "I've been looking for them for ages. We bought new ones."

I unzipped one and recoiled. Something old and green had taken over whatever forgotten snack had been inside.

Bernice snatched it from my hand. "Another one in the garbage. Yuck. How can I live like this and manage a business?"

"How many children again?"

"Three. Ten, seven, and three. A hundred school projects and a thousand mittens, no two alike." She finally noticed that tuna sandwich and bent to pick it up. "Are we beyond help?"

"Looks fairly typical to me," I said, not revealing my single, childless status. "Now that I've seen what it's like after they leave in the morning, I should see what happens before they leave and when they get home. Mind if I come by this afternoon? And one morning too."

She grimaced.

I said, "It won't hurt a bit. Let them behave as if I'm not here. It will be one morning and one afternoon, and then you'll be rid of me. I think we'll get a better plan out of it."

"If you say so," she said.

"Let's get it over with. It's not going to be a huge project, but it will have a big impact on you and the kids if we get it right," I said.

She nodded and bent forward to pick up a form. "Drat.

Here's a permission slip. There will be a total hissy fit if I don't go by the school with it."

Bernice shrugged into her jacket, grabbed her car keys, and set off down the hallway to chase the three-year-old, who had vanished. "See you," she said.

It seemed like the right time to leave.

––

Pepper had not returned my call. Was I surprised? I decided I would leave half-hourly messages with her and also try the desk sergeant at the police station. I left my cell number, although she already had it.

After I watched Bernice shoot off wildly down the street in her tan-colored SUV, I called Sally to report on the meeting, and I use the term loosely, with Bernice.

"Not sure she wants my help, but thanks anyway, Sal," I said. I filled her in on the permission slip that put an end to our interview.

"Of course, she went to the school, Charlotte. She'll want to protect that child from disappointment. Do you blame her?"

"But shouldn't the child learn to look after her own permission slip?" I said. "She'll have a lot more disappointments in her life if she doesn't take care of paperwork. Our parents didn't protect us that way."

"Don't be such a priss. Listen to yourself! Our parents were total jerks. We're lucky we're not in perpetual therapy. Bernice is protecting her daughter the same way I, as your friend, am trying to protect you from economic ruin because of your strange attraction to murder on the job."

"Oh pu-leeze, Sal," I said. "I so don't need protection."

––

I sat in the Miata collecting my thoughts; Bernice and Sally had given me something to ponder: protection. Apparently a powerful need in people when it comes to the ones they care about. I'd seen a small sample of it in a minor matter: a permission slip, not to mention Sally's desire to protect me in addition to her brood of children. Certainly, I'd experienced it myself, wanting to protect my client Emmy Lou from distress and injustice at the hands of the local police.

A sudden thought hit me: What if Emmy Lou was the one doing the protecting? And who would she be protecting anyway? Leaving aside the stuffed toy fetish, she didn't seem to be an overly sentimental person. Wasn't even in touch with her family. That left, of course, the genial affectionate new husband that she was so crazy about. The same husband who appeared to be totally inept when it came to getting past the police to see his wife and, worse, in getting his wife to talk to a lawyer. The same pudgy lothario I'd seen chasing after a beautiful young woman in a slinky red dress less than forty-eight hours earlier.

Dwayne Rheinbeck.

Where had our boy Dwayne been on the Sunday afternoon before all hell broke loose? Hanging around Wet Paint during the quiet period between lunch and dinner? Maybe. Maybe not. Dwayne would have known that I had an appointment with Emmy Lou. And he, unlike Tony and Kevin, was intelligent enough to pull off the prank call to keep me away until the damage was done. Of course, I had no idea why he would kill Tony. But since the law didn't seem to be one tiny bit interested, maybe it was time for me to find out.

I decided, as Dwayne was now my chief suspect, that I should stay close to him. I squealed up in front of Wet Paint hoping it would be open for Monday lunch. Lots of Woodbridge restaurants are closed on Mondays, but this wasn't one of them. I figured Dwayne was doing his best to build a business. That was convenient for me.

The young server who Lilith knew zipped off to the

kitchen to tell Dwayne I was there to see him. A minute later, the kitchen door opened and he barreled out. He gestured me over to a table on the side as the servers set the tables up for an anticipated crowd at lunch. Salt, pepper, silverware, napkins were being set out at speed.

"Any luck?" I said, trying to keep my smile natural.

"Luck?"

"With getting Emmy Lou to talk to a lawyer."

"Not yet."

I nodded. "How did your parents take it?"

"I haven't had the guts to tell them yet. I'll be heading back over to the jail to try to see her as soon as I finish talking to the kitchen staff. The place might have to run itself while we get this whole thing sorted out."

I fixed him with a look. "Have you thought that maybe she's protecting someone."

He stared. "Who?"

Was that a look of guilt?

"I don't know. Bill Baxter hated those two guys on the other side of you. Tony and Kevin." Of course, I didn't believe for a second that Emmy Lou was protecting her nutty neighbor Bill. I had Dwayne on the brain for this.

His mouth hung open for a second before he sputtered, "Bill Baxter? But we hardly know him. He's a neighbor. You don't let yourself get locked up because you feel sorry for the guy next door. That doesn't make sense."

"What about Kevin? Emmy Lou went way back with him."

Dwayne shook his head. "Nah. I can't imagine it. She's known him since he was a kid. And he is one weird little guy, but I would have said harmless. But if he'd killed his sleazy buddy, why would Emmy want to protect him by confessing? I could understand if she told the police it wasn't his fault. He's obviously not normal, so they're not going to treat him as a murderer. He's like a child. But that confession is bizarre. And it's not like her at all. Maybe you're right."

"We have to try to find out."

"Okay, I'll keep you posted once I get over there again."

I reached up and patted his shoulder sympathetically. A nice guy. A pudgy, gentle lump, worried about his wife. Caring, concerned, confused.

I had no problem whatsoever understanding why Emmy Lou would protect him from a murder charge.

Be prepared for disasters.
Keep your insurance and roadside assistance
policies up-to-date.

11

I didn't get far before my phone rang. I pulled over to take the call.

Pepper.

"Perfect timing," I said, "We need to talk."

"Better not be about the Tony Starkman murder."

"Why not? I don't think it's so simple. I have this theory that—"

"No."

"It will only take a minute, Pepper." I am used to getting negatives from her. But it takes more than that to stop me. If I let Pepper determine my state of mind, I would have crawled into a hole and died four years earlier.

She said, "No minute. No theory. No Charlotte involved in any way in this case. Because I have enough to deal with without you mincing around making a mess of things. Is that clear?"

Mincing? That was a low blow. I don't mince. Or make messes.

She wasn't finished apparently. "Do you hear me?"

"Yes, but—"

"Good. It will be nice not seeing you."

At that point in a "conversation" with Pepper, I usually hear a dial tone. This call was no different.

Fine.

I wasn't sure how to handle getting my idea that Emmy Lou was protecting Dwayne from my head into Pepper's, but I'd have to work on that.

———◆———

Before I could put the Miata back into gear, the phone trilled again.

"Have you heard anything?" I said.

"She still won't see a lawyer," Dwayne groaned. "She told the public defender she plans to wave her right to a preliminary hearing. He doesn't think she can get bail, even if she asks for it. Her behavior's been too erratic."

I asked myself how he could have found that out in the few minutes since I had left the restaurant. I'd had barely enough time to drive halfway home and to take that very brief call from Pepper.

"That's terrible." I feigned sympathy. No point in alerting him to my suspicions.

He said, "I can't understand what's going on. If I had my way, I'd be sitting in jail in her place." He did a very good job of sounding choked up. Maybe he'd taken a few acting classes. He added, "I'm sorry about all the trouble this is causing you."

I said, "Don't worry about me. You have to concentrate on Emmy Lou. In fact, I won't be charging for the two visits I made to your house. I wouldn't feel right about it."

Okay, that was dumb. I do have a rule that says I charge for consultations, one hour minimum fee, no matter what. I don't know why I said it.

"Why not?"

"Considering the circumstances, I can't. And you'll have legal fees and all that."

He sputtered, "But I told you she won't see a lawyer."

"I imagine she will sooner or later. I have another idea that makes more sense than Emmy Lou protecting someone."

He said, "I didn't want to hurt your feelings, but almost anything would make more sense than that crackpot notion. No offense."

"None taken. She feels guilty."

I heard a whoosh of impatience from Dwayne. "Guilty! What does she have to feel guilty about? She's an innocent woman, for God's sake. I thought you were on our side!"

"I'm not saying she is guilty. I'm saying she *feels* guilty. Maybe Tony tripped on the toys and that's how he died. Or maybe she thinks if she'd reported him to the police, he wouldn't have been in the house. Maybe he came up behind her and she pushed."

"You know, that makes sense. That's just like her. She's got such a soft heart."

"Right."

"But she's stubborn too. We'll have to find a way to make her understand she's not guilty."

I interjected. "The police don't want me to interfere with the case. You know, talk to witnesses. That kind of thing."

"They said that? Why?"

"It's a power trip. I'm a civilian, and there's a bit of history."

"But you have a lot of insight. This notion that Emmy feels guilty, it explains everything."

"Possibly." I thought: Dwayne, if you get the police to reconsider Emmy Lou's motives, you open up the possibility that she may be protecting someone. And that someone could well be you.

He burbled on. "We can work together. The police don't need to know where I got this idea. Emmy wanted this project.

It was important to her. I want you to go ahead and organize those stuffed animals. I'll pay whatever it takes. I wouldn't know where to begin. It will be something for her to look forward to. I don't mean to get rid of them or anything. I'm pretty sure she wouldn't like that. This way, I can bring her news about how the project is going. I think it will make her happy."

I thought: as happy as you can be when you're in jail for a murder you probably didn't commit but for some reason want to take the rap for, like for instance, you want to protect your husband.

He sounded genuinely pleased to my ear, not that I trusted him. "Do you think I should keep it a secret and surprise her when they let her out?"

Pepper Monahan wasn't likely to let Emmy Lou off the hook. She'd made sergeant in record time and was well on her way to being the first female lieutenant in the history of Woodbridge. Letting confessed murderers slip wouldn't fit in well with her career plan. She would have a solid sheaf of evidence for the prosecution. If Emmy Lou ever went to trial.

"There's a hitch. Actually, I can't do the project without Emmy Lou in the loop. I have to organize them to suit her. And she'll want it to suit you too, of course."

"I told you, the toys don't bother me. It's all my fault that she let the collection get out of control. You get started and we'll take it from there."

"I need an inventory. I have a colleague who can help me."

"Listen, feel free. We've got no secrets. Look everywhere. You want that in writing?"

"I do actually."

"You got it. When can you start?"

"Whenever you want me to."

"Soon as possible. I'll get you a set of keys made. I'm going to talk to the cops again. Even if Emmy Lou doesn't want to see that lawyer you recommended, I'll find someone. I have to do what I can to protect her from whatever she's trying to do to herself. So let's get going."

I said, "I'll need your cell number, in case of a hitch. Never mind. It's showing on my phone."

"Are you free this afternoon around three?"

"Sorry, I have a client booked for that time. How about this evening?"

"That won't work. I'm shorthanded at the restaurant. How about tomorrow morning around ten?"

"Sounds perfect." That gave me the amount of time I needed to talk to a few more people.

———

"Hello," I said as she came to the door. "I'm—"

"I know who you are," Mrs. Dingwall said, looking down at me. She was taller than I'd realized when I'd seen her from a distance. She looked more like a stereotypical American grandmother with her white hair in a no-nonsense blunt cut. Maybe someone from a Norman Rockwell illustration, bright cheeks matching her red, work-worn hands with their large knuckles. Today's apron was periwinkle blue cotton.

"Oh."

I wilted briefly under her stern gaze. I wondered if she'd been the person to call the police and claim that I'd threatened Kevin and Tony.

"I'm Myrna Dingwall. What can I do for you?" she said. She sounded curious, not stern.

"I wanted to see how Kevin was doing. I met him the other day with Tony, and I could see yesterday how distressed he was, when Tony was, um, found."

She nodded and let a smile slip out. "That's very kind of you. Come in. I have coffee on, if you'd like some."

She spoke softly, her words almost musical, a story-telling, child-soothing kind of voice.

I entered, feeling guilty.

"Have a seat. Be right with you." She gestured to the living room. I would have preferred to follow her, although you can put that down to pure nosiness on my part, but I sat. There was no sign of Kevin. The house was in much better shape than the Baxters', nothing patched with duct tape, although it was not at all trendy like Emmy Lou's. It seemed like a nice old family home: well worn, comfortable, and unpretentious. I sat on the sofa and waited. The room was full of framed photos, mostly of Kevin. I got up again and made my way around the perimeter of the room, studying each one: a smiling baby, held by Mrs. Dingwall twenty years younger. Another one of Mrs. Dingwall with a large-eyed, dark-haired infant. I hadn't realized that Kevin might have a brother or sister. Even then Mrs. Dingwall had been an older mother. Was that why he had problems? I wondered briefly if I should pay more attention to that biological clock. I shook my head to stop that thought. Anyway, Emmy Lou had said it was oxygen deprivation at birth, something like that.

I leaned in to study a shy little boy holding a lunch pail. A school photo, big grin despite two missing teeth. The little boy morphed into a gangling teenager. A cluster of faded photos going back generations indicated that Mrs. Dingwall cared about family.

She arrived carrying a tray loaded with coffee, cream, and sugar. I'm an old-fashioned girl. I like trays and blue and yellow china cups. They remind me of a more gracious era.

"Lovely photos," I said.

"Mmm." She hummed as she poured the coffee and I helped myself to a bit of cream. Why not? I think it reduces stress, and I certainly had been feeling stressed, facing Kevin's mother and thinking she'd accused me of threatening the boys. It was obvious from her behavior that she had no idea about what they had done to Emmy Lou or about my relationship with them. Whoever had called in that complaint, it wasn't Mrs. Dingwall. That was quite a relief to me, because it meant we could have a conversation that might produce the information I needed. I decided the baby pictures would be a good place to seek common ground.

"My friend is expecting her fourth child. She has three little girls. Maybe this one will be a boy. Kevin was a beautiful baby."

"He was a sweetheart." She was almost beautiful when that wide smile cut across her weathered face.

"I didn't realize that he had a brother," I said, pointing at the other picture in which a brown-haired, thinner Mrs. Dingwall held the other baby who stared at the camera with huge dark eyes. "He was adorable too."

The smile vanished. "That was Keiran," she said. "My first. He had a hole in his little heart. He was a brave wee fellow and he put up a good fight, but he didn't make it. Nowadays, they can do so much; they could probably have saved him, but thirty years ago, well . . ."

"I am so sorry."

She said, "These things happen more often than you'd think. People love and want their babies and they lose them, and other people throw theirs away. This world can be a strange place." She busied herself pouring her coffee. "My husband never got over it. I suppose I didn't either."

"How is Kevin today?" I said after a while. "He seemed very upset yesterday."

Her smile faded. "Not good. What can you expect? He lost his friend."

I hesitated. I wondered how much Mrs. Dingwall knew about Tony.

She said, "At least he didn't have to find Tony dead. Didn't have to see the body. I feel so sorry for you."

I blinked.

She said, "It must have been awful for you."

"How did you know that I found him?"

"The same way I knew who you were. I saw the report on

the news," she added. "Even though we were next door, you couldn't tell anything with all the police cars and ambulances and the sirens and everything. Todd Tyrell said you found the body."

"Ah yes, of course. I imagine everyone in town will have seen that. And it *was* terrible."

"Would you like a shortbread? Old family recipe."

Anyone who thinks that American women are no longer spending time in the kitchen hasn't dropped in to visit Woodbridge lately, that's all I can say.

I accepted. "Worse for Emmy Lou Rheinbeck," I said.

She frowned. "Yes. That was very strange. I can't imagine what happened there. Why would the police keep her in?"

I said, "She said that she'd killed Tony. Of course, I—"

"She couldn't have. That's impossible. They didn't mention it on the TV last night. Todd Tyrell said that she was being questioned. I thought perhaps the—"

"So you know her well then?"

"Well enough to know that she couldn't kill Tony."

"You didn't hear anything yesterday? See anything?"

She shook her head. "No, the police have been by asking the same thing. We left around noon. We went to visit my mother. She's in a nursing home half hour away, and we go every Sunday and take her a nice lunch. I wash her clothing too and I bring that back to her. The laundry at the nursing home can destroy anything in two weeks."

"That's very nice of you," I said with admiration.

"I'm happy to do it. She's a wonderful mother. She was there whenever I needed her. Now that she needs me, although she'd never ask, I plan to be there as often as I can. And Kevvie misses his grandma, so it's a special time for us each week." She paused, perhaps remembering what the question was about. "We were back in the house, less than fifteen minutes, I'm sure. I was hurrying to put the pot roast on for dinner when we heard screaming. Then sirens. Kevvie ran out to see what was going on. He was afraid something had happened to Emmy Lou."

I remembered Kevin lying grief stricken on the lawn.

"Tony didn't go with you for the visit?"

"Tony? Of course not. To tell the truth, my mother took an instant dislike to him the one time she met him."

I knew how that felt, but kept my opinion to myself.

"So he stayed behind?"

"He wasn't supposed to be here. We dropped him off at his own mother's place, down near Cherry Hill. He was going to spend some time with her. I was glad to get rid of him for a while to tell the truth. He wasn't the easiest person to be around. I think that mother of his always encouraged him to spend all his time here. But it was good for Kevin to get away from him now and then. I don't know how he got back to Bell Street. Or why."

Good questions. How and why had he come back? "And did you notice anything unusual when you left?"

"Lately, there seem to be lots of people and cars coming and going on this little street. Patti Magliaro was out walking her cat. Of course, she's always walking Princess, so maybe I'm imagining that. The people on the other side of Emmy Lou's were loading some boxes into their car at the same time we were leaving. The woman's very nice and not too well, I believe. I keep meaning to invite her for a cup of coffee, but I put it off because Kevvie's a bit afraid of the man, so he gets upset when we see them. I think their name is Baxter. Tony probably made faces at them."

More like gave them the finger, I thought.

She continued. "Emmy Lou was outside puttering around in her yard. She has a service to keep it up. I'd been kind of hoping that perhaps the boys could have done it for her, but when I asked, she'd already signed a contract with the same people who did the landscaping for her. She felt bad though about not asking them. I guess she hadn't thought about Kevin and Tony being capable of looking after her fancy plants and all that new grass. Kids like that can use any opportunity, you know. They're few and far between in this community."

It crossed my mind that perhaps that had triggered the stunts. Maybe Emmy Lou felt a bit responsible because she hadn't thought about them.

"Were they upset about it? Kevin and Tony? Did they feel cheated out of an opportunity?"

She furrowed her brow, concentrating. "It's so hard for them to find jobs. I think they were a bit disappointed maybe, once I mentioned it. The initiative didn't come from them in the first place. It was my idea. Perhaps I should never have even mentioned it."

"And when you got back? You said it was a few minutes before all hell broke out."

"I didn't pay much attention to anything until Kevvie started to scream."

"But when you drove back home, did you see anything unusual? Any delivery trucks or drivers who might have seen anything? What about Dwayne Rheinbeck? Was he around?"

She closed her eyes as if to remember. "I didn't notice Dwayne. I don't remember his car being there, but I wasn't paying attention. The same with delivery vans and trucks. You tune them out, although we don't get quite as many on a Sunday. But there was something different: a girl with very strange turquoise and black hair sitting on the curb. Kevvie was quite fascinated by her. She didn't seem to be doing anything wrong. Because of Kevvie and other things in my life, I've learned not to judge people solely on their looks."

That reminded me that I needed to talk to Lilith about who and what she'd seen. And when.

"Good thinking," I said. Seeing how I'd misjudged Kevin and Tony, I'd begun to think I needed to be less judgmental. "That was Lilith, my assistant. She was waiting for me. Someone called my cell, claiming to be Woodbridge Emergency Services and saying my house was on fire. I was late because of it. I thought my pets were stuck in a burning house. Do you think that Tony might have made that call?"

"Did you say your *cell* phone? How would he know your number?"

"I left brochures all over the neighborhood last fall. My cell number was on them. That's how Emmy Lou found me."

She shook her head sadly. "A brochure last fall? Tony probably couldn't have found your regular phone number in the phone book. And did the caller sound like an employee of the emergency services?"

"Fooled me."

"You wouldn't have been fooled by Tony, believe me. Not for a minute. He would have stammered and giggled. He wouldn't have the terminology right either. And why would he pull such a horrible stunt?" She continued to shake her head. "This is all so confusing. What was Tony doing at Emmy Lou's place? I can't imagine why he'd be in the house." She reached for her china cup.

I took a deep breath and started. "Tony had been harassing Emmy Lou, I believe."

Her hand hovered above her cup. She stared at me. "Tony? Harassing her?"

"I was starting a contract for her, to organize a collection."

"Those stuffed animals, I suppose." She chuckled. "Kevvie told me about them. Silly thing for a grown woman with a new husband too."

"And while we were there, Tony and Kevin climbed the tree outside her bedroom, with a camera and yelled and made faces in the window. Emmy Lou screamed and panicked when she saw them. They took a photo of her reaction."

Mrs. Dingwall's florid face turned white.

"I'm sorry," I said. "You didn't know?"

Shock flickered on the kind face. "Of course not. I would never have tolerated that. What a terrible thing. They could have been in big trouble if she'd called the police." She paused. "Are you sure?"

"I was there. I saw them. During and afterward on your lawn."

She was having trouble with this information. "Kevvie too? I could imagine Tony in his stupid way thinking that was funny and not imagining the consequences, but Kevvie loves Emmy Lou." Her shoulders drooped as if from the weight of this information.

"I'm sorry. This must be so upsetting. I don't know what they were trying to achieve. At the time, I thought they wanted to terrify her."

"No, that wouldn't be it. They both thought she was wonderful. It was like teasing the girl next door, I suppose. I'm not saying it was right, but it wasn't meant to harm."

"Bill Baxter yelled at them, told them to leave her alone. They gave him the finger."

"He is always yelling at them. I think he's a crank." The cup rattled in the saucer. "Emmy Lou was terrified, you said?"

"Yes, and I was angry over that stunt. But she didn't want me to call the police. She said that sometimes his jokes missed the mark."

"That one certainly did. Honestly. This is so hard. I can't deal with it."

"I got the impression that this type of thing had been going on for a while. She was rattled when I got there. And the Baxters both said that she'd been upset by the boys."

"I know my son and he would never do anything to hurt anyone."

"Perhaps he was being led astray by Tony. You can understand why I'm mentioning these things. If Tony was in her home and she felt threatened, she could have pushed him and it would have been self-defense."

"Self-defense? I can't believe anyone would need to defend herself against Tony. His looks might be enough to frighten you, but he was like a child too. Tony was harmless. I am sure of it, or I never would have let him spend so much time with Kevin. Never. I had no idea they were pulling these stupid stunts."

"Friday afternoon I spoke to Dwayne Rheinbeck. He said he'd talk to you about these pranks and ask you to put a stop to them."

She stared at me. "Dwayne didn't tell me. I saw him, let me see, leaving for work Saturday and yesterday. He seems to put in terribly long hours at that restaurant. He never mentioned anything. He smiled and waved hello, like he was real neighborly."

I raised an eyebrow. There was something very strange about that statement. "Like he was . . . ?"

"Those Rheinbecks," she said darkly, "they're not exactly what they seem." She crossed her heavy arms over her chest, and I got the impression that I wouldn't get any more than that out of her.

I said, "Dwayne has me working on the stuffed animal project until Emmy Lou gets home again. A nice surprise for her. I hope you don't mind if I drop by and say hello every now and then."

I figured it would be a matter of time until she told me why those Rheinbecks weren't exactly what they seemed.

"That'll be nice," she smiled. "I can use some company from time to time."

A *thunk* in the hallway caused us both to whirl. Kevin stood in the living room door, his eyes wide, mouth open. Freckles stood out against his pale skin. It was the first time I'd been close enough to notice them. He leaned forward and pointed a finger at me.

He shrieked. "It's you. You said we would be sorry if we didn't leave Emmy Lou alone. You killed him! You killed Tony!"

Work can clutter up your life. Make time to see friends.

12

I protested to Pepper when she showed up on Bell Street in front of the Dingwalls' less than five minutes later. I was getting into the Miata after failing to calm either Kevin or his mother.

"Of course I didn't threaten to kill him and you know that. So don't pretend." Must have been the sneer on her face that brought out my next comment. "Surely you can tell this boy is not quite normal, Pepper."

She was dressed to impress this Monday. Except for her unexpected weekend garb, Pepper always does her detective thing dressed like someone who's just stepped out of a fashion shoot. Today she had on a black-and-white print jacket, sort of a seventies vibe with a bit of sheen to it, and a pair of very stylish black "city" shorts to her knees. She had the legs for them and had obviously spent time at the tanning salon. She was carrying a large glossy purse and stood a bit taller than usual in a pair of open-toed leather shoes with high cork soles. You had to be tall and whippet-thin to pull off city shorts and a jacket like that. Pepper managed it perfectly. She'd be well aware that I would resemble a garden gnome in that outfit.

Never mind. I was glad I'd chosen a pair of silver kitten-heeled shoes. Silver was a big look this spring. I'd picked out my fave swirly little skirt and a fitted twinset in a shade of coral that looked very good on me, but, if my high school memories served, that shade made Pepper look jaundiced.

She said, "All I know is the kid claims you threatened him. He's pretty upset about it. And we'd already had a complaint about that."

"That's ridiculous. I did not threaten him. I said . . . you know what I said. I'd already explained the whole thing to you. And I can't understand why you would race out here based on Mrs. Dingwall's call and at the same time you won't even return my messages."

"Consequences."

"For what?"

"You are running around snooping. There are consequences to that."

"Listen, I went over to ask Mrs. Dingwall a few questions. I wanted to find out if she knew what Tony was up to yesterday—"

Pepper interrupted. "Exactly. Snooping. Not your job and not your business."

"It is my business, because I found the body. And don't forget my client is involved."

"I'm not likely to forget that. Let's see, 'involved'? Is that a euphemism for confessed to murder?"

"She didn't murder anyone, so stop trying to yank my chain. I couldn't even sleep last night worrying."

"And I would care about that because . . . ?"

I raised my chin. "Because I reconstructed the crime."

"You what? You went back to the crime scene? We had that house secured until well after midnight. If you did that, then your ass is grass, Charlotte Adams."

"Obviously, I couldn't reconstruct it on the spot. For one thing it was in the middle of the night. I did it, um, conceptually." I decided to omit the detail about tossing the pillow down the stairs.

Pepper rolled her eyes.

I kept on talking. "And my reconstruction told me a couple of things: one, Tony could have pounced out at Emmy Lou, pulling one of his little jokes, then, naturally, she might have panicked and pushed him away and he could have fallen. That's one scenario. The other one is that he could have really tried to get physical in some way and she could have defended herself, fought him off, with the same result: he tumbled down the stairs and . . . we know the rest."

Pepper yawned. Didn't bother to cover her mouth either. How rude was that?

I ignored that. "The third possibility is that he might have been trying to go upstairs or trying to get downstairs. Either way, he could have tripped on those toys on the stairs. He was clumsy and . . . they were all over the place. I tripped on a couple myself, and whatever my failings, I am not clumsy or accident-prone."

Pepper muttered something, but I didn't fall into that little trap either.

"So," I said, "the end result could be the same for someone like Emmy Lou Rheinbeck. She would feel responsible for his death either because she didn't diffuse the situation or because she couldn't control her compulsion to collect these toys. I know this woman and—"

Pepper said, "She's been your client for how long?"

I wasn't about to say half an hour and a couple of phone calls, although it was true. Pepper seemed to know this too. She smirked. It went well with her repertoire of yawning, muttering, and eye rolling.

I said, "It doesn't matter how long. Another theory might be that she's protecting someone that she—"

Pepper interrupted yet again. "Any word on Sally?"

I blinked. "Sally? Oh, yes, the kids are starting to feel a bit better. Little Savannah's not quite out of the woods yet. Sal's pretty tired too. We'll give you a call as soon as we're ready to get together for the sort-of shower thingie, gifts and all."

"I'm *sure* you will. And in the meantime, here's a little gift for you: you don't know anything about Emmy Lou Rheinbeck. So stay away from my witnesses or you'll be sitting in the cell next to her. Got that?"

She got into her unmarked police car and burned rubber. I guess I'd gotten to her, although I had to admit she'd won that round.

I'd been outgunned.

I hadn't had time to tell her that it definitely hadn't been Kevin's mother who called her the first time, claiming that I'd harassed the boys. I didn't know who'd done that, but although I was one hundred percent sure it was relevant to Tony's death, I had no idea how.

———

Although it was a free country last time I checked, I decided to move the Miata, in case Pepper came back to check and found out I'd continued to work for Dwayne Rheinbeck. I parked behind the giant Dumpster across the street from the Rheinbecks and the Baxters. Despite the Dumpster and the two half-demolished houses, there were no workers on the site. Not too surprising. The current building and renovation boom in Woodbridge made it hard to hang on to skilled trades. Someone else had obviously snagged this crew. The Miata would be fine there.

I checked my watch. Plenty of time before Dwayne showed up. I locked the car door and was ambling over to see Patti Magliaro when I spotted an opportunity. A stooped man who looked to be in his late sixties was emerging from the side door of the garage belonging to the well-kept house across the street from the Rheinbecks, next to the demolition site. I'd seen him before, strolling down the block and watching the scene unfold when Emmy Lou was in full hysteria mode on the street.

I approached and smiled disarmingly. Up close I could see he had large green eyes like Emmy Lou's, although I didn't detect any warmth or, in fact, any emotion in his. I felt an icy tingle in the small of my back.

"Hello," I said.

I found myself shivering under his gaze. Talk about someone who didn't like small talk. No answer. "I am working with Emmy Lou Rheinbeck. Or with her husband, Dwayne, to be precise."

His eyes flickered toward 10 Bell Street and then back to me. He knew who Emmy Lou was and where she lived.

"Am I right that she's your daughter?

I thought I saw him shake his head.

"Could I ask you a couple of questions? It could help."

He turned his back and started toward the house.

I followed him onto the paving-stone walk that led to the house. Maybe he was hard of hearing. I raised my voice. "It's very important. I need to talk to you about your daughter, Emmy Lou."

He stopped, glared over his shoulder, and said icily, "I am not deaf."

"Sorry," I said.

"But perhaps *you* are."

"What? No, I'm not—"

"I heard you the first time. Let me make myself clear. I do not have a daughter."

I stared as he turned his back to me for the second time.

"Well then," I called after him, "is her father around?"

"You're on private property. Better get yourself off it before I call the police."

He walked along the path, up the stairs, and disappeared into the house without a backward glance. As he opened the door, a tiny woman with a pinched face peeked past him for a second and then they both vanished. The door slammed shut.

Who was that woman? And why did she look so frightened?

❧

Patti Magliaro held her door wide open. "Right on. I see you met the Munsters. Of course, they call themselves the Wrights, but we know better. Come in. You'll need something to warm you up after that. Do you have ice on your ears?"

I glanced around Patti's place. I'd half expected it to be furnished in macramé, peace symbols, and hemp fibers, but it was minimalist and practical. IKEA meets The Container Store. I approved. She had several wall-mounted shelves with a collection of charming vintage teapots displayed. Several of them had a cat theme.

I said, "Almost. This Mr. Wright was something. All I did was ask if he was Emmy Lou's father. I explained that I was doing some work for Dwayne so he'd know I was all right."

"What is it the English say? A nasty piece of work? I love the way they talk, don't you? I'm a total *Masterpiece Theatre* freak."

I didn't have time to get sidetracked by Patti's many digressions. It was hard enough to concentrate with Princess wrapping herself around my ankles. I wasn't sure how I'd explain that when I got home. I said, "But he looked like Emmy Lou, especially those eyes, so I assumed that he'd be like her. Warm and chatty."

"You struck out there. He's as cold as they come. You know what? I have no idea how you can walk in those shoes. I'd be lost without my sandals. I'd tumble to my death in those. Oh maybe I shouldn't make jokes like that after yesterday. Kind of thoughtless, but I didn't mean it. Still I don't know how you can walk around in shoes like that."

My shoes had two-inch kitten heels. It wouldn't take a

circus performer to wear them. But again, I wanted to stay on topic. "He said he didn't have a daughter."

"Did he? I know for a fact that he does. I'm not surprised that he denied it, but I am a bit that he actually answered you. Never speaks to anyone, has that poor little mouse wife of his under his thumb. She looks scared to breathe. I've tried so many times."

"I got a glimpse of her. I didn't have a chance to ask her anything."

"And you won't either. She never gets out of his sight. She always looks like that, so it may not be anything in particular. She wouldn't dare contradict him about a little thing like who's a member of the family. He has a real bad aura. Did you notice it? Yours is good. Did anybody ever read it? I'm pretty good at that."

"Maybe when all this stuff is sorted out. You'd think, even if they were estranged, that they'd want to help her. She is in jail for murder and that's awful."

Patti said, "For sure. Can I get you a cup of tea?"

I'd already had coffee across the street, but I figured Patti needed to do something. Maybe it would help her concentrate. "That would be great."

"What would you like? Ginger peach? Chamomile? Sleepytime? Lemon Zinger? Green? White? Jasmine blossom?"

"You pick."

"Jasmine blossom," she said. "Special treat."

"Patti," I said, "you've lived here for quite a while."

"I've been here for more than twenty years, in this apartment. Forty years in the Woodbridge area. I was sixteen when we first set up a homestead for a long time. But after George got sick, we had to move into town. Sometimes I miss my little garden. We had carrots and radishes and the best tomatoes you could—"

Time to interrupt. "Was Emmy Lou living at home when you moved in?"

"No. She'd already left by then. In fact, I didn't even re-alize they had a daughter until she moved back in across the street this year."

"How did you know she'd lived here?"

"Emmy Lou told me. We were outside chewing the fat a bit one night, and she pointed to the house and said that's where she grew up, across the street."

"But her parents don't acknowledge her."

"Guess not. That jasmine tea is real nice, isn't it? I love the way the flower opens up when you—"

"I wonder what made her move back to Bell Street, where she'd see them every day."

"The father anyway. That mother's stuck in the house all the time. In twenty years, I've never had a conversation with her. I wonder if he knocks her around a bit. I wish I had some cookies or something for you, Charlotte, but you know I'm alone here and I get so much stuff over at Betty's that—"

"But it sounds like such a dysfunctional situation, doesn't it? Puzzling."

"Maybe she got a good price on that house. Or she thought if she was in front of them, that sooner or later she'd get a smile out of the old bastard."

"Hmm."

"Anyway, it never seemed to bother Emmy Lou any. She was always cheerful and smiling. She waved to them every day when she went out. He'd turn his head, and if the mother was around she'd scurry away. They have a beautiful garden. Did I mention how much I miss mine? Emmy Lou has done a nice job on hers too."

I rubbed my temple briefly, not that Patti noticed. I said, "Do you think deep down she wanted to reconnect with them?"

"I don't know that they were all that connected in the first place. Could be she wanted to spite them. Sunflowers, I think that's what I miss the most. That's what she reminded me of too."

I raised an eyebrow.

She said, "You know, Emmy Lou: big, bright, full of color and life. She was doing well, happy, fancy house, beautiful property. She spends hours out there. It's going to be a wonderful spot in the summer. Anyway, I don't think she had a very good childhood growing up there. So perhaps she wanted them to see that she was happy, well-off, living the good life without them. Giving them the finger without having to lift her hand, if you know what I mean. Sort of saying, you can't get to me now."

"Makes sense. And in a way, it might explain the two thousand plush toys."

———— ❈ ————

Bill was getting into his car when I strolled toward the Baxter house. He returned my grin. "How's Bonnie?" I said.

"Not so good today. Headaches. Any kind of upset is bad for her MS. After yesterday's upset, she's pretty anxious. It could take days for her to recover."

"I'm sorry to hear it."

A wave of worry crossed his face. "Yeah. She's real worried about Emmy Lou. I am too. She even feels bad about the boy, not that I can understand that. She says I was too hard on him."

"Okay for me to visit? I'm in the neighborhood."

"She'll be glad to see you. Got to say, I'm surprised you came back to Bell Street."

"I have that job to do for Dwayne. He wants it done before Emmy Lou gets back."

"Huh. Well, go on in. You'll make Bonnie's day. She gets lonely." He opened his car door, grimaced, and turned back to me. "Be careful!" he called.

"Oh, I won't tire her out or talk about anything stressful."

"That's not what I meant. I mean with Dwayne. Watch out for that guy. I don't think he's exactly what he makes himself out to be." He slid into the Dodge and spun gravel leaving the driveway.

I was still wondering what he meant by that when Bonnie limped to the door. The smell of a thousand delectable cupcakes wafted out when she opened it. "Checking to see how you were," I said.

Bonnie sighed. "Been better, for sure." Her pretty heart-shaped face was greyish today. She leaned on her cane, knuckles white with the pressure.

"Hard to avoid feeling stress under the circumstances."

She smiled wanly. "I'm not the only one. I keep seeing your face on television even though you managed to avoid the cameras."

"WINY. They're relentless, but if they come up empty, they've got file shots."

She glanced toward the Rheinbeck house. "I'm glad they're gone. WINY, I mean."

"They're probably circling the courthouse or the county jail. Or sniffing around elsewhere. Speaking of sniffing, it sure smells good here."

"Thanks. You want to try my latest experiment? White chocolate amaretto fudge cupcakes. I was playing around with new combinations to take my mind off things."

"No need to ask me twice."

Of course, my ulterior motive was not to eat cupcakes, although that was good too. It was to sound out Bonnie about whether she'd seen Dwayne the day before. All the questions I'd asked her before had pretty well flown out the window once I'd developed my twin theories: a) either Emmy Lou was protecting Dwayne because she thought he'd killed Tony, or b) Emmy Lou had accidentally killed Tony and was overcome by guilt and remorse. I hated both these theories, but I was pretty sure that one of them would turn out to be true.

The cupcakes were enough to bring tears of joy to my eyes. I said, "I want to become your best customer. Honestly."

The smile lit up her eyes. The first sign of animation I'd seen. "Thanks."

"Out of curiosity, who are your customers? I'm always interested in how other small businesses run."

"I supply some of the new cafés here and in the surrounding towns. It's a delicate balance: every café wants to have something special, so you don't want to stock two in the same neighborhood. If my health was better, I'd set up a storefront, but I can't manage it now. Can't stay on my feet that long. I get exhausted, but it's getting better with therapy. When we first came here, Bill had to carry me downstairs in the morning and back up at night. It's been hard on him, looking after me. He's getting going with his business too. It takes a while before you start making a profit after you meet all your expenses."

"Let me know if you decide to do a bit of accounting work on the side. My friend Jack could sure use someone like you. He'd buy your cupcakes too. Perhaps you remember his reaction yesterday."

She chuckled. "Yes to cupcakes. No to accounting. Been there. Done that. Burned the T-shirt. Don't need the stress."

"Oh well, for a while it seemed like the perfect one-stop shop. By the way, I meant to ask you if Dwayne Rheinbeck is a customer."

"For sure. Emmy Lou set that up for me. Wet Paint was one of the first."

"Nice guy," I said

"Nice enough. She is the friendly one."

"I've been wanting to talk to him about what happened yesterday. When you and Bill were loading the car with deliveries, did you happen to notice if he was home?"

"Home when?"

"Anytime before Tony's body was, um, discovered."

"I didn't notice, but I don't think so. Why?"

"It's probably crazy, but I wondered if Emmy Lou might

be protecting someone. And, if so, he's most likely to be the someone."

Bonnie sank back onto the kitchen chair. "I don't understand what you mean. Protect him how?"

"I had this idea that Emmy Lou might have pushed Tony by accident, or he might have tripped if he was hiding in the house trying to surprise her. Or something."

Bonnie shivered. "That's horrible."

"Yes, but not as horrible as murder."

"But wouldn't she have said it was an accident? That would make more sense. And everyone would believe her. I mean, he was huge, and if he lumbered out at her and scared her, then who would blame her?"

"Exactly. But she didn't say that. And here we are, nearly a day later, and her story hasn't changed."

"Oh boy. But it explains a lot."

I added, "Plus she won't see a lawyer. A lawyer would probably insist on finding other explanations. Dwayne told me she doesn't want that. That makes me wonder."

Bonnie's dark eyes widened. "Because she thinks he did it!"

"You got it."

"That's awful. I don't think he could have. I vote for the accident."

"Anyway, it's why I asked if you noticed him around early that afternoon."

"Oh. I wish I could help, but we were in and out, and we weren't looking out the window when we were around. Bill was giving me some extra help. We had an unusual number of special orders to yesterday. The only thing on our minds was cupcakes."

"I'm sure you're right. Dwayne wants me to finish that job for Emmy Lou, and if I'm going to work for him, I want to feel safe."

"Of course you'll be safe! Dwayne is a good guy."

"I like him too," I said, "but the thing is, Bill and Mrs. Dingwall both insinuated that things weren't as they seemed with the Rheinbecks."

"They did?"

"Yes. But you don't think so."

"Not that I know. Bill is a bit paranoid. And I've never spoken to Mrs. Dingwall. It's awkward because of Bill yelling at Kevin and Tony. You'll be fine doing that project. I hope you'll come over and see me when you're there too. I get a bit of cabin fever here."

"Be glad to. You know I shouldn't have mentioned those theories to you. I'm thinking out loud, and if I'm wrong, I'll feel like a rat."

"I hear you. Your secret's safe with me. Want a couple of cupcakes for the road?"

———※———

Here's the thing: if you have a business that requires you to be on call seven days a week, then during those seven days, you'd better make time for friends and socializing. All to say, if you have something special to eat, you'd better share it. Jack was the ideal person for camaraderie and cupcakes. The fact that he had eaten an acre of them the day before wouldn't deter him in the least. I decided to swing by CYCotics before getting on with the rest of my day. It left plenty of time to catch Lilith and do a bit more research on mudroom possibilities.

As I reached the Miata tucked away behind the big Dumpster, I did a double take. The car seemed to be sitting low on the ground. It took a second for that to compute. Ribbons of rubber stuck out in all directions. I experienced a great big "Huh?"

All four of my pricy radials had been slashed.

*Dollar-store wrappers can keep
your scattered small change organized.
Treat yourself with the proceeds. Cupcakes anyone?*

13

I dropped the box of cupcakes and dashed forward. For a
moment I thought that I might have driven over some sharp
metal debris from the demolition. But as I leaned forward
and examined them, I realized the pattern of slashes had to
be deliberate. More than deliberate: they were deep and vicious. Who would do that? Workers angry because I'd
parked in their construction site? But there were no workers,
and even though it was private property, no one had posted a
No Parking or No Tresspassing sign. This was Woodbridge
and I'd had no reason to avoid that spot.

Who could have done this?

Kevin was very angry as well as frightened of me. I
glanced over toward the Dingwall house. There was no sign
of him. But then even Kevin wouldn't hang around to be fin-
gered. He and Tony had loitered on the lawn after their crazy
stunt at Emmy Lou's window. Waiting for what? To see the
effect? I felt a chilly tingle down my spine at the idea of

Kevin with a sharp object and a grudge. Was he as damaged and innocent as his mother and Emmy Lou believed? I shivered and shook myself. I sure hoped there were other possibilities.

Random vandals? It occurred to me, a bit late, that I was alone and out of sight, blocked as the Miata was by the Dumpster. I hurried away from the demolition site and stood on the sidewalk. For once, Bell Street was empty. Not a single pedestrian. Not a dog or cat walker. No one puttering in the garden. Not even the taciturn letter carrier. As I stood staring down the street, an orange El Greco delivery car started its engine near the corner. I waved the teenaged driver over and asked if he'd seen anything.

"Your tires slashed? Whoa. That's harsh, man."

I let the "man" thing pass. "Did you see anyone?"

The kid shook his head. "But this street's getting bad, man. There was that dude got smoked yesterday. Right over there." He pointed across the street to the Rheinbeck house.

"Yes, I know. But this doesn't have anything to do with—"

"If you say so. But there was a van that peeled out from here when I pulled up with my delivery. Do you know a dude in a white van?"

"How long ago was that?"

"Ten, maybe fifteen minutes."

I would have been in Bonnie's. "Are you sure? That seems like a long time to deliver a pizza."

"Tell me about it. You get these losers that have to count out all their change. Then they don't have enough because they forget they ordered extra cheese or whatever and they got to go sticking their hands under the sofa cushions to find quarters."

"Any lettering on the van?"

"Not that I saw. A plain white van. There's a million of 'em around."

No kidding. "Thanks anyway. Can you keep an eye on me while I check something?"

He hesitated. "Okay, but make it fast. I got pizzas cooling."

I rushed back to the car as I made a call to my roadside assistance provider. When the tow was arranged, I followed up with a slightly hysterical call to Jack. Like the good buddy he is, he closed his shop and burned rubber getting to Bell Street. I reached for the note that I'd spotted under the windshield wiper, returned to the sidewalk, and waved my thanks to the El Greco guy. I was melting like an ice-cream sandwich on a July day when Jack's Mini Minor shot into the lot. He must have had it parked at the shop. He stood on his brakes.

"Stop consorting with the murderer or you will be next!" I yelled as he unbent his long frame from the tiny car.

Jack blinked. "What are you shouting about? I don't consort with—"

"Not you! That's what this note says." I passed it to him with shaky hands. Then I caught myself. "Hang on. That's kind of hokey, isn't it? 'You will be next'? Do you think it's a joke?"

Jack snorted. "Jokes are funny. Slashed tires are not. Threatening notes don't get even a chuckle. Someone was sending you a message, Charlotte."

"That's obvious. But what does the message mean? I'm not consorting with a murderer as far as I know. Unless it refers to Emmy Lou. I don't believe she killed Tony. But people who watch the WINY news probably do. Or maybe it means Dwayne. I'm going to be working for him on the project. What if someone believes Dwayne was involved? All four tires. I can't understand it. I can't begin to—"

"I know that at some point you will take a breath and then I'll get to make a point," Jack said.

"Fine. Make your point. Whatever it is."

"It is that your tires were slashed with a very sharp object. A knife. And slashed by someone who was strong enough to do that kind of job on them. So my point is that you have to be careful. Someone intends to scare you. Or worse."

"No kidding. I definitely feel intimidated."

"That's a good thing. Feeling intimidated is the mind's way of telling you not to get hurt."

"But who would want to intimidate me?"

"Any nut watching the news."

"How does this alleged nut know where I'm going and what kind of car I'm driving and where I've parked?"

Jack put his hand on my shoulder. "You have to be careful. Maybe he's not a nut."

"Then who?"

"Is that a box of cupcakes on the ground?"

"Yes it is. Pay attention to the topic."

"Wow. Lucky it didn't spill open."

"Pepper," I snapped.

That distracted Jack from the cupcakes long enough for me to say, "Pepper. She knew I was here. She wants me to butt out of the investigation and not help Emmy Lou. She knows what my car looks like. And she hates me."

"I don't think Pepper would stoop that low."

"You're not just saying that?"

"It's not Pepper. And you know what? She's right. You should keep your nose out of this whole thing. And furthermore, you have to tell her about this."

"No way. Then she'd know I stayed in the neighborhood after she told me to leave."

"Yes way. But what *were* you doing here?"

I gave him the short version, emphasizing my kindhearted visits and Pepper's mean streak. Didn't work.

"Yowza, you have more to worry about than Pepper being angry."

"Like getting charged."

"Let's cross that bridge after we've had a snack."

"Here comes the tow truck. Save the snack until we've been towed to the car dealership."

———

In addition to rescuing friends and providing a shoulder to cry on, Jack doesn't mind lending his car. His heart is way bigger than that car. After we left the Miata at the car hospital, we swung by CYCotics so he could get back to work. My cell phone began to chirp as we were pulling up in front of the shop. Sally.

"Hey!" she said. "The ankle biters are feeling better."

I said, "That's wonderful."

"I think they'll conk out early and sleep through the night. I'm feeling better and Benjamin has a meeting. So guess what?"

"Come on over?"

"You got it. See you, say, about seven? I will be fresh and fragrant and ready for big-people talk by then. I'll call Margaret and tell her too."

"Who was that?" Jack said when I clicked off. "Your client?"

"Sally. The on-again, off-again shower is on. Again."

"Hey! When do we go?"

———

I might not have been able to accomplish much for Emmy Lou at this point, but I had plenty to do, besides worrying about what had led to Tony's death and who had slashed my tires. I had four new tires to buy. Of course, I also had to worry about mudrooms. I wanted to check out what was trendy in the wonderful world of entryway storage. I swung by my apartment and took the pooches for a good long walk to tire them out. I tossed them some dog cookies and made myself a sandwich. I poked around on the Net getting some

ideas. I leafed through design and organizing magazines too.
I checked my notes from National Association of Professional Organizers courses. Truffle and Sweet Marie wanted
to play their favorite game. It was hard enough to concentrate
without playing Where's Charlotte? Truffle was particularly
miffed when I wouldn't. I immediately felt bad. My two cuddly wieners had been trying so hard to be good dogs. They'd
more or less stopped hiding keys and shoes. They hadn't
killed a sofa cushion in months. All they needed was a bit of
challenge every day. It was up to me to give it to them.

"Fine, you win. When Jack gets home tonight, we'll play
the game before the shower. It's a promise. Now where's my
other shoe, Truffle?" I flicked on the television in case there
was an update on Emmy Lou. Todd Tyrell's teeth filled the
screen. As the camera pulled back, I could see he was talking
to a rail-thin, sunken-faced woman with straggling greasy
black hair. She was smoking intensely, and Todd moved
back as she exhaled in his direction. I chuckled. I needed a
break.

"We stand here," he intoned, "with the grieving mother of
yesterday's tragic victim, Tony Starkman." For some reason
he always sounds like he's either watching a space launch
or conducting a funeral service. A long pause ensued as the
cameras scanned a run-down street, a dilapidated apartment
building, and an unbroken wave of graffiti on the street-level
walls. From the look on Todd's face he wanted out of there
before someone sprayed a gang tag on the back of his
thousand-dollar suit. "What evil has torn this young man
from the bosom of his family?"

A camera zoomed in toward the woman's chest and
zoomed out again. She inhaled once again speculatively.

"You are devastated, of course," Todd instructed her, "by
the death of your only son."

She cast her eyes down and turned away from the cameras. Todd tried again. "But this loss of young Tony is tear-
ing you apart."

Nothing.

"Do you have anything to say to the community about your son's death?"

She turned back to Todd and squinted, "Like what?"

"Like how you appreciate the outpouring of sympathy?"

"And I will too, when it comes. Are you going to put that on the television?"

"Of course," Todd said, looking like he'd like to get his mitts on a flamethrower. "And what about to the person who is alleged to have threatened your son the night before his death?"

Her eyes filled and she shook her head.

A picture of Tony, at about age ten, flashed across the screen, an awkward, smiling little boy. Horrible to imagine a child dead. The picture was followed by a shot of me. Forget mean, I looked downright dangerous. By that time I could see it coming: the visual implication was that I was the person who threatened, allegedly, the poor innocent boy the night before his death.

Once I got my breathing under control, I picked up the phone and called Margaret.

"Not much we can do about it. The damage is done. People get away with way too much by using 'alleged.' I can scare them into retracting if you want, but they'll keep airing that retraction and people will ask themselves if there's something behind it."

"Terrific," I said.

"Never mind. Hey, I hear the shower's back on tonight."

"About that, I hope the three of us will fit into Jack's Mini Minor."

"It doesn't matter. I have some running around to do. I'll come on my own. And Jack also told me someone slashed your tires."

"That's creepy, isn't it?"

"For sure. So here's a thought: maybe you should stay away from those people on Bell Street."

"I would, but I have to finish the job for Dwayne."

I had a feeling that Margaret was rolling her eyes. She said, "And you should also ask yourself why you get so overly involved with your clients' problems."

So much for sympathy.

———◆———

I arrived at my mudroom client's house just as the school bus rumbled down the street. Lucky for me, the elementary school children in this area didn't arrive home until after four. I'm sure they didn't appreciate it, but I did. Two kids tumbled off the bus and raced into the house. Shoes, jackets, backpacks, and papers went flying as they bolted through the door. They left it open. One shot off to the family room and switched on the television. The other made for the kitchen, from where the smell of something fresh from the oven wafted through the air. I smiled at Bernice from the doorstep.

She stepped outside, her arms crossed in front of her. It's a bit of body language that you learn to read quickly in this business. Usually it translates into "Game over."

Bernice said with a pathetic attempt at a fake smile, "I'm not sure this is the right time for us to take on a project like this. We're pretty busy."

The changeable client is the only constant in this business, so that didn't throw me off. In fact, I could have lip-synched that dialogue along with her; I'd heard it so often. I countered with, "Why don't we get it over with? Won't take long." I looked past her into the mudroom, where a new layer of debris was scattered.

She lowered her voice and said, "I will not be working with you. I don't want my children exposed to danger."

I blinked. "What?"

Her eyes filled. "That poor boy who was killed yesterday."

She must have meant Tony, since Woodbridge wasn't a town where children got killed. I remembered the glowering menace that Tony had presented and wondered how that could translate into fear for this trio of lively and well-loved children.

"I don't see how—"

She set her mouth in a firm line. "I am not having *you* near my children."

"You don't have to do this project if you don't want it, Bernice. But your children certainly won't be in any danger."

I attempted to make eye contact, but she averted her gaze.

"I understand," I said. "I'll send you a bill for my time. If you decide to go ahead later, we'll apply it to the contract."

It was easy to figure out who was to blame. The ubiquitous nabob of noxious news, Todd Tyrell. What did he want from me? Ruin? Disgrace? Better ratings?

I knew in my heart it wasn't personal. But I'd already made up my mind that whatever Todd wanted, he wasn't getting it without a fight.

—※—

I was feeling ridiculously dejected. That's not like me, but seeing your face flashed on the television implying that you kill children *can* get you down. I motored off to North Elm and parked at the bottom of the hill in front of the house with the cheerful yellow door. I needed to talk to Lilith about working for Dwayne. My friend Rose Skipowski, coincidentally Lilith's landlady and client, was the person to cheer me up.

Rose answered the door, as usual wheeling her oxygen apparatus. She was resplendent in a jogging suit in vivid spring green, with double white stripes down the arms and legs and a pair of blindingly white sneakers. "You're in luck," she said. "Our girl's conscious and making sense. Come on in."

I followed Rose down the short hall to the authentic seventies orange and brown living room. Her sneakers squeaked cheerfully as she shuffled along. Schopenhauer, one of Jack's more spectacular rescue projects, followed, wagging his large sweeping tail in welcome.

I looked around. "I thought your daughter was visiting."

"She was. Had to leave a bit early. Career matters and all that. She got a chance at a shoot and she was off. Once you hit forty in the movie business you take what you can get. Can't blame her. She's terrified she'll end up playing character roles in straight-to-DVD horror films."

"Oh." Every time I thought about Rose and the distance between her and her daughter, I felt a flash of guilt. I'm pretty good at dodging my own mother's phone calls, although, in fairness, it's usually because I don't want to find out that she has news, say, another husband or something.

"Don't worry about it, Charlotte. People have to live their own lives. But I have Lilith here to keep me company. She keeps me guessing. And you know what? This old gal's learning to cook vegetarian. As a matter of fact, almost all cookies are vegetarian. Not vegan, I hear, but vegetarian. I have some Toll House cookies cooling on the racks. Your favorite. Want some?"

Rose always has cookies baking in the oven or cooling on the counter. There was no way I was going to say no, or mention the cupcakes, although I had been so upset by the note on my windshield that I had left them all to Jack.

Lilith bounced down the stairs and stretched, rubbing her tousled turquoise and ebony hair.

"Good morning," I said.

Lilith laughed. Maybe because it was about four in the afternoon. "Welcome to the wonderful world of the night-shift worker."

"Have I got a deal for you," I said. "You may be able to give that shift a miss. The stuffed-animal gig is available again."

Rose, who is always up-to-date on what's going on, said, "You mean your client's out of the hoosegow?"

I said, "Not yet."

Lilith said, "What's a hoosegow?"

"Emmy Lou's stuck in jail. Her husband wants us to continue on with the project as a surprise for her when she gets out. Of course, we won't be actually eliminating any of the toys, but nevertheless, we will get started. We can take inventory—"

"Pack 'em and stack 'em."

"Exactly."

"Maybe it's the brain damage from my troubled youth," Lilith said, "but aren't we suspicious of that guy because of the lady in the red dress?"

"Yes, we are, even though when you are with him, he could—"

Rose shook her head. "It's quite terrible, that young lad dying and that poor woman being questioned. It's such a nice old neighborhood too. Not fancy, but respectable, good people living on Bell Street. I met a lot of them over the past fifty years. Now I guess it's dangerous. What do you call that? Urban decay?"

"Actually, Bell Street seems to be upgrading. I think the neighborhood's safe, but we're not a hundred percent sure about Dwayne's role. Which is why Lilith, if she agrees, will be working with me, and neither of us will be in the house alone, whether he's there or not."

"I can come too," Rose said. "I have a great scream."

"Are you serious?" Lilith said, giving her a hug. "We need you here on cookie detail."

"Oh fine. Break my heart. Better build your strength with this latest batch," Rose said.

I reached for my first one. "I hear they're full of vitamin CH."

Lilith said through a mouthful of cookies, "Chocolate's my favorite vitamin. So, you want to start today?"

"Can't. I have to get ready for a baby shower."

"A baby shower. *What!* You're not?"

I recoiled. "Me? No, not me, of course not. How would I be? I mean, I'm not even . . ."

Lilith said, "Oops, a sore point. Sorry."

"No, it is not a sore point. I am very happy with my life," I said somewhat shrilly. "I have my dogs. I have my friends. I have my job, which I love."

"Except when your clients end up involved in a murder."

"Except then, yes."

"It's starting to become a habit."

"Twice does not mean a habit. And the two situations are quite different."

"Okay, I'm going to stop putting my foot it in," Lilith said. "So whose baby shower is it?"

"Sally's."

Lilith squealed and did a little dance. "Really? That's great. I love Sally. Do you think I could come?"

"Why not?" I said. "Everyone else wants to. Seven at Sally's."

Rose cleared her throat. "Sally and I have a history, you know. Doing some joint snooping on your behalf."

"Ah yes. Sorry. I didn't mean to be rude. I never thought. Would you like to come too, Rose?"

"Wouldn't miss it. Thanks for asking. Lilith and I can get out there together. Good thing I made those cookies."

"I can run out and get something from Rose and me." Lilith seemed even more excited than Rose. They were both considerably more excited than I was.

"See you there," I said, trying not to grumble.

※

Many times your best bet is to visit the public library. This was one of those times. My next stop was the Woodbridge

Public Library. My favorite librarian, Ramona, was where I wanted her: at the reference desk. She was wearing her trademark denim. Today that meant an ankle-length slim skirt with some exotic embroidery down the side and a delphinium blue top that looked spectacular with her silver brush cut.

"Glad to see you, Charlotte," she said. "You always perk things up around here. I see you're back in the news again. So what can we do for you today?"

"I'm looking for city directories for Woodbridge. I want to find out who lived at 7 Bell Street in the early eighties."

"Sure thing, Charlotte," she said. "Lived? Hmm. We only have the current one. But tell me what you're looking for and I might be able to find it somewhere else. One of our libraries has a great historical collection."

You can always count on Ramona.

I filled her in on Emmy Lou Wright's name and the likely years.

She said, "There was a big to-do on Bell Street yesterday."

"Right."

"Coincidence? Not that I'm supposed to ask these things."

"It's probably a waste of your time and mine. We'll never find it."

"Never say never," Ramona said. "Leave it with me and I'll see what I can do. If it's public information, we might be able to track it some other way."

"What about the name of the person who owns the lots being redeveloped on that street? Can you find that?"

"Sure. That should be a matter of public record. I'll let you know."

"Thanks for everything."

"Think nothing of it. Have fun at the shower tonight."

I raised an eyebrow.

Ramona showed her wicked librarian grin. "All part of the service. We're thinking of putting up a sign: 'We know everything, including your business.' What do you think?"

Welcome back to Woodbridge, Charlotte, I thought, the small community where, if you don't know what you're doing at any given time, ask the first person you see.

<hr>

Maybe it was crazy but I buzzed over to Bell Street in the Mini. I knocked on Bonnie's door. She looked even worse than she had during my earlier visit, but her eyes lit up when she saw me. In that minute, I realized how lonely she must be, starting a new life, new business, new town, while battling MS.

"I heard about your car. That's terrible."

"Don't tell me that was on the news."

She shook her head. "No, Bill ran into your friend Jack outside the shop. I can't believe anyone around here would slash your tires. I guess I might have believed that Tony would have. But of course, he's the one person who couldn't have. It's so distressing. Is there some lunatic in the area? Maybe that's who killed Tony. We were starting to settle in and now this. Bill thinks it might be Dwayne trying to keep you away. But why would Dwayne ask you to work for him and then slash your tires?"

"You're right. I doubt that it's Dwayne. But I'm sure we'll get to the bottom of it soon. I don't think you should worry at all. The hostility seems to be aimed at me. Everyone's mad. The Dingwalls. The guy across the street who may or may not be Emmy Lou's father."

Bonnie grimaced. "I've seen him. He looks miserable. And his wife always seems like a beaten dog. If I even see him so much as raise a hand to her, I'll have the cops on him."

"It does seem awfully coincidental that my tires were slashed after I was talking to him. Of course, speaking of cops, maybe one of them did it."

Bonnie blinked.

"Just kidding," I said, "although the detective in charge does hate me. But then, so do the media. But anyway, enough about murder. Any chance you can rescue me with a supply of something fun for a last-minute baby shower? We don't know boy or girl yet."

"That's fun. And I have the ticket. I have some blueberry cupcakes and some raspberry cupcakes. So we have pink and blue, and for good measure I can throw in some nice neutral but tangy lemon meringue. How's that? And maybe a few chocolate. For good luck. This is good for me too."

Bonnie refused to take a cent for the cupcakes, although I pushed it. "You had your tires slashed on my street," she said, "and I want to make up for it in some small way."

"But—"

She raised a shaky hand. "No buts."

I left looking on the bright side. At this rate, I might never have to learn how to bake.

*Put a teaspoon of ground cinnamon
in your vacuum cleaner bag to cut pet odors.
Save time, money, and storage space.
How organized is that?*

14

Margaret's glower was the first thing I spotted when Jack and I got to the shower. She'd arrived before us and was perched on Sally's white leather sofa, surrounded by Barbie dolls and Thomas the Tanks. Her legs were crossed, and one foot was tapping dangerously. I checked around for tricky and protruding Lego projects. I hate sitting on them. There was no sign of Sally, but I heard screeching children from upstairs and the thundering of tiny hooves as the kids raced to escape bedtime.

Truffle and Sweet Marie stuck close to me, probably worried that children would materialize and pull their long silky ears.

"I thought this was the three of us, nice and relaxing," Margaret hissed. "Then Jack had to invite himself. And now Lilith and Rose are here too."

"And I thought the kids would be in bed. Anyway, what are you talking about, you love Jack."

She made a face. "Love would be pushing it."

"And Lilith is wonderful. So is Rose. Chill out," I whispered.

"I was hoping for wine and confidences, no party crashers."

"Consider yourself lucky: I forgot to tell Pepper. I've had, as you know, not the best day."

"And you forgot to tell me we were all supposed to bring some food."

"It's a shower. Everyone brings food. Otherwise there wouldn't be more than we could eat and that wouldn't be as much fun, would it?"

Margaret stared at me. "It is my first shower, so I don't know all the arcane rules."

"It's not actually a shower, as I keep explaining to you. You don't need to worry."

Margaret sniffed. "I'll worry if I want to."

I set out my cupcakes on pretty plates in the dining room, next to Rose's mountain of Toll House cookies. I wanted to give Margaret time to get over her hissiness. She seemed to recover quickly: that might have been because Lilith had made Rice Krispies squares. Margaret, Lilith, and Jack were sitting around getting ready to trash-talk anyone who wasn't in the room. I made sure to get back soon. "You should too, Rose," I said. "No one is safe from them."

Sally, who can manage to look gorgeous even when hugely pregnant, tiptoed down the stairs holding her crossed fingers to her lips.

Jack said, "Open my gift first."

I glared at him and lowered my voice to say, "You are supposed to drag it out at a shower. Not thrust gifts at people before they even know it's a shower." It was bad enough that Jack was a newbie, but a useless newbie was something else entirely.

"A gift!" Sally bubbled, shaking her blonde curls. "I love gifts! Where is it?"

"I didn't do a great job wrapping it," Jack said. "Then it

blew around a bit on the roof of the car. Kind of wrecked the paper."

"Wow, that is so thoughtful of you, Jack." Sally bent forward as far as her belly would allow her and whipped the messy paper off the lumpy present.

"Oh *really*," I muttered to Margaret. "He's lost it. The baby's not even born yet. What is he or she going to do with a bicycle?"

"It's a gender-neutral color," Jack said proudly.

I said out loud, "Yes, but a baby can't ride a bicycle. Even if it is yellow."

Jack said huffily, "It's a tricycle, Charlotte. Three wheels. And it's only a matter of time until the baby can ride it. Do you know if it's a he or she, Sal?"

"Don't know, don't care," Sally said. "Healthy baby, that's the order form I filled out."

"This is great. I've never been to a shower before," Jack said. "When do we eat?"

"What did you say? Shower? Is this a shower?" Sally squealed.

"It is now," I grumbled.

Sally said, "I love showers! So I say we eat after I open the gifts. My shower, my rules."

Margaret stood up. "Me next!"

"It's Margaret's first shower too," Jack said.

The floppy bunny was a huge hit, and Margaret shot me a little smirk. I guess I had it coming. Not everyone was as disenchanted with fuzzy plush critters as I was.

"Actually, it's my first too," Lilith said. That wasn't much of a surprise since I knew that there probably hadn't been many when she was homeless. She passed over a lilac envelope. I wasn't sure that Lilith could afford to buy shower gifts, but the girl's got heart.

Sally opened it and screamed. Nobody screams like Sal. "You angel!"

Lilith said, "I didn't know what to get you and I thought

this would come in handy." Lilith flushed as Sally passed around the homemade certificate for two afternoons free babysitting. We were all filled with admiration and probably a bit of relief since Sally would need a break and Margaret and I would be absolutely hopeless with anything babylike.

"Will you look at that! *Jemima Puddle-Duck*," Sally said enthusiastically as she got to my offering. She began leafing through the Beatrix Potter books. "I haven't seen these books since I was a kid. You had them all, Charlotte. You had so many wonderful children's books. I wasn't allowed to have books in my house. Too messy."

Oh crap. I hoped we weren't going to play the my-dysfunctional-family-trumps-your-dysfunctional-family game again.

Rose cleared her throat. "I am afraid that I stole Lilith's idea of a certificate. Mine will get you home-cooked meals delivered on whatever days Lilith takes care of your little ones. So you can rest or go out with your friends and come home and not worry about dinner. I remember what it is like to be a young mother with twenty-one meals a week hanging over my head like a . . ." She paused.

Jack said, "Sword of Damocles?"

Sally said, "Grand piano on a fraying rope?" She lurched out of her chair, lumbered across the room, and gave Rose a bear hug.

Once we'd hit the dining room and heaped plates with cookies, squares, and cupcakes, we returned to the comfortable sofas and big easy chairs in Sally's living room and the focus shifted to my latest problem. You know, the usual: dead body, client in jail, evil pictures of me flashing hourly on every television screen, possibly dangerous assignment, same old, same old. Theories flew. Of course, everyone's preconceptions colored their opinions.

Jack said, "Charlotte thinks Emmy Lou's parents live across the street. Maybe she wanted to protect them."

He would think that. Jack's parents had been a pair of

Tweedledum and Tweedledee twins, simple, warm, and affectionate. They'd been the ones with the homemade pancakes and fresh preserves. Jack's mom had treated Sally and Margaret and me as if we were the girls she'd always wanted and never had. For our birthdays we each got a special treat: marble layer cake with coins wrapped in waxed paper baked into it. And sparklers. One for each year and one for good luck. Jack's dad fixed the flat tires on our bicycles. Jack's mom wiped our tears and gave each of us misfits hugs when we needed them. One year she made everyone Halloween costumes. Our own mothers had more important things to deal with.

I shook off the memories of Jack's parents. Didn't want to blubber. I said, "Now I'm not so sure if those people are her parents."

Jack shot me a puzzled look. "But didn't Patti Magliaro tell you that they were?"

"That's her story, but you all know Patti. She's a bit . . . Anyway, when I asked the man across the street if he was Emmy Lou's father, he turned hostile."

Rose had been quiet all evening, but now she piped up. "How would Emmy Lou's confession protect them, Jack? Do you think the parents killed this boy?"

"I don't know what to think. I am trying to find out if they are, to figure what might be going on in Emmy Lou's mind. She's obviously not thinking straight."

Margaret said, "Call me crazy, but even if they are her parents, most moms and pops would want to be protected from the shame of having their daughter arrested, although that might be my mother's particular brand of weirdness."

Jack shrugged and snagged a couple of Rice Krispies squares. "Could be she thought these guys were threatening them. I mean, your parents, you'd do anything for them."

"They're not her parents," I said irritably.

Sally chimed in. "If they are and they're estranged,

I know from my own experience there'll be bitterness on both sides. She won't protect them. They won't protect her." I noticed the small pained tightening of her mouth. Lot of history in Sally's life. She added, "But what about that kid next door, what's his name? Kevin?" She glanced upstairs to where we hoped her own kids were finally sleeping. "He was the one who had the relationship with this Tony. You said she was quite fond of him, Charlotte. Maybe he did it and she's protecting him."

"I don't think so. He wasn't even there at the time."

"The other neighbor then," Lilith interjected cheerfully. "Tall? Agitated? What's his name?"

"Bill. Bill Baxter."

"Didn't he seem a bit overly involved with Emmy Lou? Like getting in a fight with the other guys over her. That's nothing if not freaky."

I had a bit of trouble with that. "I don't think he did it. The Baxters were both upset. It seems to have aggravated Bonnie's medical condition. But even if Bill Baxter had done it—and he certainly had a hate on for Tony—why would Emmy Lou ruin her own perfect life by protecting him?"

"Maybe they were having an affair," Sally said, waggling her eyebrows.

"How do you do that with your eyebrows?" Margaret said. "I'd love to be able to."

I sighed. "No. I saw how the Baxters were together. He's a nervous, irritating guy, but I'd say he truly loves Bonnie."

Jack managed to swallow his current Toll House cookie in time to add, "For sure, that was real. I liked watching them together. And those cupcakes could only come from a happy home. I worry about this Dwayne."

I said, "Exactly. He's the one with the most—"

A voice cut through the air. "You're leaving out the obvious answer."

We all whipped around to face Pepper.

The room fell silent. Even Truffle and Sweet Marie failed to bark, and they hate Pepper. She was in serious glam mode in a black and white print dress with a crisscross top that showed enough cleavage to cause a serious car accident. She held a pale yellow gift bag, decorated with happy ducks. Curled streamers in pink, blue, and yellow cascaded from the handles. She sat down and crossed her legs confidently, showing off sexy party sandals. If anything, I thought she looked more dangerous than usual. Nick the Stick was behind her, grinning like the goofball he is. I didn't pay attention to what he was wearing. Usually you can't see past his handsome, useless face. He had a bottle of red wine tucked under one arm while he hung on to a twelve-pack of Corona. "Hey, guys. The door was open. I guess you didn't hear us ringing."

I ignored him. That has always been the best approach with Nick.

Sally struggled awkwardly out of her chair. "Pepper, what a surprise! First the shower and now this."

Surprise was putting it mildly, of course. Pepper didn't have much to do with any of her old friends, including Sally, although I was the only one she hated enough to arrest.

Jack managed to produce a convincing grin. "Hey, Pepper. Nick." He gave Pepper a bear hug and jabbed Nick playfully on the arm. Jack likes a distraction more than most.

"What's the most obvious answer?" I managed to ask.

"What do you think? A woman confesses to killing a guy who's been tormenting her. There's a record of her being harassed by him. End of story. It remains to be seen what the DA will go for, but it will be serious time. But why are you bothering to come up with all these dumb-ass speculations? She's not protecting anyone. There is no secret. No conspiracy. She's guilty. Just. Plain. Guilty. Relax and enjoy it."

"So," Nick said, brandishing the twelve-pack, "let's party."

I worked to conceal my dismay over Pepper and Nick's arrival. I spent a lot of time talking to Margaret. She was busy concealing irritation as well. Sometimes you need a support group.

"Look at that," Margaret whispered as Pepper handed over her gift to Sally. Pepper had the strangest expression on her face.

"What?"

"She's got the baby crazies."

"Pepper? Oh come on," I whispered back. "She does not."

"Listen, I should know what the baby crazies look like, Charlotte. They run in my family. Big-time."

"I've never heard of the baby crazies. That's different. Your mom wants grandchildren for some obscure reason. But Pepper's a detective. What's she going to do with a . . . ?"

Sally cleared her throat and shot us a warning look. "See what Pepper brought for the baby?"

"It's from Pepper and *Nick*." Pepper linked her arm with Nick's. Possibly to keep him from bolting, although perhaps that was my imagination.

"It's great," Margaret said. "So . . ."

Jack scratched his head. "What exactly is it?"

"It's a crib mobile. And these are little bumblebee boots to amuse the baby. See the bells?" Pepper picked up the boots and jingled them a bit. That set Truffle and Sweet Marie off. We had been living on borrowed time in the good-pooch behavior department.

Jack shouted above the blizzard of barking. "Wow. That's great. The baby's going to love them."

Sally said, "Never mind the baby, *I* love them. Thank you, Pepper."

"And Nick," Pepper said.

Nick looked up from his beer. "What?" He flinched slightly when he caught Pepper's expression. "The baby. Yeah, great, great news, Sal. Really great. The best."

Jack said, "Hey, Pepper, let me show you the bike I got for the baby. How cool is this?"

Margaret leaned over to me and snickered, "It's a world gone mad."

"You're telling me. I can't wait to get out of here."

Pepper said, "What are you going to call the baby, Sally?"

"Depends on whether it's a boy or a girl, of course, but I haven't decided."

Jack said, "You have a theme going so far: Madison, Dallas, Savannah."

"How about Chicago?" Margaret said. "I like that town."

"Denver's nice," Pepper said.

"Milwaukee," Margaret said.

"Houston is good for a boy," Pepper said, giving Margaret a dirty look. Luckily Sally pretty well ignored them.

Margaret is immune to dirty looks. And she doesn't care if she's being ignored. "I'm partial to Boise."

Pepper rolled her eyes. "Macon is actually a nice name. And a real one."

"Whatever you say. Let's not forget Biloxi."

Jack said, "A name is a serious business. Sally could probably use some help."

"I'm always serious," Pepper shot back. "I like Macon and Houston."

Margaret said thoughtfully, "There's always Omaha."

I stood up and made my way to the dining room. "I think I'll get some more cookies to pass around."

I needed a break from what promised to be a litany of place-names. I arranged more treats on a plate, taking as much time as I could. When I turned to go back into the living room, I almost careened into Nick, big, handsome, clueless, and unfortunately blocking my exit. "She's on the name thing again, isn't she? She can go on for hours. Sometimes I think I'm going to pass out."

Nick responds best to crisp commands. Short words. Unambiguous meanings. Like "Go to hell." This time I kept it to: "Out of my way, Nick."

He reached over and grabbed my wrist. "Come on, Charlie. Talk a bit. You know, old times. High school. You and me. Before things got so messed up."

"Move it or lose it." Staying in the kitchen with Nick was right up there with root canal on my playlist.

"I'm having another brewski. You gonna join me?"

"No."

"Don't be like that, Charlie. Give me a call sometime and we'll go for a ride in my 'Stang."

The last thing I would ever do was go for a ride in his pride and joy Mustang, or his black Dodge Ram. Nor did I want a tour of the garage he'd built to store his "babies" or a detailed description of the security and video-surveillance systems he had to protect them. Too bad he didn't put half that energy into making his wife happy.

I lowered my voice, but only in order to sound more threatening. "Don't ever call me Charlie again. Let go of me and get out of my way, or you'll be wearing these cupcakes."

"Well," came a chilly voice from the door, "look who's here."

Nick dropped my hand as if it had ignited.

I looked Pepper in the eye. "You should feed this boy. I think he's ready to kill for dessert."

Nick managed to look pathetically grateful. "Yeah. Just one, okay? Or two? What's the good of having them if no one can eat 'em?"

I moved away from Nick, past Pepper, and toward the living room, but not before I saw the vicious look Pepper delivered Nick. I said over my shoulder, "I hold you responsible, Pepper, to make sure he doesn't clean the plate before anyone else gets a chance."

When I returned to the living room followed by a sheepish Nick and a slow-simmering Pepper, Margaret mouthed the words "baby crazy" one more time.

— ✦ —

"Haven't you ever wanted a baby, Charlotte?"

I swiveled my head to stare at Jack.

"Oops," he said, "maybe you should keep your eyes on the road."

"Maybe you shouldn't make startling comments."

"Was that a startling comment? People have been having babies forever. It's hardly breaking news. I think most people think about it. Don't you think about it when you go to Sally's? The way they're all pink and squirmy and they smell of powder after their baths? And they snuggle up and—look out for that tree!"

I swerved the Mini back onto the road and tried to concentrate on my driving. "I don't get those feelings, Jack."

"Sally does. Maybe I should drive."

"I'm fine to drive."

He said, "And I think Pepper does too."

"I noticed. I realize it's normal and a good thing. It's not for everyone. I love Sally's kids, but I don't feel ready for any myself. I'm still trying to be a grown-up."

"I guess you have to get over what's-his-name, that snake, back in the city."

"It's not about him. It's about me. I don't even know if I'd make a good mom. I didn't have such a storybook childhood. And all around me, I see so many problems. I don't want to add to them."

"My childhood was excellent," Jack said. "I'd like to be able to offer that to another little human."

"Margaret and I don't feel that way. I mean we know you had a great life, and we do know it's possible, it seems . . ."

"Don't worry about it," Jack said. "Like you say, not for everyone."

"Definitely not for Nick. Did you pick up on that?"

"Oh yeah. But I'm sure Pepper thinks he's part of her plan."

"That's my point. No wonder Margaret calls it baby crazy."

"Anyway, I think you'd make a great mother. So keep an open mind."

"I will," I said as we pulled into the driveway. "But don't start pulling your philosopher tricks on me."

"Aw shucks," he said.

"And mind your own business," I added.

Jack swiveled in the passenger seat and stared at me. "But you are my business."

Keep your shoes in boxes.
Label each box with a digital photo of the pair that is inside.
You'll save time hunting for the right shoes.

15

Tuesday morning, Lilith and Rose picked me up at home and deposited me at the Mazda dealership before they peeled off in Rose's ancient LeMans. We had an hour before we needed to meet Dwayne, and she had plans to take Rose to Hannaford's for groceries. We agreed to connect at the Rheinbeck house once I confirmed that we were going ahead with the project. I paid for the replacement tires, although I am sure I turned pale when faced with the bill. I made expensive tracks for Bell Street for my ten o'clock meeting with Dwayne. I was ten minutes early, which is the way I like things. I sat in the Mazda and waited. Dwayne's car was not in the driveway. The top of Emmy Lou's new Volvo C70 convertible, which remained parked in front of the garage, was already getting a bit dusty. I did my best to feel upbeat about working for him, especially since I'd had two other cancellations besides my former mudroom client.

At the screech of tires around the corner, I turned to see

Dwayne head down the street and then veer into the driveway on two wheels. He slammed on the brakes and barely managed to avoid hitting Emmy Lou's car. I hurried up the pathway and met him at the door.

His face was pale and pasty. Maybe I was imagining it, but I thought he'd lost a bit of the shine on his head. I caught the door before it slammed in my face.

I said, "My colleague should be here any second, but I suppose we can start."

I wasn't even sure he heard that. "You want something to drink?" he said as we entered the living room. He kept going into the kitchen and opened the stainless steel double fridge door.

"Not for me."

"This has been three of the worst days of my life." He popped open a beer, barreled out of the kitchen area, and slumped on the leather sofa.

I took a seat on the chair. "I can imagine. Have you found out what's happening with Emmy Lou?"

He took a long swig.

I waited.

"I'm back from trying to see her. She's had some kind of collapse. They have her in the psych ward. It's in a secure facility."

"Oh no!" No wonder he was guzzling beer at ten in the morning.

He ran one hand over his head. "How can this happen? How can you have a beautiful wife one week and then the next you don't know if she'll get out of jail? Or if she'll even be lucky enough to get out of the psychiatric unit and into jail. At least in jail, you can have lawyers, trials, appeals."

All of which cost a bundle, I thought. How long would the Rheinbecks hold on to their home, cars, and business if they had to fund a defense? Maybe Dwayne hadn't gotten that far in his thinking. He certainly seemed frightened for his wife. I would have believed him wholeheartedly, if it hadn't been for the nagging memory of the girl with the long dark hair and the slinky red dress, and my lingering suspicion that Emmy Lou was protecting Dwayne. Maybe he'd chosen to let her shrivel in some hideous institution for the rest of her life while he went on with his. I had no reason to trust Dwayne Rheinbeck.

"Explain to me why they moved her to a psychiatric facility."

Dwayne stared at me. "Because she's acting crazy? Saying she killed someone that she couldn't have? You wouldn't classify that as some kind of mental imbalance?"

I didn't mention that the lead detective thought Emmy Lou was guilty, not unbalanced. "But mental illness can be a legitimate defense. So it could be good news. Was she showing any signs of instability before all this?"

"No, nothing." He slumped a bit more and slammed his beer on the coffee table, spilling a bit. "But what if she was and I missed it? I keep asking myself the same question. What if she was losing it and I was too busy with Wet Paint and the expansion project to notice? You know what? Lately everything was all about me."

And maybe a girl in a red dress too, I thought. That might have been enough to send a woman over the edge.

I said, "Emmy Lou seemed very nervous and jumpy when I met with her to discuss the stuffed animals. She even had a little tic in her eye. Her hands were shaking too."

"Oh my God. She was losing it and I didn't even notice. Too wrapped up in myself." To tell the truth, he was the picture of misery. Only my suspicions stopped me from giving him a reassuring hug.

"More to the point," I added, "she said she was having memory problems. I think that's another sign of mental distress. Didn't remember buying some of the toys, that kind of thing. Could have been overload from work."

"I missed all that. I can't believe any of this is happening." He threw up his hands. "I have no idea how to handle it."

"This has been a big shock to you. Do you want to pull the plug on the project?" I asked, expecting a yes.

"What? No, no. We've got to start it. You can't back out. You have to work with me. Whatever you need. Design. Storage. Display stuff. That way when she gets home, she'll have something to look forward to."

"Oh," I said, "we can definitely do that. I was wondering about the expense when you'll have all the legal stuff to worry about."

"You know what? This is one thing we can deal with. The rest of it's a big insane unknowable nightmare. So we're going ahead. But I don't think we can get rid of any of these critters. I don't want her coming home and flipping out because some pink bunny rabbit that I've never even seen went out with the trash."

"No arguments from me. I guess you want it done quickly."

"Yep. Only thing is I usually sleep until nine or ten in the morning because I get in late. The house is yours from then on. And I'm out every night, if that helps."

"It does. I'll come up with a storage plan that's not too complex or pricey, because Emmy Lou may decide on a more permanent solution later on. I'll get some units that you could use elsewhere or sell off if that happens. And I'll have a colleague working with me, which will speed up the project. Do you want a cost estimate?"

He shook his head. "I don't care what it costs."

"Good, we'll solve the overflow for the short term and preserve her collection. How does that sound?"

"Yeah, sounds good. Whatever you want, as long as when she gets home, if she wants some particular fuzzball, she can have it. Look, I realize I sound crazy too. I know they're only plush toys. But you know what? They're the only damn thing I have any control over."

——◆◆——

Lilith got out of the LeMans as Dwayne was hotfooting it out the front door again. He nodded absently in her direction and thrust a set of keys into my hand as I introduced her.

"Don't worry," I called after him as he raced for his car.

"Talking to the wind?" Lilith said with a grin.

"Emmy Lou's had some kind of breakdown."

"That's freakin' awful. Don't blame him for flipping out," she said.

I led the way up the stairs to show her what we were faced with. "The last time I was here, there were toys all over the stairs. I guess the police removed them. Dwayne wants us to keep them all. He's worried that any change will be traumatic for her. Let's inventory the lot and figure out a quick solution to display some and store the rest."

"Makes sense."

"See if there are categories we can place then in. Make a note about which ones are where. That kind of thing."

As we opened the door to Emmy Lou's bedroom, Lilith's face lit up. "I love this. If it hadn't been for what happened here, this whole thing would be a blast. Like spending the night in a toy store. I don't even know why'd you'd want to organize them in the first place. They're great the way they are."

She didn't change her mind after we checked out the spare room that doubled as an office. "Wow, I thought there were a lot in the main bedroom. This is the best job ever."

"Good attitude, except for the don't-know-why-you'd-organize-them part. And we're going to make sure we're never alone in the magic toy store. Just in case."

"Don't worry. I'm not looking for trouble. And I haven't forgotten Tony's death or your slashed tires either. Not to mention the prank phone call and the complaint to the police."

"Right," I said grimly, staring at the giant stuffed zebra. "Let's go get our flat-pack bins and we can tackle these suckers. We can break them down into oversize, regular, and mini."

"Darn," Lilith said. "I was hoping we'd go by color. There's some great purple stuff here."

Believe it or not, the census of stuffies didn't take quite as long as I thought it would. I measured the walls in Emmy Lou and Dwayne's bedroom, hallway, and spare bedroom. I took a number of shots of the rooms with my digital camera so I wouldn't forget details. I even took a few of the down-stairs, to keep the style that Emmy Lou and Dwayne favored firmly in mind. I spent most of my time working with a layout of the rooms and furniture templates, figuring out how to rearrange the rooms to maximize the storage. As Lilith whirled through her task, I calculated the number of bookcases it would take to double-line two walls in the main bedroom. The upstairs hallway was long enough to handle four units, and the spare room could be completely lined with bookcases. Each one could hold a lot of fuzzies. If I could convince Dwayne to store the furniture in that room, then we might have a quick solution. If Gary Gigantes could squeeze me into his crowded schedule, he could attach the bookcases, put them on casters, slap on some nice trim to hide the joints, whatever I would need to make this work.

Meanwhile, Lilith had even managed to complete a sub-sort by color too. When you find a reliable, intelligent, hard-working assistant, you learn not to argue with her. Anyway, the color idea was growing on me. Dwayne had not returned by the time we left the bins full of toys, locked up the house, and started walking to our cars. This time no harm had been done to either vehicle.

As we reached the cars, I spotted Mr. Wright in his garden

across the street. I nodded in his direction. "That's the one who might be Emmy Lou's father," I said to Lilith.

She said, "Figured that. I noticed him on Sunday when I got here. And today too. He's oozing mean. Bet she didn't have any picnic growing up there."

"My impression too. If he is, what would make a smart, successful woman like her come back here? To flaunt her success in front of him?"

Lilith shrugged. "Hey, I have some of what they call un-resolved issues too. And if I *won* a million-dollar mansion across the street from my mom and her live-in, I'd let it sit empty forever. I'd torch it before I'd set foot in it."

"Ah." Something to think about.

"Looking at that old guy reminded me of why I left and why I'll never go back."

"You didn't see the wife?"

"Thought I saw a timid little person scurrying around. That's part of the pattern too," Lilith said, her face hard. "Don't ask me to go there, if you don't mind."

I left it. I'd learned early not to probe into Lilith's past. Some memories are better left undisturbed.

I put the Rheinbecks' keys into my purse and fished out my car keys. I stared at them and slowly pulled out the Rheinbeck keys.

"What?" she said.

I stared at the keys and at the front door. I said, "How did Tony get in there?"

"Through the door?"

I shook my head. "Not likely. Emmy Lou kept her doors locked, and she made Dwayne lock them too, even when I was sitting in her living room with her. In fact, when I got there for our first meeting, she unlocked that dead bolt. I had been thinking that Tony got in and frightened her. But I can't see how that would be. I can't believe she would have let him in the house. How could he get in without a set of keys?"

"We should check."

A half hour later, we confirmed that all the first- and second-floor windows were locked and showed no signs of having been forced or pried.

"So," I said, "either Emmy Lou let him in—"

"Which might be why she's overcome with guilt," Lilith said.

"Or he had a set of keys. Which doesn't make sense. What if someone else let him in?"

"But who?"

I could think of only one other person who had the keys to Emmy Lou's house. Sweet, loveable, concerned, heart-broken hubby Dwayne. Was I playing into his pudgy hands?

———

At dinnertime I made the mistake of turning on the television to see the news. What was I thinking?

Todd Tyrell loomed in my face, gleefully offering his comments on a local tragedy:

> Last night's drowning in the Hudson is the second in two weeks. WINY wants to remind our viewers that the Hudson can be unpredictable in the spring. Take good care. Elsewhere in news, no arrest has been made in the tragic death of Tony Starkman.

Tony's ten-year-old face flashed on the screen, followed by a shot of his anguished and possibly not quite sober mother, then a clip of poor damaged Kevin wailing on the lawn. I waited and sure enough I showed up too, looking as though I could give Bluebeard a run for his money.

Todd's voice over added:

> Although forty-one-year-old insurance executive Emmy Lou Rheinbeck is being held in the case, there is no word yet on whether Woodbridge Police will be questioning

Charlotte Adams again. The Woodbridge business-woman found the body in her client's home on Sunday afternoon.

"Questioning again!" I squeaked.

Truffle and Sweet Marie barked. Maybe they were upset that Todd could manage to infuse such innuendo into "Sunday afternoon."

As the phone began to trill, I braced myself for another round of client cancellations.

———

The best thing about closets is that you can always clean them out when you have to clear your mind. They're always fair targets. I wanted to take my mind off Emmy Lou on the one hand and my collapsing business on the other. It was a week ahead of my regular seasonal pruning, but hey. It helped that I was mad as hell. Tuesday's not my regular cleanup night, but I was willing to be flexible on that. I spent the evening putting away my winter gear. I cleaned both pairs of my leather boots and stuffed paper in the toes. Fifteen minutes later I snagged one of each pair from under the bed where Truffle and Sweet Marie had relocated them. The dogs love seasonal cleanups. So many opportunities to make themselves unhelpful.

I put my winter shoes in boxes and clipped to each box a digital photo of what was inside. Saves time when you're looking for shoes on the top shelf of your closet. This makes sense for people with a few too many shoes, like me. I never said I was perfect. I stuck the boxes on that top shelf and brought down my warm-weather footwear. I set my winter coat and my casual jacket aside to take to the cleaners before storing in the basement. I examined my hats, scarves, and gloves. Anything I hadn't worn in the past year went into the box for the Woodbridge Winter Warmth Fund, a charity that I support. Someone might as well enjoy them. The rest got washed and packed. Possibly I slammed the closet door a few times.

"Charlotte?"

I jumped.

"Wow, what's all this?"

"Putting away my winter gear, Jack. Of course, if a person wears shorts and a Hawaiian shirt every day of the year, then that person doesn't need to know about seasonal changes."

"That's not true. I wear cycling gear a lot. And I have lots of these shirts," he said. "I suppose I could—"

"Oh be quiet. I should rat you out to *What Not to Wear*."

"Whoa. Are you mad at me about that baby comment? I'm sorry. I was thinking about how I felt, and I shouldn't have imposed my feelings on you."

"That's very modern of you, Jack. And I guess I'm taking my frustration about this case out on you. That sleazeball Todd Tyrell keeps insinuating that I am connected to Tony's death. I've already lost a bunch of clients over it."

"Take a breath, Charlotte."

I took a breath. And another one.

Jack said, "I thought you said you had a waiting list for clients."

I made a face at him.

"Just trying to help. If you have too many clients, does it matter if you lose one? Maybe that one would have given you grief anyway."

"I reserve the right to be miserable."

"No one takes that Todd Tyrell seriously. How could they with that fake tan and those—how would you describe those teeth? Rushmore-size?"

"Todd Tyrell's cheesy chompers are not the point, Jack."

"What is the point?"

I stopped and thought. "Aside from how am I supposed to run a business if everyone in this town keeps getting murdered, I'm worried about Emmy Lou. She couldn't have done it. And yet they hauled her off to jail and now she's in the psychiatric ward. At least WINY hasn't picked up on that yet. It's enough to make you weep."

"Did you eat dinner?"

"No. Why? What's dinner got to do with anything?"

His face lit up. "An idle thought: How about pizza? My treat? I'll call El Greco."

He picked up the phone and ordered a large all-dressed double cheese. He remembered extra anchovies for me. Jack has the gift for cheering people. No wonder people drop thousands in his bike shop. Or they would if they would only walk through the front door.

He said, "And I have a bottle of red wine downstairs. Be right back."

Truffle and Sweet Marie positioned themselves by the door to wait for the El Greco guy. They love pizza, although it's not officially on their diet. They're not fooled if you spell it.

I called after him, "I might have some ice cream in the fridge. I'll kick it in."

Tails thumped on the floor.

Jack and I got in a quick game of Where's Charlotte? Truffle and Sweet Marie managed to find me in the shower, behind the bedroom door, and downstairs in Jack's apartment.

Jack said, "They're getting faster. We'll have to put a bit of challenge into this."

I could imagine myself hiding out on the roof or under the Miata one of these days. "Maybe we should quit while we're ahead," I said. "Teach them to count or something."

When the orange Neon with the El Greco sign on the top skidded to a stop outside, Jack and I were clinking our wine-glasses. The dogs set up a racket at the thunder of steps up to my door. A guy with a buzz cut and a Celtic tattoo on his neck grinned at me. I got the impression he had a pretty high opinion of himself. The grin vanished and he yelped as the dogs lunged for his ankles. Jack snagged his El Greco orange sleeve before he could tumble down the stairs.

I snatched up the dogs and tucked them into the bedroom for a five-minute time-out. It's not like I can cut off their allowances. Or ground them.

Jack's a whiz with a pizza. He cuts and plates like an artist. "Charlotte. You can't let this stuff make you miserable. Your job is to help people. Put it all out of your mind. Let it percolate. Your subconscious will take care of it. This is time to relax."

"Thank you, Dr. Jack," I said.

———

I took Jack's advice and turned my attention to another project that evening: my former mudroom client. Sure, she'd fired me. But she was merely doing her job as a mom, trying to protect her children from being in proximity to a possible killer. I couldn't blame her for that, although I could, and did, blame Todd Tyrell. Even though I knew it wasn't personal. Anything for ratings.

I decided to take the optimistic view and start up a little plan in case she got over her fears and called me again. Most of my clients who had canceled during the murderous events the previous fall had called back. Including Emmy Lou. Sometimes it took a while, but it pays to be prepared.

I studied the digital pictures of Bernice's hallway, scattered with orphaned shoes, crumpled papers, forgotten lunch boxes, coats, mittens, and more. Bernice had been overwhelmed by this, but it seemed fairly straightforward to me. I drew up a couple of principles that I felt confident she could agree with if I ever saw her again: first, every home should have a pleasant and welcoming entryway, front and rear. It sets the tone. Perhaps that seemed more important to me because I didn't have it when I was growing up. I thought the children would benefit from a sense of order and control: their permission slips would have a spot incoming and outgoing, their shoes would be easy to find, their raincoats dry, their lunch pails devoid of strange green growths.

I knew it would help if there was a place for the children to sit down to get dressed and undressed and a spot for each one to store their gear, clothing, and papers. They each needed hooks at the right height to hang up jackets. I could only estimate the heights.

I sketched away.

I figured Bernice's family could use a bench with shoe cubbies underneath, a row of colorful hooks on top, and a gadget to dry wet shoes or boots near the vent. The closet could be reconfigured to stash the odd-size sports gear so it was out of sight but still easily accessible. The opposite wall of the entryway would be ideal for a corkboard to post notices, main family schedule and calendar with key dates marked, and of course, the children's artwork currently crumpled and curling on the floor. And each child could use a container for incoming school and sports notices, treasures, information, and a separate container for outgoing signed permission slips, notes to the school, and so on. I thought those could be inexpensive magazine holders on a sturdy, low shelf. If Bernice and her children didn't like that look, we could try a variety of in-basket/out-basket solutions.

I picked up my paint color wand and put sticky tapes on several paint shades I thought would be harmonious, welcoming, and cheerful without being jarring. Color is so personal that Bernice and her children would make the choices. I'd offer them a jumping-off point.

A couple of hours later, I had drawn up a plan for first discussion, shaded in a wall color, and clipped on sample pictures of cubbies, magazine holders, in baskets, and sports-gear organizers.

I sat back and smiled. I hadn't fretted about Emmy Lou's

problems or my own for hours and I'd accomplished something. Jack tells me I'm born to help people, and I have to admit, there is a lot of satisfaction in it. Of course, I might never get to go over this with Bernice, but nothing ventured, nothing gained. I put the project in the plastic folder I'd started for it and filed it away. No matter what Bernice decided, it would probably come in handy some day. And if it didn't, I'd had fun doing what I love.

Something tugged at the back of my mind and yanked me awake at three a.m. The dogs stirred resentfully. I couldn't go back to sleep. In fact, I was beginning to wonder if I would ever sleep through the night again. This time I had Bell Street on my mind. There was something about it. But what? I shouldn't have been surprised to have a fitful sleep, after an evening of sulking, more because of the television coverage linking me with Tony's death. I lay awake and thought back to what I'd seen on the WINY coverage. I made an effort to blank out Todd Tyrell's face as I closed my eyes and tried to reconstruct the scene outside the Rheinbecks' place after Emmy Lou's meltdown over Tony's death.

The cameras had panned to the crowd that had gathered around. Neighbors. Friends. Delivery truck parked. Patti Magliaro anxiously wringing her hands. Bill Baxter pacing and running his hands through his hair. I wasn't in that footage, but I knew I'd been upset and it would have showed plainly on my face and in my actions. We'd all had the kind of confused and distressed reactions you might expect. But when I'd reached Dwayne and the restaurant and told him about Tony's death and Emmy Lou's arrest, his first reaction had been anger rather than shock. Emmy Lou's loving husband had been red faced and furious, banging the bar with his beefy arm when I gave him the news. He'd shown belligerence instead of worry. Fury instead of panic. That seemed plain wrong to me. A nagging voice in the back of my mind kept asking what Dwayne was angry about. That would be the same Dwayne who had the only other set of keys to the house. Pepper would sneer if I tried to convince her about Dwayne's out-of-character reaction, for sure, but she might take the part about the keys seriously.

I flicked on the light. Three thirty. Aak. I got a dark look from Truffle before he burrowed out of sight. I switched off the light again, tossing and turning until a soft light filled the sky and I drifted back to troubled sleep.

When you have a worrying chore, engage a friend to help you.

16

First thing in the morning, I dropped off my dry cleaning at Klean and Brite in the uptown sector. I chatted vaguely with the pleasant, blowsy woman behind the counter. Next I cruised to the outskirts of town to meet with Gary Gigantes, carpenter, painter, and all-round miracle worker. In his workshop, surrounded by tools and half-finished projects and breathing in the pleasant aroma of freshly cut wood, I showed him my designs and requirements. He saw no problem with picking up the two dozen inexpensive standard bookcases. In fact, he figured he could negotiate a bulk discount with the supplier. And he could deliver them within two days of making the order.

"It's why I have a truck, Charlotte," he said, flashing his endearing gap-toothed grin.

"Can you connect them so they look like long built-in units in each room, but still have the section slide forward to get at the units in the back?"

Gary nodded. "Nothing to it, once I figured out what you were talking about. I can attach some crown molding on top and a little flute trim to hide the joints where we stick 'em together."

"Crown molding is lovely, but the first floor of this house is very contemporary minimalist," I said. "Of course, the toy collection is definitely maximalist. I brought along these samples. There are thousands more where they came from. We think we're going to display them by color." I passed him the wedding mice and the stuffed animals that Emmy Lou had dropped on the street in her hysteria after Tony's death and tried not to laugh at the expression on his face. I told myself it was to give him an idea of what we were dealing with, but I wanted them out of my tiny home. I missed the empty space on the top shelf of my closet. I also showed him some digital pictures of the inside of the Rheinbecks' upstairs rooms, crammed with plush occupants. I followed that with some shots of the elegant, magazine-quality main level.

"Okeydoke. I got it now," Gary said. "Good to know the scope. Leave it with me. I'll use the compressor to paint up the bookcases, give 'em a professional built-in look. They won't be as classy as millwork, but they'll cost you about twenty percent what a custom job would. And the supplier I deal with, if you pay cash in advance, you can save an extra ten percent. Your choice."

"Wow. And this will be ten times faster than custom," I said. "Plus, once the collection is in place, the eye will focus on that."

"Can't wait to see this collection. To confirm, you sure you want those joined units on casters?"

"Is that a problem?"

"Not that good to look at, but I'll come up with something."

"She needs access to the items stored in the row behind."

"Good thing us guys like a challenge."

"I appreciate that. And thanks for letting me jump the gun. Are you sure you don't mind? I know you have a lineup of clients," I said.

"No worries, Charlotte. Once you told me the whole story why, I felt sorry for that lady, and this is a pretty small job. No one's going to notice they slipped two days. And if they do, too bad. You've brought me a lot of business this past year, and that counts for something."

I left a message with Dwayne asking if he was willing to pay up front to save the extra ten percent. I had an idea that ten percent was the least of his concerns. Maybe that's why he didn't call me back.

I was getting used to that. I'd left several messages with Pepper over the fact that only Dwayne had a second set of keys to the Rheinbeck house, but no response. I had a feeling none was coming either.

＊

Although I was turning my sights onto Dwayne Rheinbeck, I was well aware that I had asked Ramona to find out if Emmy Lou had lived on Bell Street back in the seventies. I didn't want her to think I was wasting her time, although I wasn't entirely sure that this question was worth pursuing anymore, so I swung by the library.

Ramona shook her silver brush cut as I entered the reference section. Her earrings glittered. "Sorry, Charlotte," she said, inserting a binder and a pile of files into an oversize briefcase, "gotta run. I'm on my way to a meeting, so I can't chat. A planning session. We're up to our patooties in planning sessions around here. No luck so far with your request. When I was at the central branch, I looked into the older city directories. Back in the day, they sometimes listed all adults living at a residence. I found that a T. Wright did live at 7 Bell Street, but no record of anyone else. But you know, you might get some useful information at the high school. Check the yearbooks around the time Emmy Lou Wright would have graduated. You might find a connection, someone who can help you, a teacher, a classmate. They keep the year-books in the library in Woodbridge High. The archives are in the dean's office at St. Jude's."

I shuddered when she mentioned St. Jude's.

"I hear you," she said. "I know the librarian at Wood-bridge High. So I took the liberty of calling her and saying that I had directed you there, because you were trying to track down an old friend. She'll be glad to help you out. I guess she doesn't watch the news."

"You're the best, Ramona."

"Not until I connect you with the rest, I'm not," she said.

"You always give me great advice."

"Here's a bit more: you might want to try to avoid the media."

"Very funny," I called after her as she strode toward the door.

A couple of library users glanced up frowning. Oops. Two dirty looks and one definite *shhh*.

Ramona laughed out loud and kept going, earrings sway-ing merrily.

Jack doesn't have creature comforts at the shop. I picked up some homemade Italian meatball soup to go and cia-batta bread from Ciao! Ciao!, Jack's Italian bistro of choice, when he can actually get out to lunch. I added espresso and tiramisu for two. He was going to love me for this. And that was good, because I needed a big favor that he would hate.

Truffle and Sweet Marie were thrilled to have a visit to CYCotics. Jack was equally happy to see them and his lunch.

I took over from Jack in the front of the shop while he wolfed the soup and bread in back. Lucky for me no one en-tered, as my product knowledge was near zero. Okay, I know that bikes have wheels and handlebars and brakes, I suppose.

But there were no customers so I made myself busy at the front desk, trying to create a little bit of order. Really, Jack had the latest point-of-sale equipment, machines for credit cards, debit payments, detailed receipts, customer files. Very high tech and snazzy. On the downside, the desk was cluttered with his scrawled notes, keys, invoices, odd bits of stock, and even a broken sandal. We had a deal that if a human being entered the shop, I was to let him know. But Jack had a customer-free zone that lunchtime.

"So," he said afterward, "where are you hiding the tiramisu?"

"Not so fast, big boy, I need a commitment from you."

"I knew this was going to cost me. But it's tiramisu from Ciao! Ciao!, so sure. I'll even overlook the fact that I'll never find anything on my workspace now that you've changed it all around."

"It's organized now. You'll be much happier. Consider it a favor. And I can do more tomorrow."

"No thanks. I liked it the way it was. I knew where everything was. What did you do with my invoices?"

I pointed to a now-neat stack in a basket that I'd rescued from under the counter.

"Where did you hide my keys?"

"They're right here. In plain view. I put them on a hook so they wouldn't get covered over. You waste time looking for them. Anyway, I don't want to argue with you. I'll put it back the way it was, if you're not happy. I want you to find out what Emmy Lou's husband has been up to with a certain beautiful young woman."

"What happened to bring this on? I thought you were working for the guy."

"I am and he seems like such a great guy, but a couple of things are troubling me."

Jack reached for the tiramisu. "Such as?"

"His wife is obviously distraught and possibly having a breakdown. What else would explain her behavior? When I first met her, she was jumpy and edgy. Even though she kept up the pretense of being so professional and on top of everything, I thought perhaps she was afraid of something, but now I'm asking myself if she wasn't distraught about her husband."

"She has a good reason to be distraught. Finding Tony dead."

"I know. But Lilith and I saw Dwayne with that gorgeous girl at the restaurant. Something's going on there."

"Can't always trust your eyes. You don't have all the background information. Maybe it was a dispute about business."

"This wasn't business. There was something so intimate in the way he touched her. So I'm asking myself: What if Dwayne was not as besotted with Emmy Lou as she was with him? What if he was faking it?"

"That seems like a big logical leap, Charlotte, based on one event, if you don't mind me saying so. Can I have that tiramisu now?"

"When I told him about Emmy Lou, he got angry. The rest of us were panicky, upset."

"Maybe he was angry with the way his wife was treated."

"She was treated quite well, considering she kept shouting she'd killed someone. The police were respectful and gentle, given the circumstances. Remember you told me to let my subconscious take care of it. My subconscious is whispering maybe he decided to get rid of her."

"Small logical flaw in the thinking of your subconscious, Charlotte. He didn't get rid of her."

"That's the problem. Tony wasn't supposed to be in the house. Emmy Lou was out and then heading home for a meeting with me. Afterward, she kept saying that she didn't know he was there."

"This is hard to follow. So you think the husband killed him?"

"I am saying Dwayne might have intended to kill Emmy Lou, who was supposed to be alone in the house."

"But—"

"No buts. Hear me out. Emmy Lou hadn't told Dwayne the kinds of dumb-ass stunts that Tony and Kevin were pulling. I mentioned it and he seemed surprised. He said he'd tell Mrs. Dingwall, but he never did. He seemed a lot less upset about it than even Kevin's mother and the Baxters. Or me. Anyway, what if this time Tony got inside the house without Emmy Lou knowing?"

"You're heading somewhere with all this?"

"I sure am. Then suppose if Dwayne had rigged up something to kill Emmy Lou, say a booby trap on the stairs. Tony could have been caught instead. See? Don't blink like that. Not a good look for you. Too owlish."

"Rigged up what? I thought the guy fell down the stairs."

"I haven't figured out what or how. Then when I came along for our meeting, I'd have found the body. I would have been part of the plan."

"Why?"

"Because I would have then told the police that the escaped toys on the stairs were a hazard and in fact were one of the signs that Emmy Lou's collecting was much more than a storage issue."

"Okay. And you think he planned to slip into the house somehow between the time she fell and the time you found her and he would have gotten rid of . . . ?"

"Exactly. The evidence. You've got it."

"Could he have done that without anyone seeing him?"

"That would be tricky on Bell Street. Patti Magliaro seems to be out all the time walking her cat and—"

"I thought you spoke to her."

"Not about this. I came up with this hypothesis overnight."

"It has a nightmarish quality to it."

I ignored that. "I didn't ask Patti if Dwayne came by. The

older man who might be Emmy Lou's father is out all the time too, but I'm sure he wouldn't help. And the Baxters were coming and going. And she has a side view from her kitchen window. I have to check with them, to be sure that no one saw Dwayne."

Jack perked up at that idea. "Try and get some more of those cupcakes if you do."

"Because Emmy Lou was screeching that she did it, she killed Tony."

"That's the part that doesn't make sense."

"It does if she's trying protect him. In fact, it's the only thing that does make sense. Maybe she realized what was going on."

"You think it makes sense to protect your husband after he tried to kill you?"

"She's crazy about him. He'd get life for this. She's going to try to work it out. She might even blame herself if things were going wrong in their marriage. This was a new start for her. A dream come true."

"Huh. Don't get upset, Charlotte, but this sounds totally ridiculous."

"There are some kinks to be ironed out. Can you go to Wet Paint tonight and see what you can find out about Dwayne Rheinbeck and the jazz singer? And even more important, find out if he left the restaurant on Sunday afternoon."

"But why don't you do it? You seem to be attuned to the subtleties that I miss."

"I would, but Dwayne will recognize me. He'll behave."

"I hate fancy restaurants. Do I have to get changed?"

"It's a pretty laid-back spot , but I think the shorts and Hawaiian shirts will stick out. Move up a notch. I'll give you the tiramisu earlier if you promise to wear socks."

Jack reached for the dessert. "Do I have to go alone?"

"Of course not. You're undercover. You need a date."

"Who?"

"Let's see now, he'd recognize Lilith."

"Margaret?"

"I told him about Margaret in the hope that she'd represent Emmy Lou. He might make the connection. She was all over the news last fall."

Jack's face lit up. "I got it! Sally. She's even nosier than you are. She'll love snooping and coming up with weird and intrusive theories about who, what, when, where, why. I won't have anything to do but drive and eat."

"You're a genius, Jack. Have I mentioned that? Take my dessert too."

———※———

If Sally hadn't been so close to her due date, she might have done backflips at the idea of spying on Dwayne Rheinbeck and his lady in red at Wet Paint.

"I love it!" she gushed. "Only one itty-bitty problem."

"Which is?"

"Benjamin's giving a talk to the blah-blah-blah society tonight."

"Not it's real name, I suppose. Don't worry about that. I'll bring the dogs over, and I'll put the kids to bed and then watch television until you get home."

Perhaps she hadn't heard me. She said, "I could ask Lilith. She gave me those babysitting coupons at the shower."

"Nope. You're doing *me* a favor. I'll do the babysitting. You save Lilith for when you need a break. I might bring along my mudroom project. Should be fun."

"You think you'll get work done while you're babysitting the kids? That's so cute."

"Don't be silly, Sally. I love your kids. I'll bring a play kit with music and crafts and stories. Maybe some bath toys. You won't have to worry about a thing."

"And I don't plan to. It's so nice not to be neurotic."
"So I've heard. See you at seven. You're a true friend."

———◆———

Sally and Jack tore off in Sally's black Jeep Cherokee. Jack doesn't believe in SUVs, but all bets are off when it comes to Sally. Jack thinks the world of her. Plus no way would Sally be able to bend into and out of Jack's vintage Mini Minor. I'd equipped them with an excellent description of the lady in red and of Dwayne too. Sally hadn't met him, and Jack, well, what can I say? Speaking of Jack, he looked almost respectable in his clean chinos and striped shirt, not tucked in of course. He must have thought the task was important. And as far as I could tell he was wearing socks under his shoes. But no one would be looking at Jack, even though he's kind of cute. All eyes would be on Sally. She was too fabulous in a sleeveless black dress, remarkably flexible to accommodate the bump. Her blonde corkscrew curls seemed even more impossibly glamorous than usual. She had a cluster of wide bangles up her arms and had found the most elegant dangling earrings and flat metallic sandals. I did my bit by applying polish to her toes, as Sally claimed not to have seen her feet for two months.

She whispered, "There's life in the old girl yet."

We waved as they left. The kids seemed overjoyed. Until the SUV rounded the corner and vanished from view that is. One by one, their eyes grew rounder. Their mouths grew rounder too. I'm not sure what came first, the gush of tears or the ear-splitting howls. Dallas, Madison, and Savannah had truly great lungs. Truffle and Sweet Marie had been little angels up until this point. Something about the wailing children brought out the devil dog in them.

The sharp sounds of barking did nothing to stop the crying. The kids have always loved the dogs, and the wieners have more or less tolerated the kids. But this was war. The screaming escalated into hysterical sobs. I picked up baby Savannah. She shuddered and shook and struggled against me. With my "free" hand I snagged Truffle and tucked him under the other arm, headed toward the back. In a second, I had deposited him in the main-floor powder room. The door muffled the barking. Sweet Marie took refuge under Sally's white leather sofa. The sofa did not muffle the barking.

Half an hour later, my single accomplishment had been to get Sweet Marie into the holding tank with Truffle. They'd make me pay in the future, I knew, but sometimes you have to look after number one, two, three, and four.

I had sung all the songs I knew. I had tried all the kids' games I brought with me. The books had already been flung against the wall, the crayons were strewn on the carpet. I had rocked, cuddled, hummed. I'd tried healthy treats, switched to ice cream, briefly considered brandies all round.

Nothing, nothing, nothing worked. Nothing. On the rare occasions when I'm watching Sally's kids, I get Jack to come with me. He plays a great game of giddyap. But Jack was on the spy mission with Sally, and I was in way over my head.

At seven thirty I caved and called Lilith. "I know you're busy, but this is a disaster."

"Whoa. What's that noise in the background? Are you at a riot or something?"

"You might say that. I'm babysitting at Sally's."

"Explains it."

"But can you save me?" I said. "I'm down on my knees. I'll crawl over broken glass."

"Reinforcements on the way."

The kids stopped in mid howl as Lilith walked through the door. Maybe it was her turquoise spiky hair. Of course, it could have been the piercings. Then again, she was toting a plate of what smelled like Toll House cookies, the universal comfort food. Could have been that. The children, shuddering and sniffing, stared. Then baby Savannah reached out for

Lilith. Dallas and Madison clustered around asking what was on the plate.

"Thank Rose too," I said.

Lilith settled everyone in minutes. And I couldn't figure out how she did it. She had the touch. Even I calmed down. A quarter of an hour later, all three rug rats were deep in sleep on the sofa. I carried the sleeping children upstairs, one by one, worrying with every creak of the stairs that a child would wake up, setting off a domino effect. Savannah's eyelids fluttered, but she snuggled into her crib, thumb in her rosebud mouth. Madison and Dallas squirmed a bit as they were tucked into their beds, but that was it. I watched their sleeping faces, still streaked with tears, for a moment and was thankful for the miracle of sleep. When I came downstairs, the dogs had been released from captivity and were curled up on the sofa with Lilith. Lucky, they hadn't chosen that night to play Where's Charlotte?

"I think we should have brushed their teeth and washed their faces, but I was afraid of what that would trigger. I'll let Sally handle it."

I stared around at the remnants of my babysitting kit. Who had I been kidding? I'd always been a lousy babysitter. Jack was a natural, Lilith was a natural. I was a natural disaster.

"So." Lilith chuckled as she handed me a Toll House cookie. "How's this biological clock I hear so much about?"

"Let's say, my alarm just went off."

—✦—

The evening out had obviously been good for Sally. She was glowing and relaxed when she and Jack returned from their mission. "Are the kids all right?"

"Sleeping like angels. As are the dogs." I was relaxing in the chair giving the impression of being in charge. Lilith departed once order had been restored. She'd left the rest of the Toll House cookies, and they had been keeping me company.

Truffle had wakened long enough to give Jack a big kiss, but was already curling up on the best chair.

"Wonderful. You want to hear about the spy mission?"

"Are you kidding?"

Sally laughed. "You were right. There is definitely something going on with that Dwayne and the singer, unless you want to call her a piano player."

"She's a piano player too?"

"She was playing jazz piano and singing kind of updated jazz stuff."

Jack said, " 'Popsicle Toes'. Diana Krall kind of stuff. She was pretty good. Sally thinks something is going on between her and Dwayne, but I didn't notice it."

"What do you ever notice?" Sally said, rolling her eyes.

"Lots of stuff."

"Brakes? Handlebars? Cycling shoes?"

"Boys and girls!" I said. "Back to the point of the exercise."

Sally slid onto the sofa. "You sure did some cleaning up, Charlotte."

"It was nothing," I said.

In fact, Lilith had insisted on helping me to get the crayons out of the carpet and pack up the rest of the disaster. She'd even run the vacuum cleaner. I owed her big-time. Not the first occasion when I'd been in her debt either.

"The place looks a lot better than when we left."

"Stop teasing, Sally. Tell me what you saw."

Sally stretched like a cat. "You were absolutely right, Charlotte. This guy seems to be besotted with that girl, whether she's a singer or piano player. And even if Jack is useless as an observer, I'm not. This girl's way, way, way too young for him."

Jack said, "She didn't look that young to me."

"Pu-leeze," Sally said.

"I did see her," I said. "I thought early twenties. Anyway, it doesn't matter how old she is. He's married to Emmy Lou. He shouldn't be . . ."

Sally's mind was made up. "That didn't stop him from putting his paws all over this chickie."

I turned to grill the second witness. "Did he put his paws all over her, Jack?"

"He gave her a couple of hugs. They seemed harmless to me. Affectionate."

"Sleazy," Sally said. "Gave me the willies."

Jack sat up straight and stared at her. "No. He seemed friendly and sort of supportive. Something seemed to be bothering the girl and he was cheering her up. Like a friend or an uncle. That's my opinion, Charlotte."

Sally snorted. "Some uncle. If ever a man had sex on his mind, he did. This is a very beautiful girl."

I piped up. "That's what I don't get. Emmy Lou's beautiful too. She's very appealing, and Dwayne gave the impression of being crazy about her."

Sally said, "Didn't look that way to me. This guy's wife is heading for either life in prison or a one-way ticket to a psych ward, so he gets to play around with the staff. That is so vile."

Even though I'd suspected it and sent out the two spies, I suppose part of me had been hoping I was wrong. "What do you mean by 'play around'? Did they leave together?"

"Not exactly," Sally said.

"Not at all," Jack added. "She left after her second set. Said good-bye to the other people there. He gave her a hug. He stayed. She went home or wherever."

I said, "I guess the jury's still out then."

Sally gave it her best sneer. "This jury convicted him."

"Guillotine at dawn," Jack said. "But I'm not so sure. I hug you guys sometimes. That doesn't make me sleazy."

"That's different," Sally snapped. "We've been friends since we first went to school for heaven's sake."

"Maybe they've been friends too. You can't jump to conclusions."

"Big age difference for friends," I said.

Sally said, "I can so jump to conclusions. I do it all the time and I'm always right."

There was some truth to all of those assertions. Sally made up her mind instantly and there was no changing it. And she was usually, if not always, right.

"I give up. But Charlotte, you might be happy to know that we have the singer's name if that helps in any way. He introduced her before each set." Jack handed me a cocktail napkin with a name written on it.

Bryony Stevens.

I said, "Looks like you're not so useless after all, Jack."

"He's quite the little detective," Sally added.

"I'm not little," Jack said. "But I did find out something from talking to the bartender."

"Wait until you hear this," Sally said. "You might not be pleased, but at least it will clear something up for you."

I sighed. "Couldn't one of you say what it was, rather than—"

"Dwayne had an alibi," Sally chirped.

"For the entire afternoon," Jack said. "I got in a conversation about bikes with the guy behind the bar and in the course of it, I asked him about the stuff that happened with Emmy Lou and Tony. It came out that Dwayne was in the restaurant all day. Never left until you showed up, Charlotte, because they were short of staff, they had some kind of disaster in the kitchen, and they had a full house at lunch. Anyway, until some chick showed up at around five, he was in full view of everyone, helping out with the cooking."

"Oh. But that's one person. Why are you shaking your head, Sal?"

"We talked to our server too. Apparently Dwayne was there. All day. Until you arrived, wearing your espadrilles, according to our server who was female and knows such words."

I sat back and pondered this. On the one hand, it was good. I didn't really want Dwayne to be guilty, even if there were some strange pesky behaviors. But it left me without a good theory to explain why Emmy Lou was acting the way she was.

"You see?" Jack said. "Sometimes you are way off base. Are those Toll House cookies?"

"I'm not wrong. I'm incomplete," I said. "Or my theory is."

Jack leaned forward, probably salivating, "Can I eat one?"

"Don't get distracted. Here's the thing: he might have been there, but where was Bryony Stevens?"

Jack's hand stopped short of the cookies. "You didn't tell us to ask about that."

Bringing flowers as a gift?
Make sure they're in a vase or container,
even if it's an empty jam jar.

17

Naturally there was no Bryony Stevens listed in the phone book. Or in the online listings. A quick Web search turned up a site and a few articles praising the jazz singer. Aside from a series of photos of Bryony at the microphone, always wearing the same red dress, the Web site didn't give much detail. Although you could click on the link and hear her sing. I did that. The girl had talent, no question about that. Her voice was smooth, almost fudgy, soft and sweet, but with a haunting edge. There was no address, no telephone number, no booking information. Nothing but an e-mail address in the contact section. If she had something going with Dwayne, I wasn't going to blow my cover by contacting bryony@bryonystevens.com and asking her what she knew about Emmy Lou Rheinbeck and Tony Starkman.

I took the dogs for their midnight constitutional, made my to-do list for the next day, brushed, flossed, set out my outfit for the morning, and hit the hay.

For once, my subconscious gave me a break. I needed the sleep, but a bit of inspiration would have been good.

My to-do list was full. I had to touch base with Dwayne to see if the bookcase project was a go with payment up front and to see if there was news about Emmy Lou. Then I needed to check back with Gary Gigantes. I wanted to follow up on Ramona's lead on high school yearbooks. I had to return Rose's plate that had contained the Toll House cookies. A trip to Hannaford's was on my list since the fridge had an empty echo. And it goes without saying, I was itching to find out all about Bryony Stevens.

When I picked up the phone to call Dwayne, I found that he'd returned my message at two thirty in the morning.

"Go for it," he said. "I'll write a check to Gary Gigantes and leave it at the house for you to pick up."

I figured that Dwayne would be sleeping when I set out, but I let Gary know I'd deliver the check later in the morning.

My first stop was Woodbridge High School. I figured I'd get a better reception there than at my old school, St. Jude's. Getting into the school wasn't the piece of cake I'd expected. In the main office I produced picture ID, and recorded my name, address, telephone number, reason for visit. Even the time. I resisted the urge to make witty remarks about how dangerous I was as I waited for Eve Renfrew, the school librarian, to collect me from the office.

"Any friend of Ramona's is a friend of mine," she remarked as I followed her to the secret hiding place of old yearbooks. She was about my age and had her blonde hair pulled back into a sleek ponytail that bobbed as we sidled past tables full of teenagers who were more interested in each other than whatever they were studying. The library was a hum of hormones. Took me back to the bad old days at

St. Jude's. Of course, that was why I'd chosen Woodbridge High for the yearbook hunt.

I found myself in a pleasant interior room where the yearbooks and other archival materials were held, along with filing cabinets and a photocopier.

"We keep them here, because they'd walk away otherwise. Kids find their parents or their boyfriends' parents. Or they find their teachers and decide to add some facial decoration with a Sharpie," she said, bringing me the books from 1978 through 1984. In case. "Have fun. Don't feel you have to rush. I'll be out here in the trenches."

I could see why Ramona liked her. Same no-nonsense approach and sense of humor. I could have used some of that.

I leafed through the old yearbooks, gasping at the hairstyles from time to time. So much mousse. So many mullets. Some of the students looked vaguely familiar to me. Woodbridge is a fairly small city and chances are some of these kids lived and worked in the area. Of course, they'd be in their forties now and if fortune had smiled on them, they had better hair. I started at the end of the 1983 yearbook and found Emmy Lou Wright almost immediately. The luminous smile and the shining green eyes hadn't changed much. Emmy Lou was heavier now and had long ago ditched the feathered hairstyle for her expensive bob. She'd wince if she saw this picture, although it was certainly the least of her problems at the moment.

Emmy Lou had been a beautiful girl. Of course, I'd already known that. I flicked backward through the pages of her classmates that year, hoping to find a familiar name, someone who might know where Emmy Lou had lived. Every one of the graduating students had completed the statement "In ten years I will be . . ." Emmy Lou had written, "In ten years I will be R.S.'s wife and the happiest girl in the world."

I flipped to the S's and began to search for anyone with the initials R.S. I gasped. A dark-haired, arrogantly handsome face stared out at me, assessing, daring. The handsome features belonged to someone called Roger Starkman.

R.S.

Well, well.

I checked through the other parts of the yearbook, the clubs, awards, record of adolescent school life in 1980s Woodbridge. I found no evidence that Emmy Lou had taken part in anything. No debating or drama club. No basketball or field hockey. No academic awards. Nothing. Knowing what I did about this high-achieving woman, that struck me as very strange. But of course, people change. Maybe Emmy Lou had been a late bloomer.

I photocopied the page with Emmy Lou's picture and the one with Roger Starkman's too. For good measure, I also copied the pages that had any faces that seemed even faintly familiar.

Eve knocked and stuck her perky blonde head into the room. "Did you find what you wanted?" she said with an encouraging smile.

"More than," I said. "I made a couple of photocopies. I realize I should have checked first."

"Hey, what I don't know won't hurt either of us."

Dwayne had already left when I picked up the check. I cashed it at my bank, dropped off the cash to Gary, and kept going. Next in my circuit was the Down Town Flower Shoppe. I chose a spray of brilliant yellow tulips for Rose and a deep pink azalea with a sympathy card. I zoomed off toward North Elm Street.

Rose opened her yellow door wearing a smile and sporting a brand-new perm and a jogging suit in an electric shade of purple. She had a fresh pair of sneakers that matched and, of course, her rolling oxygen equipment. She was accompanied by Schopenhauer, who was thrilled to see me.

"For me?" she said as I handed her the yellow tulips. "You didn't have to do that, Charlotte."

"I wanted to. Those Toll House cookies saved my life last night. I brought your plate back too. Lucky no one ate it."

"That was Lilith's doing, but I'll accept your flowers anyway."

"Speaking of Lilith, is she around?"

"She's out at one of her gazillion jobs. I can't get them all straight. But you can chat with Schopenhauer and me."

A tantalizing smell of cinnamon buns wafted by my appreciative nose. I glanced toward the kitchen and sure enough, I caught a glimpse of a tray of them, the glaze glittering as it cooled.

"Thought you might drop by," Rose said.

I made the coffee and Rose took care of everything else. That's the arrangement we have. Rose is not as gifted at coffee as she is at stuff that comes out of the oven.

I heard the follow-up to her daughter's short visit and the newly made promise of a trip to L.A. and the Universal Studio tour. I guessed that was the daughter's way of making up for cutting the visit short.

Rose said, "I'm thinking about it. Been out there before and I can't breath that valley air. Nothing to do alone in an apartment all day either. You need to drive. And the girls are all so skinny. At least in Woodbridge I can find someone to eat my baking. Never mind, I'll probably go. Family's precious."

"I'm glad you're baking," I said, my fingers twitching for a cinnamon bun.

"What's going on? I got a complicated story from Lilith before she tore off last night. I can't believe you're involved in another murder. But anyway, I want the lowdown."

I filled her in on the most recent developments.

"Terrible thing," she said. "I can't believe it happened on Bell Street."

I nodded because by this time my mouth was full.

Rose said, "I think I mentioned I knew people in that area. Of course, I used to know people all over Woodbridge. That was then. Things have changed quite a bit in my seventy some years."

I straightened up and swallowed. I hadn't thought about Rose knowing anyone on the other side of town, although I wasn't sure why not.

"So who did you know on Bell Street, Rose?"

She closed her eyes. "Let's see. Feeneys. Mrazeks. Van Loons. Lots of folks, older than me, so they're probably all dead," Rose said.

"Van Loons and Mrazeks are still alive, I heard."

"That's a good sign. I didn't know the Wrights. You were talking about them last night. I knew Myrna and Fred Dingwall. He worked with my late husband. She's about my age, but he was older. So he's long gone, of course. Why don't you ask her about Emmy Lou Wright?"

"Um, I'm not welcome at the Dingwalls. A misunderstanding about her son."

Rose couldn't muffle the grin in time.

I ignored it. "And of course, there's Patti Magliaro. Everyone knows her."

Rose chuckled. "She's a good soul and a great asset to Betty's. I don't know that I'd believe a word she says though. Smoked a bit of funny tobacco in her time. She gets a bit more vague every year. But you know, I run into Myrna Dingwall every now and then at Hannaford's. I could ask her about this Emmy Lou when she was growing up. If that would help."

"It would. Now I'm heading off to talk to someone I should have seen much earlier."

⁂

I braced myself for one of the hardest tasks I'd ever done. I waited until after lunch, even though I don't usually procrastinate. "Do the worst first" has been one of my mottoes. My heart was pounding as I rang the doorbell to Rhonda Starkman's house. I knew I should have come by earlier to express my condolences to Tony's mother. But I'd found nothing online about a service or visitation. No suggestion for donations. No fund to help the family. It was as though Tony Starkman had never existed. And, of course, I'd hated the idea of it, especially since I'd had that encounter with Tony and Kevin. I was more ashamed of myself by the minute. For sure, sudden death can bring out the coward in us.

The woman who answered the door was pallid, brimming with sorrow, and wore her despair like a heavy garment. Her eyes were red rimmed and swollen, her dark hair streaked with silver. She was slim and neat though. I never would have recognized her as the greasy-haired harridan shown in the newscasts.

"Yes?" she said.

"I'm Charlotte Adams. I'm the person who found Tony. I am very sorry for your loss," I said. I offered her the azalea and the sympathy card. I had struggled with the words to express my sympathy. She stared at the plant and finally reached out for it. Her dark eyes filled with tears. One rolled down her cheek, but she made no move to wipe it away.

"I don't know what to say. I love plants," she said. She stared at me, then said, "Do you want to come in?"

I followed her into the apartment, which was clean, homey, and comfortable, not what I'd expected. A framed photo of Tony sat on top of the television set. A Bible sat on the coffee table, next to a stack of library books. No one else appeared to have sent flowers.

"I still can't believe it," she said as she stood gently fingering the frame on the photo with her free hand.

"I didn't know when the funeral was."

"They haven't released his"—she gulped—"body yet. I guess it takes a while. I can't stand thinking about it."

I had a sharp stab of guilt sitting in this woman's living room under the worst sort of false pretences.

She sniffed. "He wasn't perfect, but he was all I had in the world."

"I didn't know him well," I said. I chose not to add that I had shouted at, and in some interpretations, threatened her son. Obviously, she wasn't the person who had phoned the police.

"Tony wasn't very easy to know. He had his problems. But he was a good boy, in his own way." She flipped open a cigarette package and lit up. "Filthy habit," she said. "Can you believe I was off these things since Tony was born? Now, look." Her shoulders slumped in defeat. "Not that it matters anymore. I felt I needed something."

I had wanted to ask her some questions, but now the raw pain of what she was experiencing caused them to catch in my throat. Finally, I managed to speak. "Eventually they'll figure out what happened to him."

She sighed. "What difference will it make? Won't bring him back. It was an accident anyway, no matter what they say."

"You don't believe Emmy Lou . . . ?"

"Of course not. She couldn't do that to Tony. Or anyone. I don't know why she's saying it. She's having another breakdown, I guess. I told the police, and I told that blockhead on the television, but that didn't get on the air. Sorry, have a seat. I'm not myself. Would you like a cup of coffee?"

I shook my head. "No thanks. I've had plenty."

"And I've had way too much." I had a belated flash of insight. This woman was nothing like the impression I'd had of her. Yet, I'd believed the images that flashed in front of me, even though I hated how they presented me: unfair, unkind, unreasonable. Looked like I wasn't the only one. "I guess the media is misrepresenting both of us."

"And everything else as far as I can see. I need to mourn my boy, and they keep showing up with the stupidest questions."

I did my best not to add to the stupid-question list. "You said that Emmy Lou wouldn't have hurt Tony. I didn't realize that you knew her." I hoped my nose didn't start to grow as I spoke.

"Emmy Lou? Sure. I've known her since Tony was a little thing. She used to go out with my brother."

"Does he live in Woodbridge too? It must help to have family close by at a time like this."

Liar, liar, my good angel said.

She bit her thin lower lip and shook her head. "Roger's dead too."

"Oh no."

"It happened a long time ago. He died a month after high school graduation—that's nearly twenty-four years ago."

"That's terrible. I'm so sorry."

So Roger Starkman was dead. I wanted to ask about the stunts that Tony and Kevin were pulling, but I decided against adding to this woman's misery. "Is that when Emmy Lou had her first breakdown?"

"Yes. Roger was killed racing his motorcycle. He could be a wild and crazy guy. Emmy Lou went to pieces afterward. They had to send her away. Then after a while she got in touch with me and Tony. Tony was about four when she started to go out with Roger. She never forgot my little boy, always sent him a birthday card. Even this year. Roger's death is what pushed her over the edge."

Of course, that explained why Emmy Lou tolerated the foolishness from Tony and Kevin. She'd known them since they were little boys. Nothing was what I'd thought. The idea that Emmy Lou's confession was evidence of another breakdown gave me plenty to think about. Of course, it didn't explain why she'd been on edge in the first place. Mind you, I kept coming back to Dwayne. If Emmy Lou hadn't been terrified of Tony and Kevin, why had she been afraid?

I took a deep breath. "And of course she has no family except for her new husband."

"I have no family either, but at least I did have people who loved me." She snorted. "Emmy Lou would have been better off with no family at all than that old bastard of a father."

"You knew them?"

"Knew of them. The Starkmans weren't good enough for the Wrights. Emmy Lou wasn't allowed to have anything to do with Roger. They had to sneak time together." She shivered. "You know, I saw her father on the television, watching while my Tony was carried out. Cold as ice, then and now. Poor Emmy Lou. I don't know why she moved back there. She might have a big job and money and a beautiful home, but she sure has been unlucky in love, starting with her parents."

<hr>

Back at home, I left a message for Lilith asking her to call me about a favor. Then I called Margaret to entice her to an early dinner at Betty's. She was at her desk because she's always at her desk except when she's in court.

"You have to eat," I said. "Or you won't be able to continue to call yourself a misfit."

"Wouldn't want that to happen. See you there."

I was grinning when I hung up. One of the best things about coming back to Woodbridge was reconnecting with Margaret. Jack and I had never lost touch, including during my unfortunate and brief engagement. He'd been there as a shoulder to cry on and a quick source of emergency ice cream. Sally had never missed one of our weekly catch-up calls, even when she was in labor. But Margaret had vanished into her Ivy League college and then law school. I wasn't sure where she'd practiced afterward, although she'd alluded to a firm where all work and no play made Margaret a dull girl. She still worked too hard, according to Jack. Why yes, that *would* be the same Jack who couldn't join us because of pressures of the totally empty cycle shop.

I used the time before the dinner date to catch up on voice and e-mails and to play around with the mudroom project, the one with no client. I used my favorite computer planning program to try out a few different wall colors. Not having a client took a bit of the pressure off. Maybe that was a good thing.

Another good thing: since I'd confirmed that Emmy Lou had grown up on Bell Street and her parents lived across the street, I no longer needed to track down any of her old classmates. I tossed the photocopies of the yearbook pages into the recycle bin. If I'd made my visit to Tony's mother earlier, I might have saved myself the trip to the high school. Not that I was overwhelmed by work. I took an hour to reschedule my more resilient clients into the slots left by those who'd bailed. I called Sally and told her I'd like to drop by after the kids were in bed to show her a project.

I had time to get ready. I woke up Truffle and Sweet Marie and gave them a brisk walk around the block. I managed to keep them out of the waves of tulips springing up on the front lawns. The dogs went back to sleep the second we got home. I barely paid attention as I was busy worrying about my new information. What if I was totally wrong? What if Emmy Lou's confession was nothing more than the manifestation of another breakdown, triggered by the accidental death of her first love's nephew? That made sense. Tragic, but logical. Emmy Lou had been showing signs of stress, and Tony's death would have been a horrible echo of Roger Starkman's, twenty-four years before. I was guessing that death would still be fresh in her mind. But how could I ever make the police believe it?

Still, I wasn't ready to shelve my suspicions of Dwayne and his girl in red. I Googled Bryony Stevens again. I pulled up her Web site and checked out the photo gallery. I picked the three best views of the singer and printed them out on my color printer. I tucked them into an envelope, changed into my jeans and new yellow leather casual jacket, and recharged my hair and makeup. I packed up my laptop and made tracks for Betty's Diner.

———— ✦ ————

Patti Magliaro slapped the menu down in front of us and grinned. "Of course, *you* always get the club with fries." She turned to Margaret. "You, I don't know."

"I'll have what she's having," Margaret said.

When Patti hustled off with the order, I said, "So what can we do about Emmy Lou?"

Margaret said, "I knew that was why you wanted to have dinner together."

"It's not the only reason."

"If Emmy Lou doesn't want me to represent her, I can't contact her. You have to accept that, Charlotte."

"But how do we know that she doesn't want you to represent her?"

"Because she said so?"

"But did she really say that, Margaret?"

"She did. Now give it up."

We went round and round that mulberry bush until our food arrived.

"Here we go, ladies." Patti slid massive plates with turkey club sandwiches and the world's best fries in front of us.

Betty makes her clubs with real roasted turkey, crisp double-smoked bacon, crunchy lettuce, heirloom tomatoes, and homemade wheat or white bread. The fries are hand-cut, fresh, and fragrant. If I hadn't had so many reasons to move back home, maybe Betty's would have been enough. Betty, who was pushing eighty, still ran the place and knew all the customers. An excellent role model.

We fell on the food like turkey buzzards.

"So back to the topic," I said when nothing but the ghosts of the sandwiches remained. "I have only Dwayne's word that she refused to see you and wouldn't talk to him and didn't want to see the public defender and didn't want any other legal assistance. I didn't speak to her. You didn't speak to her. Pepper thinks she's guilty, so she wouldn't go out of her way. Dwayne says he'll find another lawyer, but I'm beginning to doubt that. She'll come up before a judge again this week."

Margaret picked up the last lonely hand-cut fry on her plate. "These are so good, I hate to see the end of them. And as for Emmy Lou, the public defender must have spoken to her."

"Whatever. But do you get what I'm saying?"

Margaret stared back at me speculatively and munched the fry.

I said, "*He* could have asked for your advice, even if she didn't. You could push for an insanity defense. Wait a minute, can you do that even if you don't have her support? Or his, for that matter?"

"I hardly know where to start with that, Charlotte. It's certainly vile if the husband's trying to make sure she doesn't have proper legal representation. But even if he did approach me you can forget insanity as a plea. It's a tough sell even with seriously ill people. With someone elegant and articulate, there's virtually no chance. However, there's even less chance of me, with no previous connection to the Rheinbecks, butting into the case. Give it up."

"I thought people got off on insanity defenses all the time."

"A common misperception. I'd say less than one percent. And if they do, they may end up in a worse situation."

"Forget that then. What if you could demonstrate that Dwayne had reasons for wanting Emmy Lou hauled off to jail?"

Margaret massaged her temple. "Like what?"

I opened the envelope and slid out the photo of Bryony Stevens. "Like her."

"Charlotte, I know you are concerned about your client, but you're not a police officer. You're not a private detective. You can't go around making allegations about people. Pepper will destroy you."

"You know Pepper. She may destroy me anyway."

"And Dwayne Rheinbeck could take legal action against you."

"But—"

"Ah, who's the lawyer here?"

I sighed. "Margaret is."

"Margaret is also your friend. So for your own good, don't get arrested or slapped with a lawsuit."

"Okay. So supposing that I don't go around—"

"—showing the picture and asking people about this girl, which I suspect is your plan."

"But I have to do something about this case."

Margaret wagged her finger at me. "Uh-uh. There is no case as far as you are concerned. You are usually so sensible and organized and in control of your emotions. What's wrong with you? Ask yourself why you are overly involved with this client."

"I have asked myself that. I've thought about this a lot. You weren't there when I met with her. Underneath the capable exterior, she was so fragile and vulnerable. That was even before this terrible thing with Tony happened. It's haunting me. I feel she truly needs my help, maybe more than anyone ever has."

Margaret said, "Huh."

Patti chose that moment to materialize and rattle off the dessert menu without being asked. "Devil's food special, ice cream sundaes, pecan pie, and carrot cake. Same as always."

I said, "Two devil's food specials. The whole thing's on my bill."

"I hope you don't think I can be bought," Margaret said as Patti ambled away with the orders.

I said, "I know in my heart that Emmy Lou didn't kill

Tony. She may think she did because she's having a break-down, but—don't roll your eyes. Why is everyone rolling their eyes all the time?"

Patti Magliaro reappeared magically and placed two plates of dark, moist, chocolately layer cake in front of us.

I breathed in the fragrance.

Margaret closed her eyes and inhaled.

Patti nodded in Margaret's direction. "First-timer?"

"Yes."

"On the house then." Patti winked. She glanced down at the pictures of Bryony. A flicker of recognition danced across her face.

I said, "This is the jazz singer Bryony Stevens. I hear she's going to be famous one of these days. Kind of neat that she's making her name here in Woodbridge."

Margaret glowered, but Patti brightened. "I've seen her around."

"Really? Here?"

"No, near my place. When I was walking Princess. Pretty girl."

"When was that?"

"Couple of weeks ago."

"Not this past Sunday?" I blurted.

She shook her head. "No, not Sunday. But it was some other afternoon, not long ago. She was with Dwayne Rhein-beck." Patti drifted off to one of her other tables where someone was frantically trying to get her attention.

"You see," I hissed at Margaret. "Bryony Stevens was with Dwayne one *afternoon* when his loving wife was at work making enough money to underwrite his endeavors."

Margaret rolled her eyes again. "You have to stop obsessing about this. Promise me you won't go to Bell Street and ask the other neighbors about this girl. I am way too busy to haul your butt out of the slammer again."

Lay out your clothes for the morning the night before,
complete with the shoes, jewelry, underwear,
and stockings you plan to wear.
No nasty morning surprises that way.

18

"Sure, I'll do it," Lilith said when I caught up with her in between jobs. "I'll ask around on Bell Street. I'll be less noticeable."

I grinned at her turquoise tips and facial piercings. "Less noticeable than what?"

"You. I don't know how to break this to you, but on a noticeability scale of one to ten, you're eleven."

"What do you mean?"

"You know: skirt, high heels, makeup, hairdo. People notice you. City girl. And then there's that air of determination."

I held up my hand. "Never mind."

"I'll let you know what I find out."

I handed over the printed photos of Bryony Stevens, and since I had a bit of time until Sally's kids would be tucked in and dreaming, I drove to the edge of town to browse in the building supply store. To each her own. I like to see what kind of new materials they have. Especially shelving.

—✳—

On my way to Sally's that evening, my cell phone began to trill. I pulled over to take it, in case it was Lilith with a question about her undercover assignment. Rose's voice shrilled, high and hysterical. As long as I've known her Rose has been unflappable no matter what.

"What are you saying, Rose?" I said soothingly. "What happened?"

"Lilith's been hit by a . . ." Rose choked up.

"What?"

"A hit-and-run driver. Left her lying in the road."

My mouth went dry with shock. How could this be?

"They took her to Woodbridge General."

"I'll go over."

Rose said with a quaver, "Take me with you, please. This girl is closer to me than my own family. What will I do if . . . ?"

"Don't think the worst, Rose," I said. "We'll go together."

Five minutes later I picked up Rose on North Elm, which was as usual deserted. Rose had a little bit of trouble bending into the Miata, but we had no choice. Lilith had taken Rose's old LeMans. I figured it was parked wherever she'd been hit.

"I'm sorry I was out of control, Charlotte," Rose said as I gunned it down the street.

"No worries, Rose."

We squealed into the emergency room parking lot. "She has me listed as family," Rose said. "I don't know if she has anyone else."

Lilith had lived on the streets before finding an assortment of personal-care and bicycle-courier jobs in Woodbridge. She was a damaged but caring person who'd seemed alone in the world until she moved in with Rose. Come to think of it, Rose fit the same description, except for very occasional, half-hearted efforts from the daughter in L.A.

"Hard to be more real than you, Rose." I reached over and squeezed her hand.

Rose glowered. "Whoever did this terrible thing, I'd like to kick his butt."

"And I'd like to help," I said. "His or hers."

—❖—

Lilith was in surgery to reduce pressure on her brain. I alternated between pacing in the waiting room and squirming on the hard plastic seat. Rose slumped in a chair, exhausted and drawn. The purple jogging suit wasn't enough to lift the grey from her face. She'd been hauled into Emergency so many times because of her breathing and heart problems that the hospital itself probably spelled stress for her. Add to that our joint panic over Lilith and it was taking a toll. I got her a cup of what they called coffee and waited until she relaxed a bit. Then I excused myself and stepped outside the hospital to phone Sally. Benjamin worked in that hospital and I thought if I could reach him, he could help me wade through the information guardians.

As I walked past the emergency desk, a uniformed police officer was leaning over the desk, flirting with the nursing staff. He turned to ogle me. I scurried through the doors and outside as fast as I could.

Not fast enough though.

I heard his boots behind me. I turned and sighed.

"Hey, Charlie," he said, grinning.

Nick Monahan smoothed his dirty blond hair and continued to flash his smile. That smile had been the undoing of many a girl at St. Jude's when we were growing up. There used to be a rumor that Nick had the largest collection of girls' panties in New York State. Needless to say, mine were not in that collection. Nor were Pepper's, I am absolutely certain. Nick always preferred a challenge.

As much as I disliked running into him, he did present an

opportunity. And I figured Nick's tiny reptile brain would never give him the slightest hint about that.

I smiled falsely. "Do you know anything about a hit-and-run? A young woman? She was brought in here maybe an hour ago."

"Oh yeah," he said. "I was first on the scene. I was checking up on her."

"She's my friend. Lilith Carisse. What happened to her?"

He blinked. "You know. A vehicle hit her. And then took off."

Even with all the previous generations of Monahans on the Woodbridge police force it was hard to imagine how Nick had passed any of the entrance exams. Sometimes I wondered if Pepper had taken them for him. "I know what a hit-and-run is. I was wondering about the circumstances of this one."

"Like what?" he said, confirming my most unflattering suspicions.

I sighed. "Like where did it happen?"

"Here in town."

"What street?" You can't give up with Nick, even if you're fighting the urge to bang your head on the cement walkway.

"River Road, at the corner of Bell Street."

I inhaled sharply.

"What's wrong?" he said.

"And do you know anything about the vehicle that hit her? Aside from the fact that it hit her and drove off, I mean."

He frowned in concentration.

I clarified. "Car? Truck? Snowmobile?"

"Gee, Charlie. I know what a vehicle is. I told you it—"

"Was a hit-and-run. Yes, I know. But this was in daylight on a street that has lots of coming and going. So were there any witnesses?"

"Yeah. There were."

Now we were getting somewhere. "What did they say?"

"Come on, Charlie, I know you think I'm dumb, but I can't tell you that. Pepper doesn't want you involved in investigations."

"I'm not sure what that's about, Nick. I simply want to find out what kind of vehicle slammed into my friend. What harm can that do? It's not like I can track them down or anything. Ha, ha. That's your job."

His noble brow creased as he thought hard.

While he was thinking, I chipped away. "So did the witnesses see a car?"

"I guess it can't hurt. But don't you let on I told you anything."

"Cross my heart," I said, crossing my fingers.

"A couple of people saw a white delivery van, but there's a million of 'em out there."

"No license plates?"

He shook his handsome head. "Nope."

"But if it struck Lilith enough to put her in the hospital, there'd be some damage to the van too, wouldn't there? A garage might be able to . . ."

He went white.

"What?" I said.

"Don't go asking around about this, Charlie, promise me. Pepper will murder me if she finds out I told you anything."

"Frankly, any one could figure out that a garage or body shop might have repaired a white van."

"They haven't released that information. Nobody knows it was a white van. So she'd put two and two together."

"Maybe a witness told me. Anyway, she can't read minds."

"You're wrong about that. And she's in a real bad mood today."

I shrugged. Pepper had been in a bad mood every time I'd seen her for the last twelve years.

He said, "Most likely she's not pregnant again, but I didn't stick my neck out to ask. She wants a baby more than anything and it doesn't seem to be happening. We're working hard at it. We've been trying everything, even—"

I held up my hand. "Too much information."

"Huh? Oh yeah. Whenever she finds out she's not pregnant, she's meaner than a snake for a week."

I felt a rush of sympathy for Pepper. Not only because she was married to Nick, but also because I remembered the expression on her face when she saw Sally's children. Absolute agonized longing. And what was ahead for her? Either frustration and heartbreak if she wasn't successful. Or the dubious blessing of raising a brood with Nick. While I searched for the right words, Nick said, "Do you ever wonder how it would be if you and me had stayed together, Charlie?"

I didn't have to wonder. I knew darn well it would have been a slice of hell on earth. "Don't go there, Nick."

He looked down at his feet. Big, sad pistol-packing cop. Pathetic.

"Let the past go, Nick. Think about Pepper. Think about this baby that you'll succeed in having one of these days. Think about your future together."

"That's the trouble, Charlie. I am thinking about it. Pepper and me, we had a good thing going. Parties and cars and trips and great sex. A baby's going to ruin all that stuff. I'm not the one who wants kids. She's a crazy lady on the subject. Like out of her mind. It's real scary."

"We've all got to grow up sometime."

I left him standing there, moping over the prospect of growing up, not that there was much chance of that happening soon.

—✦—

When I finally got outside the hospital, I checked my cell phone. I found a message from Jack.

"Just letting you know that a guy just called me about a shipment that went astray. High-end Italian parts. I'm driving up to Troy to get them. The guy said he'd wait up for me, which is beyond the call of duty for sure. I have to go, because I have an excellent customer who's taking his bike on holiday and he's counting on those brakes for tomorrow. Didn't want you to worry. I should be back by two, two thirty latest. If you're awake then, maybe we can share some Ben & Jerry's. I'll need to get my strength back."

"Don't go to Troy," I said out loud. "I really need you. Lilith's been hit and she's in bad shape."

You know you're losing it when you start talking to people who aren't there. But Jack had no way of knowing how much I needed his support. Luckily I had other friends.

"Benjamin's tied up in surgery," Sally said when I reached her. "I'll ask him when he gets out. Where was she when it happened?"

I felt my throat constrict. "That's it, Sally. She was doing something for me. Trying to find out if anyone on Bell Street had seen Bryony Stevens."

Sally gasped. "But this was an accident?"

"The cops say it's a hit-and-run. Seems like a pretty unlikely coincidence to me."

"I'll track down Benjamin."

I choked out my thanks, hung up, and gasped.

Pepper stood behind me, waiting, the way a lioness waits for a baby gazelle to stray from the pack.

She said, "Seems like a pretty unlikely coincidence to me too."

With Pepper you have to fight the fear and simulate bravery. "Can you tell me where they found her?"

"Where did you send her?"

"What?"

"Don't dick around with me, Charlotte. Tell me what was going on and make it snappy."

I guess I'm not the type who could hold out under torture. I spilled my guts. "Bryony Stevens sings at Wet Paint. I think she's involved with Dwayne Rheinbeck, my client's husband."

"I know who Dwayne Rheinbeck is."

"I wondered if Bryony might have been on Bell Street on the day Tony died. That's all. There might be a connection."

Pepper snorted. "That's all? Let's see if I understand this. Then Lilith went around snooping?"

Uh-oh. Danger lurked. "Maybe."

"News flash: this is a police issue. There's a murder investigation going on, and you have no business sticking your pointed little nose into it."

"I thought if I could prove to you that Dwayne was having an affair with a younger woman, that might change the way you looked at the case."

Pepper's nostrils flared. "I don't need you to show me how to do my job."

"Of course not, but you had no way to know this. It was based on a glimpse, the look on his face when he talked to this girl. There was so much emotion between them. Then I started to wonder why Emmy Lou confessed so easily. Why is she freaking out?"

Pepper watched me the way I might regard a bug on my white sheets. I felt like freaking out a bit myself. Still, I continued. "So maybe she's protecting him."

She slapped her forehead. "I was too dumb to think of that. Oh wait, maybe I wasn't, being a *police* detective and all, rather than a busybody. Maybe that's why we, that would be the police, thought that her confession was a touch too hysterical. Maybe that's why we checked out Mr. Dwayne Rheinbeck. Too bad he had an ironclad alibi, Charlotte."

"I already knew that. But what if he convinced this girl to get involved somehow? I wanted to find out if she'd been seen on Bell Street that day."

"That's great. Now Lilith Carisse has fifty-fifty odds of

making it alive. If she does make it, there's a good chance she'll be a vegetable, to put it bluntly."

I felt tears well.

Pepper knows my weaknesses. She was enjoying twisting the knife.

"Congratulations," she said. "That's quite an accomplishment."

"I never thought she'd be in danger."

"You never thought, period."

"Someone tried to kill her because of this. It couldn't have been Emmy Lou because you have her locked up."

I didn't like the implication of that curled lip.

I blundered on. "Maybe Bryony has a white van. Or the restaurant might."

"What?"

Oops. "Nothing."

"Did you say 'a white van'?"

"Yeah I thought I heard something about that in the waiting room."

Pepper fixed me with her steely stare.

"Really," I squeaked.

"Maybe you heard it from a certain cop. What's his name now, Officer Shit-for-Brains?"

"No, I don't think so."

"You stay away from my husband, Charlotte Adams. He's one of the few people who knows about the white van. But he'd blab to you, wouldn't he? Anything if he thought he could get a quick grope."

"Nobody gropes me," I said. "Nick's innocent. The main thing is to check and see if Dwayne Rheinbeck or Bryony Stevens had access to a white van. They're the main suspects."

"Here's the bad news about your so-called suspects. I have checked them out. They're not having an affair. And your client? She's a nutbar. Maybe Lilith Carisse got run over for nothing. Live with that while you learn to mind your own business."

"How do you know they're not having an affair? You didn't see how close they were to each other. Not a working relationship. More like—"

Pepper curled her lip again. "How about like father and daughter?"

Take digital photos of your home and valuables.
Store this record on a CD off-site.
If you have a fire or robbery, you'll have an accurate
inventory that's much better than your memory.

19

By eleven o'clock, we learned that Lilith was out of danger but unconscious. When the news came to us in the waiting room, Rose and I clung to each other in relief. Afterward, Rose dozed from time to time, but I had too many things buzzing in my mind, not only intense guilt about Lilith but also the news that Dwayne was Bryony's father. Where did that leave all my theories?

At least the hospital staff gave us occasional updates about Lilith. I was pretty sure that knowing Benjamin had made a difference in the speed and quality of the information we received.

Toward midnight, Rose said, "I'm spending the night here."

"You need your rest. And you shouldn't be alone. Tell you what, I'll go get Truffle and Sweet Marie, and you can have a houseful of guests tonight. Schopenhauer loves the girls. Tomorrow I'll come over and we'll spell each other off."

Rose shook her head. "My heart's not so good. I might as well stay here as go home and get hauled back in by ambulance. I never sleep anyway, and I can't even think straight. I would appreciate it if you got Schopie and walked him, maybe take him home with you. Then in the morning, you can do a shift if you'd like."

—••—

It wasn't easy squeezing Schopenhauer into the Mazda, but he was willing to cooperate. Fatigue washed over me as I drove from North Elm to my place. I hate to come home to a dark house. As I turned the corner and slowed, two small bright-eyed creatures raced across the street, barking.

"I must be tired, because my eyes are playing tricks. If I didn't know they were safe inside, I would have sworn that was Truffle and Sweet Marie," I said to Schopenhauer. He licked my hand.

I parked in the driveway and hurried toward the house. Although I'd lived happily by myself for seven years in New York City, now that I'd come back to Woodbridge, I hated when Jack wasn't home.

I stopped at the front door. It stood open. The hallway and staircase lay in darkness. Schopenhauer barked. "Jack? Did you get back early?" As I stepped inside, I realized Jack's dung-colored Mini Minor was not in the driveway. I squinted up the long flight of stairs leading to my apartment. I knew even before my eyes adjusted that my door would be wide open too.

"Burglary!" I shouted into my cell phone. "In progress!"

"Your name and location, ma'am? Oh wait, is this Charlotte? Mona Pringle here."

"Mona. My door is open, my dogs are gone. I have to find them, but what if he's inside my apartment? What if—"

"Your place, Charlotte?"

I hurried along the sidewalk frantically searching for

Truffle and Sweet Marie. I huffed and puffed as I confirmed the address.

"Unit's on its way," Mona said. "You're having a lousy week."

I snuffled. "Craptacular."

"I heard about your friend, Lilith. That's rough."

"I have to find my dogs. They ran away."

"Not such a good idea. You should get in your car, lock the doors, and start her up. Wait until the police arrive."

"They were running like crazy. They're not afraid of cars. They could be hit! Truffle! Sweet Marie! Come home!"

Mona Pringle raised her voice. "Charlotte? Please get in your car."

I was hunting for the dogs when the first police car swung onto the street, red and white roof lights flashing. It was joined by a second one coming from the other direction. That was reassuring. The police officers got out of the cars, and at almost the same moment two small dogs scampered recklessly across the street half a block away and raced off in the opposite direction.

"Mona? Tell them I'll be right back!"

Five minutes later, two panicked dogs continued to shake as I carried them under my arms. With Schopenhauer as a guard by my side, I joined the cops. Naturally, one of them had to be Nick. It was nearly midnight. Was he working overtime?

"Nice place, Charlie," he said.

"It was," I said.

The other cop stepped over the devastation that was my tiny perfect apartment. Cushions lay on the floor; the sofa was upended. The wooden legs of my pretty occasional chair were broken. The upholstery was slashed. The contents of my closet lay scattered across the floor: skirts, jackets, even my new white shirt that I hadn't even worn once.

"Please don't step on that," I said to the new officer.

My dresser drawers had been dumped. Nick regarded my

underwear with interest before I hastily swept it out of his sight. Someone had pulled the sheets and comforter off my bed and dumped them in a heap. My supplies had been tossed from their shelves, along with out-of-season clothing. It was a measure of how much they'd been traumatized that Truffle and Sweet Marie didn't each grab a roll of toilet paper and play Make Some Clouds. Luckily the burglars hadn't emptied my jewelry box.

In the kitchen, things were worse: the doors of my perfectly organized cupboards were open. Pans, cans, strainers, cleaners, dry goods littered the floor. My spices were no longer in alphabetical order. My last container of Ben & Jerry's sat melting sadly on the counter. A broken jar of Dijon mustard was splattered everywhere, yellow streaks staining my pretty cream-colored cabinets. I picked up the dogs so they didn't cut their paws.

Next I checked my small office area, which is nothing more than a section of my bedroom hidden by a screen. I was followed by the officer I didn't know and even more closely by Nick. The first thing I noticed was the upturned trash can and the paper recycle bin that seemed to have been flung at the wall, denting the drywall.

"I guess they took your computer," the other cop said.

I shook my head, feeling a bit overwhelmed. "At least I had my laptop with me. I worked on some projects while I was waiting at the hospital today."

I wondered. Could Nick have done this as an excuse to get into my apartment? He knew I was at the hospital . . . No. Too much like a plan for Nick.

I turned my attention to my poor, still-cowering little dogs. I covered them up with a blanket, gave them a reassuring pat, and told Schopenhauer to watch over them. It was time to check out Jack's place. Sure enough, it had been turned over too. But there was less to trash, since his parents' furniture was in storage, he had absolutely no food, and what burglar is desperate enough to steal a collection of Hawaiian shirts? I explained that I wasn't sure whether Jack had money or bike parts in his apartment. His books lay sprawled from wall to wall. Nick bent over and picked one up. "Can't see anyone ripping off this stuff."

Jack's prized CD collection had been dumped out of the holders. There was a crunch as Nick stepped on a couple of the jewel cases.

"Why would anyone do this?" I sniveled.

The cop I didn't know gave me a strange look. "Burglary, ma'am. Theft."

"But of what? They didn't take my jewelry. Some of it's valuable. And they didn't take Jack's CDs."

Nick said, "I dunno, there's a lot of jazz. And way too much classical and opera. Weird and screechy in languages no one can understand. No fence is going to touch them. You can't give that crap away. Now if he had tools or something, that'd be different. You think he did?"

"We'll have to ask him. He'll be back from Troy later." As the words flowed out of my mouth, I wanted to claw them back.

Nick cleared his throat. "If you don't mind me saying, Charlie, you shouldn't stay here tonight."

"I'm staying. I have to clean up! I can't leave my home like this."

"It might not be safe."

"Why not? The so-called burglar's gone. Why would he come back? And how would he get in if I'm here?"

"With a key. The same way he did before."

"What?"

Nick said, "With a—"

"I heard you. But how would he get a key? The only people who have a key to the front door and my door are me and Jack."

Nick smirked.

"Well, I didn't do it."

Nick said, "Maybe Jack flipped. And trashed the place. Insane jealousy or something."

I stared at him. "Are you smoking dope, Nick?"

"Hell no. I'm on duty."

"Okay. I have my keys, so someone must have Jack's. He's gone to Troy." A hellish world of possibilities unfolded in my brain. I babbled in a panic, "What if Jack picked up a crazed hitchhiker? What if he was robbed? What if he's been tied up and left to die?"

Nick and the other cop gawked at me as if I'd started speaking in tongues. I pulled out my cell phone with shaking hands and keyed in Jack's number. To my surprise, he answered.

"Where are you?" I shouted.

"Be home in half an hour," he said. "Why do you sound like that?"

"Where are your damned keys?"

Long pause.

I tried again, "Well?"

"Last time I looked they were in the ignition. The car is moving."

"Oh."

If Jack's keys were in his ignition and mine were in my purse, what keys had been used to break in?

Nick looked at me with pity. "Somebody probably copied them. Have you left your handbag out of your sight recently? It doesn't take long for a pro to take an imprint. If they know your name, they can find your house. Of course, usually, they steal your credit cards too. Or they get the numbers and make copies. Any unusual activity on yours lately?"

I spent the next half hour on the phone with my two credit card companies. No one had done anything with mine. To be sure, they put a hold on both cards. Jack doesn't even have one, so I guessed we didn't have to worry about that.

"That's good," Nick said. "But weird. It's a lot easier to make purchases with forged cards than it is to break into houses."

"That's the problem," I said. "I don't think this a break-and-enter. This person was searching for something."

"I can understand that," Nick leered.

"But what?" I said, ignoring him.

Nick finally took my statement and waited until the twenty-four-hour locksmith arrived. I spent the waiting time picking up the mess. I worked fast and kept a jump ahead of Nick. "Nothing is missing. Is that usual?"

"It's sort of weird." He edged a bit closer.

It helped to mention Pepper's name once every second sentence. Sort of like hosing down a dog that's out of control. When the locksmith arrived, Nick gave up and went back to work.

By the time Jack got home, the locks had been changed on both our doors and I'd made a big dent in the disorder. I handed him his new set of keys as he reached the top of the stairs. "My treat."

He stood in my doorway, staring. "Temper, temper, Charlotte," he said. "I wasn't that late."

"Let me guess. Your trip to Troy? Was it a wild-goose chase?"

"Honk honk," he said.

———

It would have been the perfect night to sleep through. But my subconscious sounded a gong at the preferred time of three in the morning and told me why two of Emmy Lou's classmates looked familiar. They were no longer teenagers with bad haircuts; they were women in their forties with jobs around Woodbridge. Not that it mattered, because now I knew that Emmy Lou had indeed lived at number 7, that the man who denied being her father was indeed her father, and that she'd known and cared about Tony Starkman since he was a small damaged boy. Not that I understood what any of this signified, but you can't have everything. The same subconscious didn't offer insights about who might have hit Lilith. It was equally silent on my break-in. But it did remind me that I hadn't made a to-do list the night before and suggested that I add the following items to that list:

+ *Visit hospital to see Lilith*
+ *Double-check to see if anything is missing after break-in*
+ *Get LeMans back to North Elm Street for Rose*
+ *Talk to Gary about progress with shelves*
+ *Bring Dwayne up-to-date on shelving*
+ *Pick up dry cleaning*
+ *Call Sally*

I was blasted from a deep sleep by the first shrill ring. Luckily my cell phone was by the bed.

Ramona said, "You sound groggy. Did I wake you?"

"It's okay," I yawned.

"I know the old joke: you had to get up anyway to answer the phone. Of course, it is ten in the morning, not that it's any of my business. Can't talk long, we're up to our patooties in pesky patrons here. But I checked with the city system and the properties at 9 and 11 Bell Street, for your information, are owned by a T. Wright. Same name as the person you were looking for. Hope that helps. Gotta go."

Rose called from the hospital as soon as Ramona hung up.

"I slept in, but I'll be there as soon as I can," I said.

"No rush, they've wheeled her off for tests," she whispered. "She won't be back for an hour and a half at the earliest. I'm going to get some shut-eye."

I was halfway through my very late cup of coffee when my brain clicked in and I realized that the man who denied being Emmy Lou's father was probably the person who

slashed my tires. But slashing tires was a big step up from ignoring my questions. So why would he want to frighten me
off?

———❦———

Jack was passed out when I knocked on his door. I heard a
muffled groan from inside and then the door opened. "Please
tell me it's the middle of the night," he said.

"It's the middle of something." Of course, I had the ad-
vantage. I'd walked the three dogs, showered, done my hair,
and put on a pair of slim brown dress pants and my yellow
leather jacket. All in top speed so I could get going fast and
make up for lost time.

I'd had breakfast and three cups of coffee. I was ready to
run rings around him.

"I'd like to get over to the hospital to see how Lilith's doing this morning. Maybe we should get the LeMans. One of
us can take Rose home afterward."

"Boy." He had the wide-eyed look he gets without his
glasses. "You're talking awfully fast. I can take Rose home.
And I'll be happy to spend time with Lilith. Do you want me
to come with you now?"

"Thanks, Jack." I felt my chin wobble.

"And Charlotte?"

"Hmm?"

"I can close the store for the day. Whatever it takes."

———❦———

I had time to swing by Klean and Brite on my way to the hospital. As I walked through the door, I felt a tiny tickle from my
subconscious. Of course. The pleasant blowsy woman behind
the counter had been one of Emmy Lou's classmates, clearly
recognizable despite the fifty pounds she'd added. Her hair
seemed stuck in the eighties style, but maybe that was the hu-
midity. It was a long shot, but after all, high school is such an

intense experience, some people have every person in every class etched in their brains.

I slid my claim slip across the counter and said, "This might be a weird question, but do you remember Emmy Lou Wright?"

"I remember everyone from high school," she replied. "It's taking tonight's dinner from the freezer that I forget. She was a beautiful girl."

I leaned forward and said in a conspiratorial whisper, "I heard she had a breakdown."

"Who wouldn't?"

"What?"

"Wouldn't you have a breakdown if you were forced to give up your baby?"

"I'm sorry. Did you say give up her . . . ?"

"That was the rumor going around. I know she was in bad shape after Roger Starkman died, but I always wondered if the real breakdown didn't happen after they snatched that kid from her. Hang on, I'll get your cleaning for you."

"Wait! Did *everyone* know about Emmy Lou's baby?"

"Her family tried to hush it up. That was crazy. So many girls had babies back then. Anyway, you can't keep something like that a secret." She paused and frowned. "I don't *think* it was a story. Emmy Lou left town, and she didn't come back for years. Can't say I blame her. It was a real surprise to hear she moved back to Bell Street. I'll tell you one thing: I would never want to see the people who did that to me. I'd never forget and I'd never forgive."

*Keep a simple project in your briefcase or handbag
in case you find yourself with a long wait.*

20

When I found Rose in the relatives' lounge, she looked as drawn and gaunt as any patient in the trauma unit.

She said, "Don't try to talk me into going home. I can catnap here and be good as new. Lilith's off having tests for the next while."

"Fine. Let's go to the cafeteria. At least you can have some food and coffee, and we'll have a chat. I can swing by your place later and get you a change of clothing."

Rose didn't put up any resistance. Over what the hospital optimistically called "food" and "coffee," I filled her in on Emmy Lou and the baby she may have been forced to give up.

"That's a terribly sad story," she said.

"Yes, it is. Now I have to figure out what it means. It answers some questions but raises just as many." I'd thanked my subconscious, of course, for the connection. I could hear little pieces ringing deep in my brain, like a wind chime. The only problem was that when the pieces fell into place, they didn't make sense.

"So, Rose, you know Myrna Dingwall. You said she was your age."

Rose managed a weak chuckle. "Yep. Just another kid into her seventies."

"But Kevin is only twenty-three."

"These things happen."

"But did it happen in this case, Rose?"

She bit her lip. "I wondered about that too. When the other baby died, Myrna went into a real depression. Didn't come out of the house, didn't get out of bed. It lasted an awful long time. Fred still worked with my late husband then. He was beside himself. Then after a while, he sent Myrna away to visit family somewhere out of state for a while. When she came back, she had her beautiful new baby boy. That's all I know."

"Emmy Lou Wright was forced to give up her child at about that time."

Rose twisted her hands. "People gossiped, of course. I never liked that kind of talk. I was happy for her. It's not the kind of thing you question."

"There's no question that Mrs. Dingwall loves Kevin. And so does Emmy Lou. Here's what I think might have happened. I think Emmy Lou never got over losing Roger Starkman, her boyfriend, and then having her baby taken away. I think she came back, not to aggravate her horrible father, but in spite of him. She wanted to be near to her son. I think being so close to Kevin was driving her to the brink. And Tony Starkman was her boyfriend Roger's nephew, a reminder. They played stupid stunts, but she would have been on edge all the time anyway. Imagining things, having trouble concentrating, forgetting things."

"That might send anyone up the wall," Rose muttered. "Especially if it was a secret. These are more open times, Charlotte. It used to be that every family had secrets; every neighborhood was full of them. Babies born and whisked away, girls who left suddenly and came back sad, if at all, affairs, double lives, battered wives, abused children, so many things we pretended didn't exist."

I said, "Perhaps some of those old secrets are causing grief."

Rose said sadly, "If Kevin was Emmy Lou's child and she was estranged from her family, it must have been horrible for her. Especially keeping that secret from Kevin himself." Rose glanced over sharply. "Do you think her husband knew?"

"He's a smart man. He has his own daughter. But I doubt that he'd have a problem with Kevin."

"And who is she protecting?"

"It must be Kevin. Perhaps he and Tony were clowning around and Tony fell. But Kevin was away with his mother, visiting the grandmother. He couldn't have done it. Unless . . ."

Rose's gnarled hand shot to her bloodless lips.

I said, "Unless Myrna Dingwall is lying about when they drove away."

"To protect him. Same as Emmy Lou."

I met her gaze. "Or to protect herself."

"You think she killed Tony, accidentally or even deliberately?"

"She wasn't too fond of him, and she didn't believe he was good for Kevin. Afterward, she would have made sure that Kevin was out of the way. I doubt if he'd have been aware of the time. She was the one who told me when they returned."

I watched Rose's kindly face crumble. "But she would be setting Emmy Lou up in that case. That's a very wicked thing to do."

"She had no way of knowing that Emmy Lou would scream out a confession in front of everyone. And if she hadn't, Tony's death would have probably looked like an accident."

Rose said, "And where is Lilith in all this?"

"I don't know. But if it's a coincidence, it's a huge one. Lilith was asking questions on Bell Street when she was hit. Even though the questions were about Bryony Stevens, maybe someone didn't realize that."

Rose shook her head slowly. "I don't believe that Myrna would run down an innocent girl like Lilith because she was asking questions. I think you're wrong about that, Charlotte."

"Let's hope so. There are delivery vans speeding up and down there all the time. Maybe one of them hit her. But even so, I feel responsible for what's happened."

After I left Rose, I left a message for Nick Monahan, asking if the witness who'd mentioned the white van had actually seen the van hit Lilith. I wasn't sure if he'd have the guts to call me back, but I had to do something.

—※—

Lilith was still unconscious when she was wheeled back to the room. Her spectacular turquoise tips were a thing of the past, replaced by sterile bandages. I spent the rest of the day by her bed, alternating with Rose, who was catching up on her sleep in the relatives' lounge. Rose tiptoed in from time to time, looking ten years older, wan and worried. I used the time during Rose's visits to step out and call Sally and bring her up to speed. I phoned Dwayne and let him know the project would be a bit slower because Lilith was in the hospital. Finally, I told Gary Gigantes the news about Lilith and also my break-in.

"That's too bad, Charlotte. I heard about that hit-and-run, but I didn't make the connection with your friend. You do what you gotta do. I'm ready anytime," he said. "The trim's cut. Got good deals on the bookcases, so I used the savings to get you some lighting to show off the collection. Won't take long to install. You're number one on the list, so whenever you're ready, give me a shout. Even if I start another job, I'll slot yours in. I'll let the next client know right up front."

"You're amazing, Gary. As soon as Lilith's out of the woods, I'll be able to concentrate. I have a lot to do, because of my break-in and everything else."

"I'm here."

In between visits from Margaret and Jack, who both wanted to be in the loop, I kept an eye on Lilith's sleeping form and did a bit of work to take my mind off my guilt over putting her in that situation. Logic told me the hit-and-run had to be connected to Tony's death and Emmy Lou's situation. Lilith's presence had stirred up Tony's killer in some way.

I fiddled with notes and diagrams. Tried to remember what Patti had said about who lived where. Made mind maps. Drew arrows connecting people. I proceeded with a few assumptions. First, the chances were good the person was connected with Bell Street and specifically with Emmy Lou. Second, that all or most of our bizarre experiences over the last few days were linked.

I did a little map of the block.

On one side:
- *Numbers 2 and 4: Demolished, now vacant lots*
- *Number 6: The Van Loons, a housebound couple in their eighties*
- *Number 8: Kevin and Mrs. Dingwall*
- *Number 10: Emmy Lou and Dwayne*
- *Number 12: Bonnie and Bill Baxter*
- *Number 14: Someone away on road trip*

On the other side:
- *Number 5: The Mrazeks, a couple in their late seventies*
- *Number 7: Mr. T. Wright and Mrs. Wright, who probably had a name too*

✦ *Numbers 9 and 11: Vacant properties being demol-*
  ished. Owned by Mr. T. Wright and possibly Mrs.
✦ *Number 13: Patti Magliaro upstairs*
✦ *Number 13: Downstairs, Patti's landlord, Ralph—*
  visiting his son in Florida
✦ *Number 15: Vacant—sold but not yet occupied*

Fine. What about Mr. Wright? A bully? For sure. Heart-less? Sounded like it. A child growing up without a pet or even a stuffed animal. A man who would disown his daughter. A man who would coerce her to give up a child she wanted. A man who appeared to dominate his timid wife. Would such a man kill Tony, the nephew of the boyfriend who set things in motion? Mr. Wright owned the property where my tires had been slashed. He'd seen me asking questions of people on the street. He was obviously hostile. Did he have something to hide? He could have made the call to Pepper saying I'd threatened the boys. He might have overheard, perhaps even from an open window. He would have seen Lilith outside the house with me. My face had been all over the news. My address and phone number were listed in the phone book. He could have trashed my house. One more way to frighten me. A major question was how he could have obtained a key. But for all I knew he'd been a career lock-smith. I wrote "KEY????" next to his name.

He was the most appealing villain, hands down. But why would Emmy Lou lie to protect such a vile person? Did she still love her father in spite of everything? Did she want to protect him? That seemed likely.

I moved to another house on the list: number 8. Kevin might have accidentally killed his friend, or even been at the scene, but Kevin was no conspirator. Bonnie and Bill had seen the Dingwalls leaving around noon. But we had only Mrs. Dingwall's word about when they'd returned. For sure, she would have lied to protect her son if he'd caused Tony's death. But it was more likely that she had done it. Ridding herself of a troublesome bad influence in her son's life. I closed my eyes and recalled our conversation in her living room. She had a deep voice. She'd have no trouble sounding like a man on the phone. She was close enough and strong enough to slash the tires on the Miata. On the other hand, I was pretty sure she hadn't been a locksmith or a burglar, and anyway, she hadn't had any opportunity to get her mitts on my keys.

It was fairly obvious that a demolition team had been working on the site of numbers 9 and 11, but I hadn't seen any of them. Still, tradespeople were in short supply with the renovation boom in Woodbridge. On the other hand, those properties are owned by T. Wright. I put a "?" next to them.

Across the street at number 10 where I'd started, there was Dwayne, seemingly loving husband. I had suspected he might be better off with Emmy Lou out of the way, although now that I knew he was Bryony's father, not her lover, I found it hard to give that idea any weight. And he certainly wouldn't be better off with Emmy Lou on trial or in a mental hospital. In fact, the legal costs would probably bankrupt him. However, unlike Mrs. Dingwall, he could have easily copied my keys when I was checking out the house. He'd been alone in the room with my handbag. Unfortunately, I couldn't come up with a plausible reason for him to trash my house or slash my tires.

Also at number 10 was Emmy Lou herself. But Emmy Lou was locked up in the psych ward, which was why I was so upset in the first place.

Was I wasting my time? I bit my lower lip and stared at what I had so far. A moan from the hospital bed distracted me. Lilith's eyelids fluttered. I dropped my papers and stood up.

"Lilith?"

"Sorry," she whispered.

"Nothing to be sorry about. I'm so glad you're back." I squeezed her hand.

The eyes closed again.

"Lilith," I said, "who ran you down?"

Soft breathing, then a raspy, "Don't know."

"Who did you see on Bell Street? Did you talk to Mr. Wright? Mrs. Dingwall? Bill and Bonnie?"

A soft, soft, "Yes."

"The workers at the demolition sites?"

"My head hurts."

What was I doing? Lilith had regained consciousness. The medical staff had to be informed. Rose needed to know. I leaned over and rang the bell for the nurse.

"You rest," I said.

Lilith whispered again, "Needed distraction. Talked about the toys. Tried to trick them . . . about Sunday."

At that moment the nurse bustled through the door. "What can I do?"

"She's awake."

"I'll get the doctor."

21

Rose settled in and prepared for another night at Lilith's side, claiming she'd slept all day and was completely re-freshed. One look at her told me that wasn't true. She frowned and said, "There's something I'm supposed to tell you and darned if I can remember what it is."

"That's the stress of worrying about Lilith, Rose. It's hell on the concentration. Whatever it is, it will keep."

"Hope so. I feel like an old fool though. And this old fool is staying here."

Before I could put up an argument, Margaret arrived.

"You look worse than Rose does, if that's possible," she said. While I was recovering from that comment, she added, "Hit the road and get some sleep. I have a lot of files to catch up on, might as well do it here. Don't argue."

On the way out, I called Jack and told him I was on my way home from the hospital.

"I walked Truffle and Sweet Marie. And Schopie," he said. "The four of us will be waiting for you. Make that the six of us. I replaced your melted Ben & Jerry's New York Super Fudge Chunk with two new tubs."

As soon as I hung up, the phone trilled again.

"Charlotte?" A vague tremulous voice.

"Yes."

"This is Patti. Patti Magliaro?"

"Oh, Patti, of course. What can I do for you?"

"Sorry to hear about your friend. But something weird is going on across the street. Can you hear me? I'm whispering."

"What is weird? Are you okay, Patti?"

"It's hard to explain. Can you come over? I'm home. It's my night off. Because I worked an extra—"

Before Patti could head down a dozen conversational bypasses, I intervened. "If you're worried, you should hang up and call the police."

"It's probably nothing or I would call them, except I don't like them much."

Understood. "Can you tell me what is happening?" I refrained from adding, "It's late and I need to get home."

Patti sighed. "It's probably nothing. Dwayne will be home soon anyway. Sorry to bother you, Charlotte. Don't worry, Princess, I'm coming."

"It's okay, Patti. Just tell me what it is and . . ." I waited. "Hello? Hello? Are you there? Oh for Pete's sake."

Patti was vague enough to hang up on me and go about her business, but I would worry about it all night if I didn't know. I checked my phone so I could call her back. "Unknown Number." Truly unhelpful.

I snapped off the phone, jumped in the Miata, and broke the speed limit getting to Bell Street. I decided that the dogs, the ice cream, and Jack could wait a few minutes while I checked out Patti's problem. I would make it up to them with extra cuddles and treats. The dogs anyway.

As I pulled up in front of Patti's place, I noticed her half-hidden behind her evergreen hedge, beckoning. I rolled down the window. She put her fingers to her lips.

I bit back my words. Patti is sweet even if she's totally ditsy. She pointed across the street to number 10. I opened the passenger door so that she could stumble into the Miata.

"Do you see that?" she murmured, pointing across the street again.

"It's okay, Patti. We don't need to whisper in the car."

Princess apparently didn't care for my tone. She hissed at me. I had a feeling the next message would contain claws.

Patti gave Princess a soothing stroke. "So do you see that light?"

"I do. Is that why you called me over?"

"Well, yes. Don't you think it's strange?"

No, I thought. It's a light inside a house. "I imagine Dwayne is home getting ready for bed."

"Did you see Dwayne's car when you drove past?"

I frowned. "I didn't look."

"You wouldn't have seen it if you had looked, because Dwayne's not home."

"Maybe his car is in the garage."

"Emmy Lou's car is parked in front of the garage, blocking it. Dwayne has to park in back of hers. Anyway, the light is flickering."

She was right. It did look more like the flicker of a flashlight than normal interior lighting. "Oh, I see. And you think it's . . . ?"

"Burglars."

It was my turn to blink. "So why didn't you call the police? I don't handle burglars, although I would put them in the category of people who need to be cleaned up."

"That's the thing. I'm not so good with the police. There are issues."

Wacky tobaccy issues maybe.

"You can make an anonymous call," I suggested.

She shook her head violently. "I don't trust them. What if they have my phone bugged?"

No point in wasting my breath on that. I'd obviously upset her.

"Tell you what, *I'll* call them. I'll say it looks suspicious, but it could be the homeowner. Maybe he blew a fuse or something."

She said, "Except his car's not there."

I had a thought. "What if it's Kevin? I'd better say it might be the kid next door and not to shoot him by mistake."

Patti gasped. "That would be real bad."

"No kidding."

"Hey? Who's that?" Patti said, leaning forward and squinting.

"What? Where?" I paused, my fingers hovering over the 9 on my cell phone.

A furtive crouching figure scurried alongside the Rheinbeck house. As I watched he—or she—dashed across the lawn and into the Baxters' backyard. Another figure followed. They would have been invisible if it hadn't been for the glow of the brilliant full moon.

"We can't let him get away," Patti gasped.

"I don't intend to tackle a pair of burglars, but I'll see where they go. Maybe they're planning to break into Bonnie and Bill's place next." I thrust the phone into Patti's hand and hopped out of the car. "Patti, call 911 and tell them what has happened. Do not mention my name whatever you do, but tell them to check number 12 too." I closed the Miata door softly. I wanted to see where these creeps went and then spring back to the safety of the car, which was just a few yards away.

I scurried across the street toward the Baxters' place. I hugged the wall and made absolutely certain I had time to dash back to safety if the break-and-enter artists spotted me. Even though I know that burglars aren't usually dangerous, my heart was pounding. But I knew that Patti had called 911 and the police response was very fast in Woodbridge.

Particularly if I was in the vicinity. Usually that wasn't such a bonus. Tonight it would be.

I edged to the far end of the exterior wall of the Baxters' house. I peeked around the corner and smothered a gasp. Two figures were huddled by the back door. I could hear their whispered voices. The smaller one kept looking around, nervously. I pulled back. I hadn't got even a glimpse of their faces.

I could hear them fiddling with the lock. In a minute or two they'd be in the house. I had to warn Bonnie and Bill. I was approaching the front of the house when my nose began to twitch. That damn white mulberry tree. My eyes watered. My nose twitched harder. I pinched it to stop the sneeze.

Too little, too late.

A giant sneeze wracked my body. It sounded like someone had fired off a twelve-gauge. I glanced behind me. A head appeared by the side of the house. I started to run. Feet pounded after me. I put every scrap of energy into sprinting back to the safety of the Miata. Too bad my princess heels were not built for this. One shoe slipped off my foot, throwing me off balance. I sprawled forward onto the grass, knocking the breath straight out of my body.

"What the hell are you doing here?" the voice behind me said.

I scrambled to my feet and thudded forward wearing only one shoe. I kicked off the second shoe and ran like hell. I heard heavy feet behind me, gaining.

Talk about adrenaline.

As my stocking feet hit the sidewalk, I squeaked in horror. Where was the Miata?

There was no sign of my beautiful, safe little car. Or of Patti Magliaro and Princess.

I froze. Which was not the best idea under the circumstances. I felt a rough hand grab at my shoulder and yank hard at my jacket. Bell Street stood empty. Except for Patti's the houses were in darkness.

Since flight seemed pointless, it was time to turn and fight. I whirled and yelled in the face of my pursuer. Loud enough to scare him, I hoped. Or at least to wake up the neighborhood. Of course, with Dwayne out and Patti gone and Mr. Wright being who he was, that left the Baxters.

"Bill!" I shouted as I caught sight of his face.

He recoiled.

I laughed out loud. "What a relief. I thought you were a burglar because—" Because he had just come out of the Rheinbeck house. How was that for a because?

Bill eyed me warily. I assumed he was trying to figure out what I knew. I did my best to fool him. "The police are on their way. Patti called them. Someone's trying to break into your house. I hope Bonnie's not in there alone."

I don't know who was more surprised by this, Bill Baxter or me. I stood my ground. The hooded person with him crept up alongside him and tugged at his arm. Bonnie. But why would little Bonnie have a weapon in her delicate hands?

"Bonnie?" I said, stunned. "Is that you? What were you doing in the Rheinbecks' place?"

Sometimes you find yourself in a tight spot and the stuff that comes out of your mouth isn't the most brilliant. In this case, I'd almost have to plead insanity. If I could have grabbed the words back and swallowed them, I would have.

"Jesus, Bill," Bonnie said. "We've got to shut her up."

"Shut me up?" I squeaked. "Why?"

Bill ran his hand through his hair.

"I think I hear the police now," I said. Of course, I didn't hear anything except my heart thundering. The cops had been everywhere this last couple of days. Where were they now that I needed them? Patti had had plenty of time to make the call.

Bonnie barked, "Be quiet."

Bill laid a restraining hand on her arm. "Give me a minute to think."

"What do you mean, shut her up?" I said loudly enough

to be heard across the street, if anyone was there. "I thought we were friends, *Bonnie*. You too, *Bill*."

She sneered. "Like hell you did. You were messing with my head to find out what you could."

"What? What did I want to find out?" I said.

"Nosy bitch. Bill, take care of her."

He bent over and started talking back to her, whispering, pleading: intense, conspiratorial, appealing. She glared up at him, arguing back hoarsely.

I thought fast. How far to the nearest house? Too far. Where was my car with my cell phone in it? No idea. What would I do to Patti when I found her? Something bad.

In the meantime, I began to back up, imperceptibly. There was always so much traffic on Bell Street. But where the hell was it now that I needed it? I stepped into the street, the same second an El Greco pizza delivery vehicle rounded the corner and slowed in front of the Dingwall house.

"Help!" I howled, racing toward it. I zigged and zagged in case one of the Baxters fired a shot. Of course, if they had any brains, they'd get away rather than taking potshots at me in front of a witness. But at this point, I wasn't sure if they did have any brains. Plus, I was pretty sure I'd left mine at home.

In the distance I heard the heartwarming music of police sirens.

"They're trying to kill me! The Baxters! Bonnie and Bill! They broke into the Rheinbecks' house and . . ." I checked behind me to see if Bonnie and Bill were following. But they had slithered across the street and into the demolition area, next to the Wrights' garage. I turned back to the orange Neon and was thrilled and relieved to see my own familiar pizza-delivery guy staring at me, astonished. I hoped he'd forgotten that my dogs almost knocked him down the stairs. "Let me into your car."

Instead he jumped out, leaving the driver's door wide

open. He whipped across the street after the Baxters. "No," I shouted. "Wait for the police!"

What if Bonnie shot my Good Samaritan? I could not let the Baxters harm him because of me. I hightailed it across the street shouting to the pizza guy to stop. "Let them go. They have a weapon. The police are coming," I shouted, but he had already disappeared behind the Dumpster. I could only hope that my bluff would fool the Baxters.

The pavement shredded my stockings as I ran. I was limping as I reached the vacant building lot. I heard no voices, although I might have expected to hear the pizza guy confronting the Baxters. I sneaked up toward the Dumpster, careful not to make a sound, not even a bleat because of the pain from my damaged feet. As the sirens drew closer, I stuck my nose out. The delivery guy was sprawled by the chain-link fence next to the Wrights' garage. His body lay on the piece of plywood I'd last seen leaning against the fence, but his head had come to rest in the dirt. Behind him I could make out a white van, parked in the shadow of the old oaks at the back of the lot. It looked as though Bill was about to open the door of the van. He was holding a piece of two-by-four like a weapon. I had started to creep backward toward the street when Bill jerked his head around and spotted me. This was truly a night gone wrong. Where were the police? At a glance over my shoulder, I could see the pulsing flash of lights. The troops had arrived. Of course, if Patti had called the police, she would have directed them to the Baxters' house and not behind the Dumpster across the street. Never mind, I turned to slip toward the street. My arm was nearly yanked out of its socket as Bill grabbed me. I struggled and yelled as he dragged me back behind the Dumpster.

"I told you so, you idiot," Bonnie said. There were streaks down her cheeks. "You are going to blow everything again."

Of course, I was the idiot, but I didn't bother to say so. The delivery guy groaned, and Bill whacked him again.

"Look!" I said, pointing behind them. "The cops!"

As they both whirled, I sprinted toward the street shrieking my head off. I didn't get far. Bill tackled me and I found myself on the gravel, flattened by his weight.

"Where are they?" he said.

I managed to grunt. "Can't breathe."

I gasped for breath as he stood up. He yanked my jacket and pulled me to my feet. He spun me around. I found myself staring into Bonnie's eyes. She continued to hold the gun, quite steady. I thought those things were heavy. Out of the corner of my eye, I could see that the delivery guy was passed out cold.

"Where are they?" Bill repeated.

"They're across the street, and you can't get away with this. They'll be here in a second. People have heard me. They heard your names."

"Nobody heard and if they did, they're not going to be here in time for you. Don't play stupid games with us." Gone was Bonnie's gentle voice. This one made the hair on the back of my neck stand up. "Where are they?"

"I'm not playing games. I don't know who you want. Just put it in words and if I know I'll tell you. I'd like to get out of here."

"Emmy Lou had something belonging to me. You have it now. Where is it?"

"I don't have anything of Emmy Lou's. What could I have? Except for a bunch of stuffed animals."

"That's better. Maybe we won't have to kill you."

I tried hard to make this compute. Was I dreaming? Hallucinating? "You want the toys she had when she ran out of the house after Tony died?"

I twisted to look up at Bill. He was watching Bonnie. She kept her eyes on me. How had I never noticed how cold and hard those eyes were?

"You know what I mean."

"I don't have anything else." I don't know anything about

guns, except that they can kill you. The one Bonnie was holding seemed terribly big. Huge. But they hadn't shot the delivery guy, so maybe they were bluffing, maybe it was a replica. Maybe they didn't want to take the chance of a gunshot waking the sleeping neighbors on Bell Street.

"Do you believe we won't shoot you and him too? Don't delude yourself. Tell me where the mice are and you'll get out of here alive."

"The wedding mice? That doesn't make any sense at all."

Bonnie turned to Bill. "I guess we should shoot her."

I said, "The police will hear that for sure, and there's only one way out of here."

Bill said, "You can see that Bonnie's under a lot of stress. Why don't you tell us where they are? When we have the safety deposit key, we'll leave you alone."

Bonnie exploded. "What are you blabbing about that for? You are so stupid, Bill. I should shoot you too."

Safety deposit key? My mind whirled.

"I'm sorry," he said. "I didn't mean to blab. This isn't easy, you know."

"But I don't have them anymore. They're with the book—" I snapped my mouth shut. I didn't believe that Bonnie would shoot me while I had information that they needed.

"Where?" Bill said. The menace in his voice sent an icy chill racing down my spine. How could I have thought these people were pleasant? How could I ever have wanted to help them?

"They're gone," I said. "I didn't want them. I never keep stuffed toys."

"You said with the book," Bonnie said, narrowing her eyes.

"I'm an organizer. I clear surplus items out all the time. I took them to the Goodwill, along with some books." That seemed safe. The Goodwill was closed. Even if they went in waving their gun, no one would get hurt.

Bonnie turned to Bill. "That girl was talking about book-cases yesterday. For Emmy Lou's project. *Bookcases.* Some-one was building them for you. Is that where they are?"

"No," I said shrilly. "I told you, Goodwill. You can check in the morning. Trust me."

"I trust that you're lying. I can see through you. Where are the bookcases and the mice?"

I thought fast. I'd witnessed the brutal way Bill hit the de-livery guy. I'd observed the merciless expression on Bon-nie's face. I'd seen Lilith lying near death in the trauma unit after she'd been run down by a white van. As much as I wanted to save myself, I couldn't send them to a defenseless Gary Gigantes.

"Promise me you won't hurt my friend," I said.

Bill yanked my hair. "Look at me," he said. "Bonnie's up-set. If we get the mice, we're out of here. No one will get hurt."

I tried not to turn and stare at the wounded delivery guy. A board across the head would do more than hurt. Was he alive? And even if he was, I didn't believe that Bonnie and Bill would leave me around to describe that assault to the police. There wasn't much I could do for either of us. I did my best to stay calm, keep my heart rate under control, keep my breathing natural. After all, they hadn't shot him. Maybe they wouldn't shoot me either.

"Tell you what," Bonnie said. "If you lie to me about this and I don't find what I'm looking for, I will kill your friends one by one until you tell me the truth. Then I will take you somewhere that the sound of a gun doesn't matter. Under-stand?"

Bill said, "Bonnie, please."

I felt a wave of anger and hatred toward this woman. How many people had she harmed? It hit me like a board across the head: Bonnie had come from the Rheinbecks' house. She must have had keys. She'd been searching for the wedding mice. Who owned the key Bill had mentioned? Emmy Lou?

Whatever I didn't know, I was sure I was staring at Tony's killer. Had Bonnie been driving the van that hit Lilith? Did Bill have the cruel edge to do it?

"Shut up, Bill. She's sitting on our ticket out of here." She focused on me again. "You heard me. The girl in the hospital. I'll finish her off this time. The old lady. Why not? Your friend Jack. Right between the eyes."

It was essential to keep calm, rational. I said, "But why?"

Bill turned to Bonnie. "I told you it was crazy hiding it over there. They're never going to track us down here. You're really paranoid about that. Now we really have to go into hiding again. But we can't kill people. If we have to, we can say the other thing was an accident."

Bonnie said, "It was an accident."

The other thing: Would that be poor dead Tony? Or Lilith?

Bonnie's voice sliced through me. "I need those goddamn mice. Don't argue. Pull yourself together. You're either with me or you're history."

"I'm with you, Bonnie. Always. No matter what. You know that."

I tried to see something I could use as a weapon, but there was nothing but the Dumpster, the demolition site, and the Wrights' garage. There were no windows in the garage, and even if there had been, no one was there to see us. That's the problem with garages, I thought, they're—An idea rocketed through my brain. I tried to keep the hope off my face.

"And this one knows where they are. Now, Charlotte, talk or else."

"All right," I said, taking yet another calming breath. "I gave them to my friend because she's having a baby. They were with some baby books, *Jemima Puddle-Duck*, *Mrs. Tiggy-Winkle*, the Beatrix Potter collection. They're painting the baby's room now and she's stored everything in her garage, with the baby equipment she's been collecting," I babbled on. "They don't know if it's a boy or a—"

"Stop stalling" Bonnie said. "Just give me the address."

I raised a hand in entreaty. "Okay, okay. She's on Old Pine Street. Let me think, um, number 42. Everything's stored in the garage. It's a separate building, to the left of the house."

"You'd better be telling the truth." She raised the gun. This time her hand shook, but that only made her seem more dangerous. "You're staying here. Bill, take care of her until we get it."

Bill whipped a roll of duct tape out of his pocket.

"Remember, better be telling the truth," Bonnie said.

Behind her I saw the delivery guy stir. The moon was so bright I could see the blood trickling down the side of his head, but his eyes had opened. His hand slid silently toward the board he'd been hit with.

I had nothing to lose by my question: "I told you what you wanted, now tell me, why did you kill Tony?"

She snorted. "That creepy Neanderthal jumped out at me, screaming and cackling. Enough to scare a person to death. I gave him a good shove and down the stairs he went. Better off dead anyway."

The delivery guy was inching forward, behind Bonnie. Bill grabbed my hands and held them together in front of me. He wrapped the duct tape expertly around them. "For your friends' sake, I hope we find it. She's not kidding," he said. He pulled a box cutter out of his pocket to sever the ends of the tape.

I tried not to let my eyes drift to the injured man's progress. Inch, inch, inch.

My back was to the Dumpster, with Bonnie's gun trained on me. I willed myself to be still. I looked at Bill and tried to hold eye contact with him as long as possible, so that he didn't see the delivery guy rise silently to his knees and then into a crouch behind Bonnie.

I said, "I see you have the white van everyone's talking about. I guess it belongs to Nerd on the Spot. I suppose you were driving that when you slashed my tires as I was talking with your wife. I just want to know why."

Bonnie bent over and said, "Why do you think? Because you're a nosy, meddling busybody and you were going to ruin everything for us."

I figured stalling was the only tactic I had left. Perhaps Patti would come back before Bill finished wrapping that strip of duct tape twice around my ankles. "Of course, it's all clear now. No wonder she was edgy. You sneaked the stuffed mice into her house, maybe other stuff too, knowing that she didn't even remember half the ones she bought but would never get rid of any of them. I imagine Emmy Lou told you she was bringing me in. So you had to get rid of me and you had to get in the house and get back your mice and whatever else you had there before I sorted through and perhaps discarded them. I guess it was easier to get a copy of Emmy Lou's keys than it was of mine. I am guessing that Bill got his mitts on Jack's while they were sitting on the counter in the bike shop. Jack's so trusting. Did he tell you about the customer waiting for the delivery of the brakes, so you could make a call and send him on that wild-goose chase to Troy?"

"These things are easy when you know how," Bonnie said snidely.

"Speaking of phone calls, reporting me for yelling at Tony and Kevin was real cute. And staging the false fire call to my cell phone to delay me. You had me fooled for sure. I guess we'll learn that Emmy Lou got some kind of an emergency call to get her out of the house so you could retrieve the wedding mice, but they were already gone. Tony died for nothing. And you burgled my house for nothing too."

"Just shut up," Bonnie said. "Make that happen, Bill."

With the box cutter, Bill sliced off another strip of duct tape, and though I turned and twisted my head to avoid it, he slapped it over my mouth. I told myself that they couldn't shoot me until they had the wedding mice in their hands, and with luck, that attempt would blow up in their nasty murdering faces.

Behind them, the delivery guy got to his feet and reached into his pocket.

Just as my hopes soared, Bill leaned forward and picked me up. I weigh ninety-five pounds, but he merely grunted and heaved. All that practice lifting his wife when she was ill had paid off for him, but not for me. I struggled hopelessly as he tossed me over the sides of the Dumpster.

As I landed inside, Bonnie yelled a warning to Bill. A shot rang out. And then another. The slippery bag I'd landed on seemed to collapse. I felt myself falling. A sharp pain. Then nothing.

When faced with an overwhelming task,
break it into small manageable bites.
Do one at a time.

22

I awoke in the dark. Where was I? Dead? If so, I definitely hadn't made the cut for heaven and who could imagine that hell would smell so disgusting. A million bags of doggy do might have added up to this.

I stirred. What was wrong with my arms? I struggled to move them, without success. The memory of the Baxters flooded my brain. Of course, duct tape. Were they still outside the Dumpster? Was there any point in screaming? But obviously, the duct tape across my mouth prevented that. My feet weren't any better off. My ankles were bound. And my soles were paying the price for running without shoes.

A cloud drifted past, uncovering the splendid full moon. How long had I been out cold? And speaking of cold, the night air had developed a nasty chill. I had to get out of there. Had to call the police. Had to see if the delivery guy was lying in a pool of blood. Had Bonnie shot him? The moon was bright enough for me to see that debris and garbage bags were piled deep in the Dumpster. That was good. If I could reach a higher mound of refuse, perhaps I could fling myself over the top. Lucky for me the Dumpster wasn't empty or I would have been four feet down. That thought was replaced by a chilling realization

What had Patti said about the garbage? That they emptied it every second Friday and this was the week? My heart began to pound. What would happen in the morning? Would the workers toss in another load of drywall and decayed wood? Maybe an old toilet or a length of antique wire? Did anyone check Dumpsters before the contents were tossed into some garbage-crushing vehicle?

I tried to get my mind off that. I had lots to think about. I took a long time to ponder where Patti Magliaro had gone in my car. I wouldn't have been on Bell Street if it hadn't been for her call. She'd definitely been on the scene for all of my visits. She had the most harmless way of getting you to tell her everything you knew. She kept an eye on the street and all its inhabitants. Surely Patti must have known that the Baxters were up to something. Was she involved too?

How long would it take the police to find the empty delivery car? Or the guy's body? If he were alive, he could tell the police where I was. But what if he was in the Dumpster with me? Maybe Bonnie and Bill hadn't killed him, just injured him. Maybe . . . It was time to find out. Duct tape can keep your mouth closed, but as I soon found out, a determined person can make a bit of noise. "Help! Help!" turns into a high-pitched humming sound, with a pathetic hint of whimper. I made as much noise as I could. Then I lay there, listening for an echo.

Nothing.

I tried again several times, pausing and waiting in between muffled yells.

Where were the police?

Thank heavens they hadn't blindfolded me. Perhaps I could make that work in my favor.

I tried to sit up. Bad move. The debris kept shifting under my back. Okay. What was nearby? Mostly jagged bits of drywall. I moved my knees and hit something hard and round. Pipes, I decided. I tried the other direction. I felt a sharp pain in my shin and pulled back. I yelped, not that it made any difference to anyone, since the yelp was muffled by the tape. My shin throbbed. Glass? Shards of glass. I froze. Where else was it? If whatever I was lying on shifted again, would I find myself impaled next time? I lay there long enough to watch the progress of the moon. Every time I decided to try to move, my nerves failed me. After a long pep talk, I inched along, moving as slowly as I could, trying to gauge where the glass was. I'd already learned how sharp it was. I needed to position myself to use that glass to slice through the duct tape binding my wrists. Could I do that without slicing an artery at the same time?

After what felt like an hour, I talked myself into slithering ahead. If I waited much longer, my hands would be too numb to maneuver. My bladder throbbed. So what the hell did I have to lose?

Plenty as it turned out.

After nine or ten gentle shuffles forward over the slippery garbage bags, I heard the dreaded crunch of glass. I froze again. I had to remind myself of how much worse it would be when the compactor truck collected me in the morning. That was motivating.

Something shifted underneath me. Unstable bags? Loosely packed debris? I had no idea, but every panicky breath I took seemed to cause the rubble to sink. I squeaked. I heard the worst sound in the world: breaking glass.

Where was it? I shifted slightly to the left. A jagged shard bit into my upper arm. I bit back tears. I steeled myself to reposition toward the right. More shards. I heard them crack.

I was well and truly trapped.

"Is anybody out there? Mmmph hyoo mmm hhhhhrrr?" I tried again, louder and louder. Useless, useless. But you can only play the cards you've been dealt.

I jerked at a sound. What was that? Could it be sharp little barks?

I listened intently.

Yes.

Truffle and Sweet Marie.

Of course. Jack would have worried when I didn't show up. He probably figured out I'd gone to Bell Street.

I heard another round of barking or two. A man's voice shouted, "Shut that dog up!"

That brought on a blizzard of barks. Except for Jack's, Truffle and Sweet Marie did not care for men's voices. Especially telling them to shut up.

My brave feisty little dogs. I'd never see them again. I would die so close to them and to Jack, the best friend anyone ever had, not that I had mentioned that to him in a while. There was a good chance no one would ever know what happened to me. I tried my duct-taped scream again, useless as it was. As loud as I could. As long as I could.

I heard the man's voice call out again. "That's it. I'm calling the cops."

Jack yelled back, "Go right ahead." He sounded close, although the acoustics weren't all that great.

I gave it my best shot. My muffled yells: "Where's Charlotte! Wwwrrrrsssssssssslllllllddddd!"

"What is it? What's wrong, you guys?" Jack hollered. "Where are you going?"

The barks came closer, turning to high-pitched yips. Or so it seemed. My throat was raw from forcing out the sound.

"What is wrong with you two? Wait? Is it Charlotte?"

The Dumpster shook a bit, thumped on the outside.

"Charlotte?"

"Hhhhlllppp!"

Jack's face appeared overhead. The sight of his glasses glinting in the moonlight brought tears to my eyes. "Holy crap. You are in here. Don't move. I'm coming to get you."

I shook my head frantically. If Jack jumped in, he'd slice his legs and probably bleed to death by my side.

"No, no, no!" There is no way to shout intelligibly with duct tape on your mouth. Truffle and Sweet Marie continued to yip in triumph, which didn't help communications.

"Wait a minute," Jack said, "Don't move. Looks like this sucker is full of broken glass. I'll be back in a second. I'm calling 911. And I'm getting help too."

Seconds later Jack tipped the battered plywood sheet from the lot into the Dumpster, making a bridge to safety for both of us. Apparently, he did not find me heavy.

I wasn't sure how much time elapsed since I'd been pulled out of the Dumpster. I was trembling, sweaty, and dizzy. My mouth hurt from having the duct tape removed, even though Jack did his best to be gentle. Myrna Dingwall hustled over almost as soon as we emerged. She was wrapped in a plaid dressing gown and lugging a blanket and a pillow. Behind her Kevin, in pajama bottoms and a T-shirt, eyed me warily. Jack sent Myrna rushing back home for a pair of scissors. He sat me down on the pillow and draped the blanket tightly around me. Truffle and Sweet Marie climbed onto my lap and snuggled in.

"Don't try and talk," he said.

I snuffled. "I have to talk. Bonnie and Bill did this. They are looking for something in one of the stuffed animals. Oh, Jack, I told them it was in Nick's garage. He has heavy security to protect his stupid cars. I figured if they tried to get in, then Nick would hear them and . . . But what if that backfires? What if they try the house? What if they're over there and—They've had enough time."

"Where's Pepper and Nick's house?" Jack pecked at his

cell and spoke rapidly to the 911 operator. He passed on the address as soon as I croaked it out. He clicked off the phone.

When Myrna returned, Jack unwrapped the blanket and cut the duct tape. I said, "How did you know where I was?"

Jack said, "Patti Magliaro showed up at the house in your car, hysterical. She told me she didn't know how to use your cell phone, so she came to get me."

"Why didn't she go ask someone here on Bell Street?"

"She claimed 'they' saw her, whoever 'they' were and she panicked. She got in the driver's seat and took off. She said it was real lucky she remembered how to drive after all these years. Patti and I burned rubber getting back to hunt for you. I drove, you'll be glad to hear that. When the police showed up, there was no sign of anyone at the Rhein-becks' or the Baxters'. We couldn't find you anywhere. Now I know why. I went home again, expecting you. Then I couldn't relax and I came back with the dogs, in case they could help, although I left Schopie at home. I knocked on every door. These people were helping search for you," he said, pointing to Myrna Dingwall, Kevin, Dwayne, looking more rumpled than usual, and a sheepish Patti Magliaro. They'd formed part of a small, hovering crowd.

"How long was I in that thing?"

"Not that long, I don't think."

"It seemed like forever. Thank you for the blanket, Mrs. Dingwall. I'll probably ruin it. I stink," I said, staring at the small crowd and beyond it to the white van still parked on the site. I wondered if Bonnie and Bill had escaped in the old blue Colt or in the delivery vehicle. Where was the de-livery guy? My head swam with shock and confusion.

Myrna said, "It will wash."

I beckoned her to come forward. She knelt, wincing as she bent. I whispered, "You have to talk to Emmy Lou about Kevin. She's paid a terrible price for that secret."

She swallowed. "I realize that. I ran into Rose Skipowski in the hospital cafeteria today and she broached the topic.

I kept silent so long and now that it's out, it's a relief. I was so afraid I would lose Kevin to Emmy Lou, but in my heart I know it was wrong. I should never have listened to my brother. He's a harsh and unfeeling man."

"Your brother?" *Clink, clink.* Another piece of the puzzle. That must have been what Rose couldn't remember. "You mean, Mr. Wright?"

She nodded. "I don't know how Emmy Lou could bear to live right across the street from him. He never spoke to her after she became pregnant. I couldn't believe it when she bought the house next to me. She must have been desperate to be near Kevin."

I kept my voice low. "Don't worry. Emmy Lou must know how much you love Kevin and what good care you take of him. I believe you and Kevin will gain something, and so will Emmy Lou. Let's hope it's not too late for her . . . stability."

She stumbled to her feet, blinking away tears. "Yes."

Meanwhile, Dwayne, oblivious to our conversation, shook his shiny head. "I can't believe all these weird things keep happening on Bell Street."

"I think it's over. And we have proof Emmy Lou didn't kill Tony. Now I know that Bonnie Baxter did that. She was searching for something in the house, and he saw her and she pushed him."

"Shhh," Jack said. "Don't get agitated."

Myrna gasped. "Bonnie Baxter?"

At the sound of the name, Kevin jumped up and down and tugged at her sleeve. "I told you, Ma."

Patti Magliaro stumbled forward, a vision of guilty panic. "I'm so sorry, Charlotte. I wanted to help. Sorry about the bumper too."

"Don't worry about it, Patti," I said. Turning to Jack, I pointed toward the white van. "Bill beat the El Greco guy. Then I think they must have shot him. Can you look and see if he's in there?"

Jack said, "You've had a horrible traumatic experience. Maybe you're imagining—"

"Listen to me. They must have dumped his body somewhere. Maybe he was even in there with me," I snuffled, staring back at the Dumpster with a shiver. "Maybe he's only injured. We have to find him."

"He can't be in the Dumpster. I would have seen him."

"Then please check the van."

I shivered as Jack strode toward the van, checked the driver's side, and then yanked open the rear door and stuck his head in. I watched, frozen, as he leaped back and was sick on the gravel. Myrna grabbed Kevin and hugged him close.

Jack staggered toward us, stabbing in 911 on his cell phone and shouting something that I couldn't make out.

"They're coming. It might take a while," he said when he reached me. "Mona Pringle said they've had a dozen 911 emergency calls about events at the other end of town. Mostly false alarms, but they have to check everything. All the first responders are stretched. And it's way too late."

I said, "The delivery guy, is he . . . ?"

Jack shook his head, "Not him."

"What? But—"

"It's Bonnie and Bill, Charlotte."

Just when I thought my heart couldn't race anymore, it turned out I was wrong. "They're in the van? You mean they're dead?"

"Oh yeah. They'd have to be."

"But if Bonnie and Bill are dead, where is the delivery guy? Why didn't he call the police? Why didn't he send—?" I glanced at the circle of faces, stopping with Myrna and Kevin. They'd been asleep earlier, their house dark when the El Greco guy pulled up. Who delivers pizza to a house where everyone's asleep? The last pieces fell into place. "He shot *them*. And now he must be . . . Jack, we have to stop him."

Jack squeezed my hand. "Be calm. The paramedics will

be arriving any minute. They'll treat you for shock. You have to go to the hospital."

"There's no time. We have to get to Pepper's! Try 911 again and tell them to forget Bell Street and get the hell over to Old Pine Street before someone else is killed."

———※———

As we rocketed toward Old Pine Street, I felt nothing except fear. The delivery guy had killed Bonnie and Bill. And he had heard me give the address for Nick's garage, which was next to Pepper and Nick's home. I'd tried to lay a trap for Bonnie and Bill, but what if Pepper and Nick were caught in that trap?

Pepper's cell phone went straight to message. I dialed 911 yet again.

Mona Pringle must work the world's longest shifts. "I hear you, Charlotte. And I heard you the last time. And the time before. The call is out, but all our units have been deployed at the far end of town. You know that. But we've got personnel heading to the Monahans'. Just calm down and stay where you are."

"We'll be too late," I said as I hung up. "I know it. Why did I waste time talking to people after you hauled me out of the Dumpster?"

Jack said, "Because you were in shock and bleeding and you needed medical attention. And you still do. We'll check Pepper and Nick's place just to be on the safe side. Then I'm taking you to the emergency room, and I don't want any more arguments."

"I wasn't thinking clearly, but that's no excuse."

Jack listened as I explained once again my desperate ploy of sending Bonnie and Bill to Nick's secure garage to find the wedding mice. "Not your fault. Get used to that," he said. "Guy must be a psychopath to do what he did to Bonnie and Bill. His fault. Their fault. Not yours."

I babbled endlessly. "He was badly injured. Bill whacked him a couple of times with the board. I don't see how he could drive. Maybe he'll have lost consciousness by now. Maybe he wouldn't make it all the way to Old Pine Street. But anyone who gets in his way could be in big trouble. We have to call the police and tell them to be on the lookout for an orange Neon. Unless, what if he changes vehicles?"

Jack slid the Miata to a stop in front of Pepper and Nick's house. All seemed normal. Quiet. Lovely, sleepy streetscape. Nice houses, nice hedges, dark yet tranquil.

Jack said, "Huh."

I said, "Oh. Well, good. Still, I have to wake them and tell them what I've—"

An unfamiliar car crept around the corner. The new-looking black Acura sedan skidded to a stop, half on the sidewalk. Jack and I ducked down out of sight. A crouched loping figure slipped from the car and staggered toward the garage.

I said, "He must have stolen a vehicle. You keep an eye on where he goes and I'll wake up Pepper and Nick."

"No, you stay here and lock the car door and I'll—"

"I'm going, Jack. This is my fault."

"You are hurt and I can't—"

The shriek of an alarm cut through the night. Motion-detector lights on the garage lit up the street. The figure ducked out of sight into the hedge by the side of the Monahan property.

"He has a gun, Jack. If Nick comes out, he's in danger."

As the alarmed wailed, Nick exploded through the front door of the house, a weapon in his hand. I jumped out of the car, just as Pepper appeared at the door, pulling on a bathrobe. I didn't dare shout as the delivery guy was out there somewhere. Jack and I crept closer to the house, hugging the shadows. We had to warn Pepper.

Nick swaggered toward his garage. He must have flicked off the alarm with a remote, because, suddenly, everything went silent. Nick opened the garage door and peered in, checking his babies. Jack slipped toward Pepper. I watched as a dark shadow detached itself from the bushes and inched toward Nick, behind his exposed back.

The shadow darted, raised an arm.

"Nick!" I yelled. "Look out. He has a gun."

Shots, flashes, breaking glass, shouts. Who was screaming? Pepper? Me? Both? Who knows?

The shadow crumpled, tumbled to the ground. Nick Monahan bent to examine his would-be attacker. He stood up again. I watched as he ducked into the garage to check on his precious vehicles. It seemed as good a time as any for me to pass out.

⸻⸻

The worst thing about the hospital was finding a television set near my bed. My friends had provided it as a favor, since I fussed a lot about being kept in for observation. And the worst thing about the television set was Todd Tyrell's face. This time his gelled head was visible in front of Pepper and Nick's house on Old Pine Street. He intoned with obvious pleasure:

It was a wild night of murder and mayhem on the streets of Woodbridge. On this quiet street, last night Officer Nick Monahan risked his life to stop a killer.

A shot of Nick, in uniform, looking handsome and almost intelligent, flashed on the screen. I considered putting my pillow over my head.

In a terrifying home invasion, Officer Monahan, a third-generation member of the Woodbridge police force, defended his pregnant wife against an attack by a crazed killer.

I sat up fast enough to make my head spin. Pregnant
wife?

Pepper's picture flashed across the screen next, followed
by a shot of Nick's garage, with the windows shot out.

The fourth image was our own El Greco delivery guy.
He looked older and harder than I'd remembered. Maybe
because of his goatee and his darker hair in the picture. No
arrogant flirtatious grin there. Then again, it was a mug
shot.

> *Ex-convict Waylon Favreau was wanted by the FBI on
> several charges, including a contract killing of three peo-
> ple in Syracuse last year. Favreau died in an exchange of
> gunfire as he attempted to gain unlawful entry into the
> property of Officer Nicholas Monahan and Sergeant Pep-
> per Monahan. The Monahans were lucky to escape injury
> or worse. Their attacker was pronounced dead at the
> scene. Less than an hour earlier, Favreau is suspected
> of having shot Woodridge residents Charlotte Adams,
> and Bonnie and Bill Baxter. Adams is recovering at
> Woodridge General Hospital. The bodies of the Baxters
> were dumped on a Bell Street construction site, before
> Favreau—what's that? Oh right, allegedly broke into the
> Monahans' property to continue his rampage. Favreau
> has also been linked to the hit-and-run that hospitalized
> twenty-year-old Lilith Carisse yesterday. This begs the
> question of whether Waylon Favreau was also responsi-
> ble for the death of Tony Starkman last Sunday. Follow-
> ing these startling developments, an unnamed police
> source is quoted as saying that Emily Louise Rheinbeck
> should be released from secure custody at any moment.
> In the meantime, Nicholas Monahan remains a hero for
> our town.*

A shot of me being loaded into the ambulance followed.
Not surprisingly, I looked like I'd spent the night in a Dump-

ster. Something told me that would be the new stock shot of me in the WINY files. I was followed by another shot of Nick Monahan outside his home.

"Nobody touches my baby," he said.

At least his Mustang was safe, although I might have been one of the few who made that connection. There was no mention of my role or Jack's.

Todd Tyrell's day was made as he added:

Police chief Maurice Eaves has called a press conference for this afternoon at two p.m. Stay tuned to WINY for this breaking story.

I glanced over to the door where Jack was now standing, holding a bouquet of blue irises. He was more like my idea of a hero. I hoped he hadn't sneaked the dogs into the hospital since I'd had my share of trouble so far. On the other hand, they were heroes too.

―――

Sally couldn't have picked a better time to have her baby. Half her friends were already stuck in Woodbridge General; the other half were already visiting. Even Margaret had ducked out of her office to visit Lilith. Very convenient.

No surprise, there was a partylike atmosphere in her private room in the Mother and Baby Center. Pink flowers filled the room, including a giant bouquet from Jack. He was very disappointed that the hospital had a no-balloons policy.

"Don't worry, Jack," Sally said. "We'll make up for that when I get home. No latex allergies there."

Lilith was out of danger, relocated on the fifth floor near me, and surprisingly well enough to be wheeled in to see Sally and the new baby. She smiled vaguely and briefly before she was whisked away back to her room. Word was she had a good chance of a full recovery. Rose, of course, remained by her side, although she had promised to sleep at home that night. I felt a lump in my throat at how close my friends had come to seeing Bonnie Baxter on the wrong end of a gun.

"Hey, Charlotte," Sally said. "Bernice called just as we were leaving for the hospital. She mentioned that she'd like that mudroom project after all. What a ditz."

There was so much going on in my head that, for once, I couldn't think about work.

I jumped when I spotted Pepper at the door. Without a glance in my direction, she swooped in on Sally. Her skin glowed, her eyes shone, she looked quite magnificent, although in the magnificence sweepstakes, no one can ever top our gal Sal. I watched and waited as Pepper pecked Sally's cheek. I thought I spotted a special bond, the mothers' club.

I felt a wave of guilt and shame as I watched Pepper. I had sent Waylon Favreau to invade her home, well, her husband's garage, but close enough. How could that ever be forgiven?

Sally said, "Meet Shenandoah."

"Shenandoah," Pepper said, leaning over the pink bundle and reaching down to stroke the tiny cheek.

"Did you wash your hands?" Jack said.

Pepper said, "She's so beautiful, and that's a lovely name."

Sally shot her an impish grin. "Should be. Jack thought of it."

My injuries were catching up with me; the adrenaline from Shenandoah's arrival wasn't enough to keep me up much longer. I left them all cooing in the room and stumbled into the hallway. The granite-faced detective stood there, sipping his Stewart's coffee, waiting for Pepper. My mouth fell open as I spotted Margaret advancing toward him with a can-do look in her eye. When Pepper emerged from Sally's room, I said, "I urgently need to talk to you. I've been leaving messages."

"And I've had a few things on my mind. Anyway, every time I tried to contact you, you were tied up with the doctors or getting X-rays or whatever."

"I guess that's true. First, congratulations. You will make a terrific mother."

"Thank you."

I swallowed. "Second, I want to say how sorry I am that I put you and Nick in danger. I hope you can forgive me. I felt I had no—"

She raised her hand. "Forget it. Worked all right. No one in his family or the police force ever took Nick seriously. Now he's a hero, all over the news. People are asking him for his autograph. Best thing that ever happened to him."

"But won't he be investigated? There was a death."

"I'm not worried. Nick was defending himself and me. With what this Favreau pulled off? Murders, assaults, hit-and-run, plus there's a lot of outstanding stuff against him. It will be ruled a clean shoot. When it's over, he'll probably get a commendation."

"Oh, that's good."

"Yeah. It's hard for him to get respect. This will change things."

"I hadn't thought about it that way."

Her eyes shone. "Everyone's always so disappointed in him: his father, his uncles, his brothers. Now he showed them. I knew he could do it.

"Right." He was a vapid, underperforming, womanizing child in a man's body. But hey, whatever turned her on. Maybe the combination of hero status and fatherhood would make a difference. But any suspicions I'd had about her relationship with the granite-faced detective vanished. There was no one for Pepper but Nick. If only that could work both ways.

She said, "And your friend Emmy Lou's out now. We got that one wrong."

"I think you can both be heroes. All the family. I believe

you'll find the missing piece of the puzzle about Bonnie and Bill, or whoever they really were—"

"Fugitives."

"This will sound crazy, but if you go to Gary Gigantes shop and check out the toys I left there, you'll find a little bride and groom mouse. Somewhere inside them, there's a safety deposit key to something that the Baxters were willing to kill to protect and Waylon Favreau was willing to kill to get. I don't know where the safety deposit box is or what's in it, but I wanted to tell you. At least you might get credit for something."

I took some satisfaction in watching Pepper's eyes widen. "Safety deposit box? Beautiful. I bet I know what's in it. We've been working on this all night. Your Bonnie and Bill Baxter were actually Brenda and Bob Billings. There are posters of them down at the station, FBI most wanted. They were implicated in a bank heist, along with a partner. The partner went down, died in jail. Money was never found. Feds have been looking for Brenda and Bob ever since. No way they'd get out of the country. I guess they were lying low, building a life and some businesses to launder their money."

I refrained from saying I wasn't sure how much money you could launder through a cupcake and computer-repair business. "Becoming part of a community."

"Right. After a while they'd blend in, get older, change their appearance some more. Heat would die down."

"How did the delivery guy fit in?"

"Favreau was the partner's cell mate. Maybe the partner filled him in. He was paroled recently and vanished after committing a flurry of contract killings."

"He'd tracked down Bonnie and Bill. I think he was stalking them, getting a part-time job as an El Greco delivery guy. He was looking for his chance to search the house and find that money. Bonnie had a gun and she had no problems killing. He must have known that from the partner.

Maybe have had some kind of plan to get the loot from them."

"Yeah, we'll never know. Three more lowlifes off the streets. Thanks for the tip about the key. We'll get our ducks in a row and check the banks."

I nodded. "If you're lucky, you'll be in time to add to the press conference this afternoon."

"Or else the next one."

Maybe it was relief. Maybe I was happy because Pepper and I had reached a truce of sorts. Maybe my meds were wearing off. For whatever reason, my head whirled. My knees started to buckle.

Pepper said, "Are you all right?"

Jack popped out of Sally's room, grabbed my elbow, and said, "Charlotte has to go back to her room now. Too much excitement. Anyway, the nurse has kicked us out."

"We'll talk," Pepper said as Jack bustled me down the hall. "Take care."

I barely managed to nod.

As Jack propelled me back out of the elevator on my floor, the second elevator door opened. Dwayne and Emmy Lou Rheinbeck emerged, followed by a whippet-thin young man with sideburns. Emmy Lou looked drawn and exhausted. She was easily ten pounds thinner than a few days earlier when she'd been stuffed into the police car. Her red hair had lost its shine, her skin sagged somewhat, but despite that she radiated joy. Dwayne was holding a massive bouquet of spring flowers: daffodils, bearded iris, forsythia, tulips, even lily of the valley. Over the top, just like Dwayne himself.

Dwayne said, "Emmy should be home resting, but she wanted to express her appreciation in person for a moment."

Emmy Lou beamed at me. "I know you found who really killed poor Tony. I was so afraid Kevin had done it by accident. I could never let them arrest him. Myrna told me that she spoke to you and that she understands how much I need to be near Kevin. And Dwayne told me how you fought for me. I am sorry for all the trouble you've had. Thank you for helping me connect with my son in a real way."

I said, "Perhaps you'll talk to Tony's mother too. She'll be glad to have a living connection to her son and her brother."

"Already done," Emmy Lou said.

Dwayne thrust the bouquet into my arms. "And we've re-connected with my daughter too. Although that would have happened anyway. It's a bit easier now that we're both in the same situation. Should never have had secrets from each other."

At that moment, I recognized the young man standing be-hind him, the server from the restaurant. "They've moved Lilith," I said. "She's down the hall in 512 now."

He vanished down the corridor, leaving Jack and me to say good-bye to the Rheinbecks'. "I hope you'll like what we've decided to do with the stuffed animal collection," I said.

I caught a glimpse of the old Emmy Lou when she re-sponded, "Even though Dwayne has already paid, I've de-cided I never want to see them again. I'm giving them all away. But thank you for all you've done."

Dwayne mouthed "sorry."

As the elevator door closed behind them, I snuffled. "All these happy endings. It's a bit too much for me."

"And more to come," Jack said. "When you're ready."

Mary Jane Maffini is a lapsed librarian, a former mystery bookseller, and a previous president of Crime Writers of Canada. In addition to creating the Charlotte Adams series, she is the author of the Camilla MacPhee Mysteries, the Fiona Silk series, and nearly two dozen mystery short stories. She has won two Arthur Ellis awards for short fiction, and *The Dead Don't Get Out Much*, her latest Camilla MacPhee Mystery, was nominated for a Barry Award in 2006. She lives in Ottawa, Ontario, with her long-suffering husband and two miniature dachshunds.

Cozy up with Berkley Prime Crime

SUSAN WITTIG ALBERT
*Don't miss the nationally bestselling
series featuring herbalist China Bayles.*

LAURA CHILDS
*The Tea Shop Mysteries are the
toast of Charleston, South Carolina.*

KATE KINGSBURY
*The Pennyfoot Hotel Mystery
series is a tea-time delight.*

**For the armchair
detective in you.**

penguin.com

WELL-CRAFTED MYSTERIES
FROM BERKLEY PRIME CRIME

- **Earlene Fowler** Don't miss this Agatha Award–winning quilting series featuring Benni Harper.

- **Monicca Ferris** This *USA Today* bestselling Needlecraft Mystery series includes free knitting patterns.

- **Laura Childs** Her Scrapbooking Mystery series offers tips to satisfy the most diehard crafters.

- **Maggie Sefton** This popular Knitting Mystery series comes with knitting patterns and recipes.

SOLVING CRIME CAN BE AN ART

penguin.com

GET CLUED IN

Ever wonder how to find out about all the latest Berkley Prime Crime and Signet mysteries?

berkleysignetmysteries.com

- See what's new
- Find author appearances
- Win fantastic prizes
- Get reading recommendations
- Sign up for the mystery newsletter
- Chat with authors and other fans
- Read interviews with authors you love

MYSTERY SOLVED.

berkleysignetmysteries.com

Penguin Group (USA) Online

What will you be reading tomorrow?

Tom Clancy, Patricia Cornwell, W.E.B. Griffin,
Nora Roberts, William Gibson, Robin Cook,
Brian Jacques, Catherine Coulter, Stephen King,
Dean Koontz, Ken Follett, Clive Cussler,
Eric Jerome Dickey, John Sandford,
Terry McMillan, Sue Monk Kidd, Amy Tan,
John Berendt…

You'll find them all at
penguin.com

*Read excerpts and newsletters,
find tour schedules and reading group guides,
and enter contests.*

Subscribe to Penguin Group (USA) newsletters
and get an exclusive inside look
at exciting new titles and the authors you love
long before everyone else does.

PENGUIN GROUP (USA)
us.penguingroup.com